The Nine Irony

by Tom Rieber

A Nick Thomas Novel

©2009 by Tom Rieber
Published by American Imaging
Cover design: Ikoneast.com
Format and packaging: Peggy Grich

Printed in the United States of America

ISBN: 978-1-60743-748-2

This book is a work of fiction. All characters in this book have no existence outside the imagination of the author and have no relation whatsoever to any-one bearing the same name or names except where permission has been granted.

This work is dedicated to the many who believed in me but especially to my loving wife, Kibbi and my dear mother, Marie.

Without their encouragement and faith I would never have finished this incredible journey. Also I want to thank my good friend, author and mentor, Jacqueline DeGroot, and my dear friend Monty Winters, my spiritual advisor and the brother I never had, who helped me believe all this was possible.

I thank all in my life, my God and my sobriety.

T.N. Rieber

The Nine Irony

Chapter 1

Wellfleet, Cape Cod

The lone woman worked with a fury at her computer in the rear of the dark warehouse, lit only by a single, harsh fluorescent lamp that hung suspended by two rusty chains over her desk. The rest of the damp, humid chamber was shrouded in musty shadows. Bits of odd machinery and pallets loaded with various sized crates littered the concrete floor.

The woman seemed nervous and kept looking back over her shoulder as if she were expecting someone. She'd shiver and stop typing every so often to peer back into the darkness, shading her eyes with her hand. Then, after a moment, she'd return to her screen and resume working. The only company she had was music from an oldies radio station that cut into the heavy silence.

The dark-clad figure found the door to the warehouse unlocked, as he knew it would be, and entered through the loading bay without a sound, closing the metal door softly behind him. The front half of the huge room was pitch black and he paused to let his eyes adjust and his senses tune in to his surroundings. The intruder smelled the musty air from the August humidity inside the old warehouse along with the fishy smell from the small marshy harbor outside.

He glanced at his black diver's watch confirming that it was 8:15 p.m.—well after closing time. He had to be done with this by 8:30 and he knew going in that no variations from the plan would be acceptable. Every detail had been carefully timed and planned. So far all was going according to schedule.

He heard the steady tapping of the woman's fingers flying across the keyboard and the soft music coming from her radio somewhere in the back by her desk. He had parked across the lot at the busy restaurant and patiently watched everyone else leave as he had many times before. He was very thorough at his little game. He was the hunter, patiently stalking, and she was the unknowing prey—the lion and the lamb. Nothing was left to chance. He had become totally absorbed into the role and it excited him beyond expectation, creating a high that money couldn't buy. The intruder even knew that the woman's partner, Shawn, was blissfully working on his second or third cocktail by now and would never consider going back to the office.

The man smiled and thought to himself, "He'd better have a good time tonight because tomorrow's gonna be a whole different story."

He advanced slowly and could see the back of the woman's head bathed in a harsh pool of light from the overhead fixture. She had long, fierce black curls that cascaded down the middle of her back. She was short but well built, and had a deep, natural color.

She wore a turquoise tank top and white shorts, which accented her skin and her well-defined body. He had no doubt that she had to die. It was just a shame that's all.

He had seen her face a lot lately, even as he slept, and he would wake up sweating with his heart pounding wildly, gasping for breath. He had even fantasized about being with her many times. Finally, she belonged to him and the union soon would be complete.

This was a test and he knew it. Part of him wanted to turn around and forget this whole thing. She hadn't seen him yet. But no—it was too late. He was committed and had no choice but to follow through and do it right.

He felt his hands sweating inside thick leather gloves as he crept forward slowly and silently in his black rubber soled shoes to where she sat at her computer terminal. He watched her sitting straight and noted the strong lines of her jaw as she concentrated on the screen before her. He continued to inch forward blending in with the shadows around him. He picked his way around a large packing crate and was almost in plain view. She would see him if she turned. She was only about ten feet away now. The announcer on the radio was telling of more sweltering heat to come. He swallowed hard, reached back, and found the butt of the large revolver that was tucked into his waistband in the small of his back. Just as he tightened his fingers around the smooth butt, his foot struck an object that was lying on the darkened floor in front of him, making a loud metallic clatter on the cement.

"Shit!" He exclaimed loudly, startling himself as well as the woman. He fought the impulse to run.

The woman whirled around in her chair and looked straight at him, startled and scared. Her eyes were large and round, and her mouth was open, ready to scream.

"What the . . . You scared the hell out of me!" She sighed and then smiled at him nervously, but with obvious relief. "Hang on a sec. I'll be right with you, OK? I just want to finish what I'm working on. It'll only take a minute." He nodded as she turned back to her screen, then wiped the sweat from his forehead with the back of his sleeve. She didn't appear to notice or question his thick gloves or dark clothes.

He felt a moment of uncertainty. She didn't seem so bad, he thought, and boy she really was a looker! His heart was racing and his mouth was dry. He'd heard that she was always pissed off at somebody. But she was nice to him now. Were they wrong? Could be. He smiled his best smile and reached down to pick up the object that so rudely announced his arrival.

"Take your time," he answered her thickly, trying to be casual as the heavy revolver dug into his back. Heart racing, he tasted the cocaine in the back of his throat. Maybe he shouldn't have done any till this was over. Oh well, it was too late now and nobody would know! Plus, he loved the warm surge of ecstasy the coke gave him, deep in his belly. He stared at the object in his hand and almost laughed aloud when he saw that it was a golf club. All the planning in the world just went to hell in one second because of a stupid golf club—a game for the fat and lazy. He studied the club for a brief moment and noted the detail as if to ease his anxiety. It had a long chrome shaft with a wedge on one end and a rubber grip on the other. The number 9 was stamped on the wedge end. He hefted the club and tossed it back against his right shoulder, smiled, and walked towards her, much the same way a soldier marched with a rifle.

She'd already turned back to the computer and was totally absorbed in her typing when he came up behind her.

The scream froze in her throat when she saw the reflection of the steel shaft descending in an arc towards her head on the screen in front of her . . . a fraction of a second, and a lifetime, too late.

He watched with a mix of fascination and horror as he buried the club into the dark mass of curls. He'd never hurt anyone before. Not like this anyway. It was like an out-of-body experience in which he was the spectator.

The club partially deflected off her arm when she raised it to ward off the blow. But it still landed hard against her skull sending her sprawling sideways out of her chair and onto the cement floor. He knew she must at least be dazed because he heard a nasty sounding crack when her head hit the floor. Her eyes rolled back and her mouth stayed open.

Now he just wanted to get out of there fast, but he knew he had to finish the job he had started. She had seen his face and could identify him. How could he have gotten involved in this nightmare?

"Why?" he looked up and asked God aloud.

God chose not to answer him.

The attacker looked down at the club and saw that the wedge was covered with blood and some of her now-sticky black hair, and then he stared at her. She wasn't moving, and he didn't see her breathing. There was a large gash just above her right ear that was open, bleeding, and very ugly. There was a stirring deep in his loins and he felt a hot rush of excitement.

He raised the club over his head, closed his eyes, took a deep breath, and then stopped himself. She was already dead, he thought.

He watched her prone, lifeless figure. There was no sign of breathing and he wasn't about to touch her. She looked dead all right and that was good enough for him. He glanced down at his watch. 8:23 p.m.

He felt weak and sick to his stomach. It was way too late now! He knew he had to keep a level head or else he would go to jail for the rest of his life. He just prayed it would all be worth the risk.

He checked himself and saw blood splattered on his pants and shoes. He would get rid of these clothes tonight. He leaned the bloody club against a nearby desk, picked up the phone with his gloved hand, and punched out a memorized phone number. He knew that he had done what he came to do, even though it didn't go exactly as they had planned.

He put the receiver to his ear and listened as it rang once, and then again. He heard a click and then silence. He spoke softly into the receiver, and quickly hung up, not expecting a reply.

He stared down at her motionless body once more and shrugged his shoulders. He did what needed to be done. No time for regrets now. He picked up the bloodied club and headed out of the warehouse the same way he came in. He looked at his watch and noted that it was 8:26 p.m. His mind raced. She wasn't supposed to die by a golf club! Now what to do with the club? He told himself to stay calm over and over.

He was aware of his own breathing and heard a loud thumping that he realized came from his own heart. All he had to do was to get out of there without incident, and he was home free.

He pushed open the metal door a crack, looked outside, and scanned the large lot carefully. There was the usual activity at the restaurant next door and nobody seemed to be looking his way with any interest.

The front half of the old building was an art co-op that had been there for years and was closed for the evening. The only car parked next to the building was the woman's black Acura. This was a normal sight because she always worked late. He slipped out the door, pulled it closed behind him, and then leaned the bloody golf club against the door.

He smiled to himself thinking that this was a true stroke of genius. The next person to go into the building would have to touch the club and leave their prints. In the semi-darkness the blood and hair on the other end wasn't visible so at first glance, the club wouldn't seem too out of place-just careless. The man smiled again knowing that his prints would not be found.

He felt the .357 Smith & Wesson Combat Magnum in small of his back that he was supposed to have used on her, but things happened a little too fast.

He didn't want to toss the gun as he was instructed to do, because he didn't use it on the woman. He decided to hang on to it until he could figure out what to do with it, besides it might come in handy and it was a nice gun. But it was not something he wanted to get caught with. The gun already had a history and with a little diligence it might somehow be traced back to him.

He took one last look around the parking lot and,

satisfied that he was unobserved, went around the side of the building, and disappeared quietly into the night. He didn't see the darkened patrol car parked in the shadows near the restaurant.

Chapter 2

It's funny how quickly your perspective on life can change when you find yourself sitting in the back of a police cruiser with your wrists handcuffed behind your back while your blood is being drained by hoards of relentless mosquitoes. It certainly made me realize how much our fate depended on the cards Lady Luck decided to deal us on any particular day. All it takes is one split second in the wrong place at the wrong time; one innocent misalignment of fate, and any one of us could find ourselves knee-deep in an honest-to-goodness nightmare. That's when we realize how fragile our little self-important existence really is. Some say we need crisis and pain to appreciate the good things in life. Personally, I think that philosophy is OK—as long as it applies to someone else. I don't happen to be that evolved.

It was quiet except for a lone foghorn rumbling low and deep in the distance. The sky was starless and the night eerie as the parking lot lights barely cut through the heavy mist. It seemed like I'd been cooped up in the back of the cruiser for hours, but I wasn't sure how long I'd actually been sitting there.

What I did know was that I was miserable. It was a humid, windless August evening, and the fishy smell from the bog that bordered the parking lot was heavy from low tide.

I rolled my head and shrugged my aching shoulders in an attempt to ease the cramped, stiff muscles in my neck. All I had on was a thin tee shirt that was sweat-pasted to my body, bluejeans, and topsiders without socks. Had I known that I'd be the guest of the Wellfleet Police Department, I'd have dressed more appropriately.

The windows of the Ford were only cracked open about two inches on both sides, and it felt like an oven in the back of that car. I bet they thought I was going to pick the locks on my cuffs, slide out unnoticed through the crack in the window, and disappear into the night. How did they know?

Let's get real here. I'm not a black belt, and I'm not an ex-SEAL or an exotic weapons expert. I've never learned how to kill with a rolled up newspaper or a paper clip. My name is Nick Thomas. I'm a moderately successful writer of mystery novels, who, by good intentions and errant judgment, occasionally gets involved in some very strange situations. This topped the list so far.

I was covered in a sticky sweat, and those very lucky and very hungry mosquitoes were having a feast at my expense. I was beyond miserable; I'd skipped over pissed-off and shifted right into teeth-gritting, industrial grade nasty! The mosquitoes must smell Carla's blood on my clothes and hands. I took some satisfaction in knowing that they'd die soon after they drained my blood. The two Wellfleet cops who had stuffed me in the back of the car didn't exactly extend me a whole bunch of courtesy, even though they knew who I was. In retrospect, I might've been a tad mouthy with them. OK guys, I got the point already.

Chris, my love and my best friend, says that I need to be more sensitive and more in tune with the feelings of those around me. But I didn't like being cuffed, and my serenity, that I was so proud of, was gone at this point!

I needed to reach Chris so she wouldn't worry. That's a joke, I thought. Of course she's going to worry, especially after I explain to her that I'll probably be charged with the attempted murder of my ex-wife.

This evening had disaster written all over it, and I wasn't overloaded with gratitude. I was starving and would've killed for a cup of coffee, probably not a great choice of words, given the circumstances. But there's such a thing as cruel and unjust punishment. Earlier, one of those flabby cops came back with a tray of coffee and a bag that I just knew held donuts.

Let me back up a bit. It all started when Carla, my ex-wife, called me earlier about our court date on Tuesday. She was nice and sweet on the phone, and I believe she used that alien word 'reasonable'. That should've set off all my internal bells and whistles. She always felt that she got shafted in our divorce and, now that I was making some money from my books, she was entitled to her "fair" share. She said she had a way that we'd both win and that maybe we could finally work things out. Optimism sees no enemy, so I agreed to meet.

I hopped in my old MG and drove down to Wellfleet after dinner. Carla's black Acura was the only car in the gravel lot, so I parked next to it and went up to the darkened warehouse. The path to the door was overgrown and littered. I remembered kicking a *Budweiser* can into the bushes, and when I got to the door there was a golf club leaning against it. I grabbed it and tossed it into the bushes in an unseen act of defiance. Shawn, Carla's partner, was always leaving his shit around, so it'd serve him right to lose a club.

Inside the warehouse, I saw the overhead light on back by Carla's desk and heard some soft music coming from her radio. Otherwise, the silence was heavy in the big dark building. That was when I found her lying on the cement floor bleeding from a huge gash on the side of her head. She had on a turquoise tank top and white shorts in contrast to her well-tanned skin. Her raven hair was splayed out on the dirty cement floor and there was blood—a lot of blood.

She looked dead to me, but I felt her neck like they do on TV and found a weak pulse. Her breathing was labored; she was in bad shape and fading fast. I wrapped her head in a sweatshirt that was on her desk and then sat with her head cradled in my lap while I tried to process what had happened. I knew I should've picked up the phone and called 911, but I was frozen and just sat there not knowing what else to do. I was scared, shocked, and not thinking rationally. I remember being stunned by the fact that it was only a matter of a minute or two before I heard sirens coming in my direction, an unusual sound in this area. I didn't call them, so how could they know? Cars skidded to a stop outside—how many I couldn't tell you and there were muffled voices. I was in a vacuum and everything was happening in slow motion. I was lead.

The warehouse door flew open, and two cops

entered with their weapons drawn with more behind them. And there I was sitting there with Carla's head in my lap, her breathing short and raspy and her blood warm and sticky on my fingers.

The greeting I received was less than friendly. "Get on the ground. Now!"

"Officer, please. She's hurt badly. You have to . . ."

The cop crossed the few feet between us, motioning for the other cop to come over and tend to Carla, and grabbed me by my arm and pulled me up, cuffing me in the same motion.

"Hey what the . . ."

He pushed me back down and said, "Shut up and stay down!"

I did. And that was how it all began. I figured that we'd straighten out this misunderstanding fairly quickly, and they'd apologize to me for being so rough. I still believed in Santa Claus and the Easter Bunny, too.

I found out later that they'd received an anonymous tip that a woman was being attacked in the parking lot. That same thoughtful caller went on to say that the woman broke free and tried to get away from her attacker. They said they saw a man wielding a golf club, who by the way fit my description, chasing her into the warehouse and that they heard a woman screaming. Come on! That was bull! But the fact of the matter was that when the cops arrived I had blood all over my hands and clothes. I also had a sneaking suspicion that the golf club I found by the door had something to do with all this as well. They just haven't found that out yet. God, please don't die Carla. They are going to think I did it. There was no doubt in my mind about that!

I looked out toward the building and could see that things were starting to heat up.   In addition to the Wellfleet Police and miscellaneous official-looking people, I recognized a couple of reporters that I knew from the Times. A squeaky clean, high-tech sound truck with a satellite dish and a camera crew had arrived a few minutes ago. It had a big <u>Action 6 News</u> painted through a yellow sun on its side. A few people from the State Police violent crime CPAC unit had arrived and immediately took charge of the crime scene. That was how things worked on the Cape.

It was then that I realized that my night was going to get a whole lot more intense once a certain larger-than-life Captain Artus Q. Peck arrived. There was no question that once he heard that I was involved, he'd want to pay his respects in person. Captain Peck was an old friend in a manner of speaking, but I knew that he'd crawl over a mile of broken glass on his hands and knees to see me handcuffed. It'd be fair to say that I had caused him some anxiety in the past, but we did become friends of sort when I sobered up and stopped being a menace to his little kingdom.

My attention shifted back to the crowd of nosy curiosity seekers that had pushed closer to the building to see what had happened in their peaceful little hamlet. The chopper that had airlifted Carla out brought them all out of their beds. This was an event to behold because there is very little violent crime here on the Cape.

My heart sank even further as I looked over to the news truck. Standing there was a ghost from my past, Katlin Ross, with a camera crew getting ready to smear my life all over the airwaves. Kate Ross and I had dated a few lifetimes ago, but I broke it off when I saw her ambition and agenda was less than ethical. She wanted to do some in-depth stories about the people of Alcoholics Anonymous and figured that I would help her. I informed her it was called anonymous for a reason and that it would be in poor taste to exploit the people in AA for personal gain and glory. She laughed in my face and called me an idealistic idiot and a loser. We didn't exactly part as friends after that conversation.

I stared out the cruiser window and watched the local traffic back up as more people came to get a better look. Most people are ghouls at heart. They want to see bodies, or at least think they do, but when they actually see one, they wind up in therapy from the trauma.

The Wellfleet cops tried to keep the road clear, but it was a losing battle. A chubby uniformed cop, who looked like he was barely old enough to shave, was in the road blowing his whistle and gesturing at the crawling cars. He looked like he was either going to pull out his gun and start shooting or cry. After a few frustrating minutes he did the prudent thing and retreated into the building. I cheered inwardly at the small victory for the masses. The end result was a major traffic jam along East Commercial Street complete with a lot of honking and swearing. This was all happening on a road that would normally be deserted at this time of night, even though it led to the town pier and harbor.

I was detained and restrained in the parking lot of CAPE DISPATCH, INC., my ex-wife's place of business. Carla and her business partner, Shawn Kiley, ran a shady, but somehow bonded courier service that catered to local artists and galleries. I never had a burning desire to know much about it, because I always had the impression that they operated in some pretty gray areas. And I couldn't stand her partner, Kiley who I strongly suspected was a lot more than a business partner The aroma of cooking food emanating from the building next door began to make me hungry. The parking lot was large and unpaved, and also served a local eatery called the Lobster Shanty, complete with fishing nets and lobster traps that adorned its weathered outside walls. It was a local favorite, and the food was good. It also had a small, busy bar that looked pretty good right about now.

Two floodlights mounted on a pole near the restaurant and another pair mounted above the loading dock at Cape Dispatch illuminated the dirt and gravel parking lot, casting shadows over all the nooks and crannies of the building. It was an old red wooden structure with peeling white trim that housed several businesses besides Cape Dispatch. Cape Dispatch was at the rear of the structure where a rickety loading dock adorned with an old Pepsi machine stood dimly lit against the night. A few threadbare tires, a couple of crates, and a bunch of broken pallets were piled up against the side of the building amongst the weeds and tall grass. The light over the main entrance was either off or broken, but harsh light spilled from inside through the high windows and the now open loading dock.

The only two vehicles next to the building were my old MGB convertible with its top down and Carla's gleaming, black Acura. I've always believed that cars were a true statement of our personalities. I rest my case.

I turned in my seat and watched several officers

doing something I couldn't recognize up on the hill above. They wore nice bright blue windbreakers like the ones TV cops wear with POLICE stenciled on the back in huge white letters. I could almost feel their excitement. I watched the scene unfold before me with macabre facination, in spite of my mood and predicament. It reminded me of the classic Arlo Guthrie ballad, Alice's Restaurant and Masacree, where the cops mobilized S.W.A.T. teams, helicopters and dogs to find out who dumped the garbage on Thanksgiving Day. That's how ridiculous this all seemed.

My stomach rumbled and reminded me of where I was and instantly refueled my wrath. A small coffee wagon had pulled into the parking area by the restaurant and opened up. I couldn't believe the cops let him through, except that they'd be his best customers and, more likely than not, he was probably related to one of them. Whatever the case, the coffee wagon was an oasis in the desert to me. I leaned my head against the window and closed my eyes. I could smell the fresh coffee brewing and the distinct wonderful aroma of greasy hamburgers and onions frying side by side with the much maligned, but ever loved, side of bacon. And that damn truck was a good thirty yards away. Now that's talent and focus. I looked over at it the way a young man in love would look at his lady fair from the deck of a departing ship. I'll get there yet, I promised myself, sitting back up straight. It became a new priority. One needed goals in life.

The cops didn't ask me my thoughts on who tried to kill Carla. There was no doubt in their minds. But they didn't ask, and they were quite rude about me talking to anybody before my lawyer got here. But they did let me make my call from inside where I was informed by a woman at his answering service that my beloved lawyer was in Aspen on business. This must be my lucky day. If he was in Aspen it wasn't business. But that still left me in a bind. I pleaded for one more call and was granted one minute. I left a message on Chris's machine. I knew she was out on the *Ulysses*, one of the Woods Hole research ships. It was due to dock early the next morning, and I wasn't about to hail her over the ship's radio. I hoped this mess would all be sorted out by morning.

I leaned my head back against the window, closed my eyes, and sighed. What a freaking nightmare and I still had my little chat with Captain Artus Peck to look forward to. He'd be here sure as taxes. What makes life so interesting is that the only thing you can predict is unpredictability. Each new day holds many surprises and the bad stuff usually has a habit of rearing its ugly head when you least expect it.

Chapter 3

A big police-type Crown Victoria, with a serious cluster of antennae waving in the night, wheeled into the lot spraying loose gravel and rocks as it ground to a stop in front of the main entrance of Cape Dispatch. The powerful sedan was a spotless ebony with tinted windows and bright chrome wire wheels. I groaned inwardly because I knew that car well. There was no doubt in my mind who was going to climb out of that car growling like a grizzly bear with a hornet's nest stuck to his ass. It was none other than Captain Artus Q. Peck, head of the Massachusetts State Police CPAC unit, and I was about to be his supper.

Peck slid his huge bulk from the car, smoothed his crisp blue suit, straightened his tie, and then finally acknowledged the presence of the two cops that had rushed up to his car as he parked.

One of the cops handed him a Styrofoam cup of coffee that quickly disappeared in his massive paw.

Peering through the cruiser window, I watched the three of them closely. There was a lot of talking going on over there, and I saw one of the cops jerk a thumb in my direction and shrug his shoulders nonchalantly. Peck scowled at them and gestured toward me angrily, his lips moved quickly and his eyes shone white. The two cops looked at each other in desperation, wishing they were somewhere else. It was safe to assume Peck was having them for an appetizer. Peck threw his hands up in disgust, turned on his heel, and stalked in my direction, shaking his huge head and talking to himself. I knew then what a matador must feel like with a murderous bull charging at him, only I didn't have a little sword hidden under a pretty red cape. And a matador could always run. I took a deep breath and tried to gather my cool.

Captain Artus Peck was a very large, very loud, extremely savvy black man who'd lived on the Cape all his life. Over the years he had become very protective of his little kingdom by the sea and took any intrusion of the status quo personally and very seriously. He'd arrested me in my formative years for numerous misdemeanors that usually involved alcohol.

He stood about 6'5" and probably weighed in at 270, with a large head of closely cropped gray wool and sharp, dark raven eyes that missed nothing, and he always dressed like a bank president, boardroom perfect even at ten-thirty at night.

Tonight, as he neared the cruiser, a wide smile lit up his broad face. I was glad he was entertained. He stooped down to the window and peered in.

"Had to make sure it was really you, Thomas. It's little pleasures like this that I go to church on Sundays for," he said in his deep baritone.

I swallowed hard and sat back in my seat. He was enjoying this.

"Hello, Captain. Think you could find your way

to letting me out of these cuffs, huh?"

His face was inches from mine, separated only by glass, and he looked me in the eye for a few hard seconds. I felt like Faye Ray with King Kong staring in the window. Apparently satisfied, he grunted and yanked open the door of the cruiser.

"Those gentlemen over there say you gave them a bunch of shit, Thomas. I see you're still exuding that magical personality of yours. If it was up to them they'd forget you were out here and see how much of your carcass the bugs left come morning. Personally, I like the idea a lot," he said.

My whole body ached. I was drenched and dirty with sweat from the god-awful humidity. My arms, legs and back will never be the same. My sense of humor was long gone, but I knew it was time to grovel a bit.

"Come on Captain, I didn't expect to be cuffed and thrown back here. They were out of line first, and I didn't hurt Carla. You know me better than that. Hell, I'd be the first one you'd look for if something happened. We both know that."

He didn't answer, so I continued. "What happened was that I went to see Carla on some business, at her request I might add, and found her on the floor unconscious and bleeding. I wrapped her head and that's when the cops came in. Come on, Captain, let's be real. If I did do it, I'd be long gone by now."

Peck cleared his throat and set his coffee on the roof of the cruiser. He reached in, grabbed my arm, and pulled me out of the car as if I were a child. My knees buckled slightly when I tried to stand, so I steadied myself against the back fender. I'd been cramped up in there for at least two hours.

"Thanks," I mumbled and turned around so he could take my cuffs off. Instead he pushed me hard against the car and pinned me with his huge body from behind. I smelled his expensive cologne, and I felt his breath in my ear as he spoke softly and slowly.

"Thomas, if you so much as breathe the wrong way, I'll snap your neck. Do we understand each other?" I nodded attentively.

"You will not make me look stupid and make me regret taking these off, right?" He gave the cuffs a quick tug that sent needles up both my aching arms before he unlocked them.

I gritted my teeth and kept nodding vigorously, fighting the urge to eulogize his mother, and concentrated on restoring feeling to my limbs. It felt wonderful as my fingers began to tingle once again. Being handcuffed is not high on the list of self-esteem builders.

"Thanks, I won't do anything to piss you off. I promise," I said, massaging my wrists.

"You already did. You took me away from a real good book, my only cigar of the day, and a nice snifter of imported brandy. If you think I'm happy about that, think again. Those were precious moments in life that I'll never get back."

Leaning back against the cruiser, I managed a weak smile and looked at him. Artus Peck actually was a great street philosopher, and he was a fair man.

"Captain listen, we gotta talk. What do you say to us getting a couple of hot coffees, maybe a doughnut or two and sit down and talk like two rational men. Honestly, I had nothing to do with this. Let's clear this up and let me the hell out of here so I can check on Carla. I'm not sure if she's even alive. Nobody here will tell me squat. And if you ask me, which I know you won't, my money's on her partner; one Mr. Shawn Kiley. Now there's a real card carrying dickhead if there ever was one."

Peck looked at me closely and after a long moment said, "Carla's still alive, Nick, but just barely. From what I hear she's in rough shape. It doesn't look good for her and quite frankly it really doesn't look too good for you either. Everything points to you, my friend." He held his hand up to stop my indignant protest. I stayed quiet.

He still had me against the car, and had my full attention. "First, you're going to tell me exactly what happened here in my nice quiet town where tourist families come and spend lots of cash." He got closer, his voice lower. "I think you know where this is going."

I found myself nodding at his every word like one of those little brown slinky dogs in the back of a car window.

Peck cleared his throat and then said, "Come on, let's find somebody to take your statement, and then I'll decide whether or not you'll be our guest this evening." Maybe he missed the part about coffee and donuts. I kept my mouth shut.

Cameras flashed and a blurry sea of faces shouted at me from behind the barriers as we approached the building. I kept my head down and just kept walking straight ahead.

"Hey, Nick!" a female voice yelled. I looked up and there was my old friend, Katlin Ross, pushing toward the front with a cameraman following closely behind her. Kate loved those cameras. She gave me her TV smile and hollered over to me, "Got a statement for us, Nick? Or do we go with what the cops gave us?" I could feel the heat from the bank of lights surrounding the camera and there were little spots where her face was supposed to be.

"The story is that the police have you on attempted murder and that your ex-wife is barely holding on. What do you say, Nick?" Kate played dirty, and I knew that she'd twist anything I said, so I kept it simple.

"Just this, I'm innocent," I called out to her and anybody who'd listen. Then I shut out the ensuing roar of questions and catcalls.

Peck guided me through the warehouse door, out of Kate's web and into his.

This was one of those rare moments in which I thought about a drink, actually many drinks. I knew with all my heart and soul that it wasn't an option, but when the shit hits the fan like this and I find myself standing in front of it, my disease likes to rear its ugly head. I made a note to find an AA meeting first thing in the morning.

Chapter 4

We entered the now brightly lit warehouse, and I paused, not really wanting to go in. Peck growled behind me and navigated me around a makeshift barrier the police had set up in the middle of the floor. I looked closer and saw that the main attraction was the mess from a bag of spilled take-out food and a cardboard tray that was either thrown or dropped onto the floor. The bright red and white bag was from the restaurant next door, and it looked like fried clams and French fries had spilled from a rip in its side. A large empty cup of soda was tipped over next to its sticky contents that formed a pool on the warehouse floor. I didn't remember seeing it there when I came in before, but this part of the loading dock entrance was usually dark at night and Carla didn't keep the cleanest place in the world. I could have stepped right over it and not noticed.

Peck watched me look at the spilled food with a raised eyebrow, he asked, "Yours?"

"No, not mine, and I don't remember seeing this when I came in before, but I could've missed it. It was dark in here, and the take-out food is not out of character either. Carla always ordered dinner from next door when she worked late. She'd rather starve than cook."

"Easy enough to check," he grunted and then guided me toward Kiley's windowed office in the rear.

We passed close to Carla's desk, and I saw the white chalk outline of her body before the paramedics took her to a waiting medical helicopter. The dark stain of her blood was still on the floor. I felt a queasy stab in my gut. Carla and I didn't get along, but I never wished her any harm. As much as we'd battled, I was sad for her. She was never truly happy. I don't think she ever stopped long enough to sit on the beach and enjoy the good things in life. It was a waste, and I couldn't have lived like that. Life is too damn short.

I promised myself I'd find out who did this. I owed our failed marriage that much. The *who* part I thought would be easy. But I'd have to convince someone else of that fast, before they tried to pin this on me.

At the back of the shabby office I saw Shawn Kiley, a large, white-haired Irishman in his fifties who was, or should I say still is, Carla's business partner in Cape Dispatch Inc. He looked like he'd be at home selling cars on the local cable channel with a white suit and a cowboy hat. "Come on down-suckers!"

I had seen him pull up in the silver company van about an hour ago and stagger inside. Good, I thought. He looked red-faced, which was probably the result of his liquid supper, and disheveled. He was probably trying to look all shook up. I had to laugh.

Peck looked back at me as we walked toward the back.   "Something funny, Thomas? I ain't laughing."

"No Captain, it's not funny. But that clown on the other side of that glass is. Kiley's probably in there telling those guys how worried he is about Carla. He hated her worse than I did. He's a bullshit artist and a complete jerk, and I'll bet my last dollar that he's the one behind this. Mark my words."

"Thanks for the character analysis," Peck answered.

"Anytime," I said trying to sound cheerful.

I flexed my still cramped fists. Kiley was a gold-plated jerk. It was no secret that Carla and he did not see eye to eye on how their business should be run, or what day it was for that matter. Carla sucked him in because she thought he had money, but come to find out that all he had, with the exception of bad credit, was a good line of crap. By then, they were already playing hide the salami, while scheming to make millions. The joke was on Carla that time. She reached for the brass ring and came away with a big, greasy bag of hot air.

Kiley was a drunk, quick with bad jokes, but even quicker with his temper and the company credit card. And he thought he was a lady's man. He usually forgot about Karen, his wife of thirty-one-years, who was stashed away conveniently in Wellfleet. I think Carla had the goods on ole' Shawn and was about to leave him in the street. She had alluded to this a few times when she was full of herself and bragging. Knowing her, she probably threatened to tell his wife, Karen, just to blackmail him.

Peck rapped on the dirty glass door and opened it. Kiley was seated behind his filthy desk and a detective was questioning him in earnest. The detective had a hand on the back of Kiley's chair and was leaning toward him as he spoke. Kiley sat looking at his thumbs. I could tell the cop was one of Peck's boys; mature, in shape, and serious.

Peck addressed the cop as Jacobson, who was tall and thin with short wavy white hair, had steel gray eyes, and wore a fancy suit like Pecks.

All violent crimes on the Cape came under the jurisdiction of the State Police CPAC unit who worked out of Troop D in Yarmouth. They operated in conjunction with the locals on these cases.

Kiley and the cop looked up as we entered the office. Peck motioned me to the chair against the wall and put his finger to his lips. Then, he signaled for the detective to continue.

"Just got started, Captain. He's been a bit testy."

"Hell, I've been sitting here for a long time with my dick in my hand. I just want to go home," Kiley whined.

Peck glared at him and Kiley went back to examining his thumbs. "Go ahead, Jake, I'll take it from here, " Peck said.

Jacobson nodded and left. Peck grunted and stood with his huge hands clasped behind his back, rocking forward on his heels. Peck was the consummate waiter. He could out wait a stone statue.

Kiley eyed me with contempt. "What's he doing here? Thought he was already in jail. What gives?" His words came out thick and slurred.

I gave him my best smile and kept my mouth shut. I wasn't going to trade insults with this half-in-the-bag slob. I looked at Peck and he nodded. He was glad I'd kept my mouth shut, too.

"Mr. Kiley, I suggest that you don't worry about Mr. Thomas.   Just answer the questions," Peck snapped.   I knew what Peck was up to.   He once told me that he liked to put two suspects together in the soup and see what happens.   He was a shrewd man, and if it weren't me sitting there, I'd be full of admiration.   Yes, I would.

Kiley nodded.   He appraised Peck and decided wisely to cooperate.

Peck took a deep breath and continued, "Mr. Kiley, I know it's late and you must be tired, but there are questions that have to be asked and answers that need to be given and until those two things happen you're not going anywhere.   Do we understand each other, Mr. Kiley?"

Peck was sizing up the man seated before him, much the way a big cat watches a fat little mouse he is about to devour.

Mistaking Peck's tone as being friendly, Kiley got brave and said, "Hey, Captain, I got an idea.   Why don't we hold a press conference?   I'm getting sick of repeating myself to you people."   Kiley smiled.   The Captain didn't smile back.

Peck towered over Kiley.   He put his hand on the back of Kiley's chair and spun the Irishman around to face him squarely. The chair made a loud squeaking sound that got all of our attention. Kiley stopped smiling.

"Listen Kiley, you can do this here or you can do this from a cell, I really don't care which.   Actually, I'd prefer you in a cell at this point, and I've just met you."   Peck hissed, "So, if I were you I would sit up straight and start answering my questions or you're going to spend the rest of the night at my house."

The room suddenly shrank, and you could cut the silence with a knife.

Kiley swallowed hard and looked up at Peck. I was thoroughly enjoying this. The Captain's unwavering stare bored a hole through Kiley's sweaty forehead.

Kiley licked his fat lips and said, "Sorry, I guess everyone's nerves are wearing a bit thin. Let's not get off on the wrong foot here. I'll tell you whatever I can." Peck seemed to have made his point. I wanted some popcorn. Outside, I noted several cops, including Jacobson, keeping an eye on our little trio.

A minute later the door opened and a woman entered.

"Kiley, meet Detective Carol Russo, our psychological officer.

"Hey, a good looking shrink. This ain't so bad after all," Kiley babbled, then he realized what he had just heard.

"Wait a minute here. You saying I'm Nuts?"

Russo nodded quickly to Peck, eyed me coolly, and then turned her attention to Kiley.

Detective Russo was an athletic looking woman, in her late twenties. She leaned up against the credenza, swept her dark hair back with one hand and crossed her shapely legs at the ankles. Her eyes never left Kiley's face. Kiley zeroed in on her legs immediately, like Pavlov's dogs.

Russo didn't appear to notice, or care. I swore I saw a little spittle forming at the corner of Kiley's mouth.

I watched as I always do, being ever the writer. Eddie Kane, my alter-ego in my novels, would flip over this dame. Eddie is a hard-boiled, kick-ass, private investigator who is blessed with charm, savvy, and a lot of luck.   So naturally, a lot of those thoughts I blame on him. Chris doesn't buy into it for a second.

My trained eye also noticed that Peck and Russo worked together, like a well-oiled machine. He'd be the aggressor, and she'd watch for reaction and evaluate.   It was unnerving to be watched by a psychologist, even one as pretty as Carol Russo.

Peck perched his massive ass on the corner of the desk next to Kiley's chair, pulled out a notebook and pen, and calmly addressed the now cooperative subject.

"Carla Thomas is your business partner, is that correct?"

Clearly flustered by Peck's now quiet, probing manner, Kiley fished out a rank-looking handkerchief and dabbed at his forehead. He had a hard time looking straight at Peck, who was one of those men who could be very focused and intense, and accomplish a great deal by saying very little.

"Yes sir, we started CDI together about nine months ago, and she was/is a full partner." Kiley answered proudly. But his voice was up an octave. The slime looked scared as he fidgeted in his chair, waiting for Peck to continue.

"How close are you to your partner?"

Kiley watched an ant climb out of an open can of Planter's Nuts that was on his desk. "I...uh...uh...close enough, I guess. I mean, we were friends before we were partners."

I coughed back a laugh. Peck shot a look at me, and then went back to Kiley.

"Were you intimate with her?"

"Hey, what are you trying to pull?" Kiley whined, "I thought you already said Thomas did it." He jerked a fat finger in my direction. "I heard you found blood on him and all that."

Peck poked Kiley's chest. "We're just trying to get the facts, Mr. Kiley. Somebody attempted to kill Mrs. Thomas here tonight, and I'm going to find out who and why. I'm not going to play games with your ass. Either you start getting real helpful in a real hurry or we haul you in for questioning. A night in the drunk tank would do wonders for your attitude. You make the call."

Peck held up his huge finger. He looked over at me sitting against the wall and said, "Maybe I'll put you and Thomas in the same suite. You two can be roomies." Ross snickered, and I shook my head and leaned back against the wall. Funny guy.

"OK already, I'll answer your questions," Kiley said, his eyes following the ant that had traveled down the can of Planter's and found a small pile of something else edible under some papers. "There were rumors. I'm sure you'll hear, but there was no truth to them, I swear." He didn't look up at them as he spoke.

"Look, I can't do this with him in here, OK. There's got to be a law or something," he snorted, finally looking over at me. "Know what? I think I want a lawyer before I say anything else."

I took the cue, stood up, and said, "Look Captain, There's a chair outside and I'll just go and sit. I'm not going anywhere. I promise."

Peck looked at me, cocked his finger, and said, "I'll shoot you myself if you so much as get an itch. Got me, Thomas?" He fired an imaginary round at me and blew the tip of his finger. The man watched too much TV if you ask me.

"Yes, sir!" I straightened up, saluted and went

outside the office and plopped down in a gray metal folding chair right beside the door. I moved the chair back and angled it to see what was going on inside. It was perfect. I looked over and noticed several cops were watching me with curiosity. I smiled warmly at them, and then turned to watch my good friend Kiley squirm some more.

Peck's voice came clearly through the closed door. "What rumors, Mr. Kiley? Who's going to say what?" Peck pried, brushing an imaginary speck of dirt from his sleeve. Kiley nodded in my direction and said in a lower voice, "Her old man, Nick, for one. He accused her of having an affair with me from the first day I met her."

Peck shook his head. "Why did he think that, Mr. Kiley? Just where did you meet Mrs. Thomas?" asked Peck, watching Kiley like Kiley was watching that ant.

Kiley shrugged his shoulders. "Hey, we met in a bar and we hooked up. You know, we became friends. We hung out and got to talking and stuff." He moved the small pile of papers on his desk and squashed the ant with his beefy hand, and then wiped his hand on his pants.

"What bar?" Peck asked.

"Montego Ray's, up in P-town. I'm sure you guys know where that is. Cops hang there, too, sometimes."

Peck ignored the allusion.

"What do you suppose a married woman was looking for there?" continued Peck while Russo watched Kiley intently. She hadn't even moved her little toe the whole time. There goes my trained eye for detail again.

Kiley was flustered. "How the hell should I know

what she was looking for? Look you guys, we shared a few beers, a few laughs and found out that we had something in common. O.K.? Is that a crime?"

Where was your wife while you were having all these laughs?" Peck asked. "She doesn't like to laugh, Kiley? My wife loves to laugh. Thing is we laugh together. You like to laugh, Russo?"

Russo nodded affirmatively, still looking serious.

"Hey, we don't need to drag my old lady into this, do we?" Kiley cried. His eyes darted toward Russo almost apologetically. Maybe he thought he had a shot with her, too. How pathetic.

"That all depends on you, Pal," countered Peck. "What time did you say you left the office tonight?"

"I already told you," hissed Kiley. "It was about six, and I went down to Montego's for a cocktail to unwind."

"No doubt for some of those laughs. Any witnesses?" asked Russo. Kiley turned and looked at her not answering. She repeated the question. "Did anybody see you in there, Mr. Kiley?"

"Did you call your wife?" pressed Peck.

Kiley's head went back and forth like one of those little dogs on a spring in the back window of a car.

I saw him run a beefy hand through his thick white hair and look from one cop to the other, then pause to catch another look at Carol Russo's legs. It seemed to rejuvenate him. She didn't budge.

He licked his thick lips and took a deep breath. He decided to get brave again. "Look you guys, we finished up business at the usual time. I put on my coat, said goodnight, went outside, got in my van, and took off. End of story. Now, if you've got something specific you want to hang on me then go

for it. OK? But I can prove where I was all night.
That's the bottom line."

This was great. Peck looked like he was going to
squash Kiley like the bug he was.

Russo asked, "What was Carla doing when you
left?"

"She was on the phone with her ex-husband.
Your buddy out there." I assumed he meant me.

"How do you know it was her ex-husband?" fired
Peck, leaning a little closer to Kiley's red face. Better
him than me, I thought. I remembered that Kiley
always smelled like Maalox and sweat. Probably
some exotic brand of aftershave he found at a tag
sale, I mused.

Kiley cleared his throat, licked his lips again, and
continued, "Well I heard her ask him to come by,
and that she had a few things to discuss with him. I
could tell she was talking to him by her tone of voice.
She had a special one just for him. Ya know what
I mean?" Kiley made a weak attempt at another
smile. He looked over at Russo for support, but she
was eyeing him much the same way one would view
a nasty stain on an expensive carpet. He looked
away quickly, but not before he got another glance
at her legs.

I slapped a mosquito and looked back in at Russo,
who was still leaning against the desk. She had on
a light beige skirt and blazer with a pale blue silk
blouse, bare legs and beige peep toe pumps. Russo
was a woman who turned heads. Yes, indeed.

"Did you ever hear them argue?" asked Peck.

"What do you think? They weren't getting
divorced because they were in love. She was pissed
about the book money. She wanted a piece of that
bad. She told me more than once that Nick would

suffer every day for the rest of his life unless she got her cut. And trust me, she meant it, pal. She could be a ruthless asshole."

"What book money, Kiley?" asked Peck, ignoring the "pal". Peck looked over at Russo who shrugged her shoulders.

"You know, from those Eddie Kane books he writes. Real trash, if you ask me, but he's gotta be a millionaire or at least close to it by now. Carla figured that he owed her even though they weren't together when he started writing them. She thought it was her prodding that pushed him to write. Nick told her to take a hike." Kiley laughed. "Actually, he told her where to stick the money—one penny at a time." Kiley thought this was funny.

What he was saying was no state secret. It was the reason Carla and I couldn't put an end to our miserable relationship. I couldn't see clear to giving her one stinking dime of my book royalties, and my lawyers concurred. It's not as if there were millions there. Far from it. The life of a writer who's reaching for the stars is full of rejection, revision, and work, lots of work, and not as much moolah as everyone seems to think.

Seeing his chance to clear himself, Kiley was more than willing to fill in the details on how I hit it rich when my first book sold and refused to split the take with Carla.

You see, when we first legally separated, Carla made me sign a document saying that whatever we did from then on was untouchable by the other, so that when she struck it rich with Kiley, I couldn't come after her for money. She had no idea that I had talent.

Kiley went on to tell Peck and Russo about my

cottage on the ocean and my sports car. What he neglected to say was that when Carla and I split, I left with the clothes on my back, a battered up old car, and nothing more than self pride and sobriety. She got the condo, the bank account, and everything else.

A patrolman waddled past me and opened the door. He motioned to Peck, who followed him outside the small office. They spoke in low tones a few feet away while Peck eyed me.

Peck thanked the cop, strode past me and opened the door to Kiley's office.

"Carol, Mr. Kiley can go for now." He held up one finger to Kiley. "Make sure we can get a hold of you at all times, Kiley. I don't want to have to look too hard. That would piss me off."

"Always at your service, Captain," Kiley chirped and slithered out the door and past me without so much as a glance. Russo looked at me then at Peck.

Peck gave her a tired smile and said, "I'll handle Mr. Thomas, Carol, you see how things are going out there. We'll wrap it up soon." He jerked his thumb toward the warehouse. "Oh, and I want to know all there is to know about our esteemed Mr. Kiley: family, friends, money problems, the works, OK? I want to turn over some of his rocks. I just know something slimy lives under them."

Russo laughed and went off to take care of things, her high heels echoing on the cement floor.

Peck motioned for me to come inside. It was my turn. I was so excited! He closed the door and sat down in the well-worn, red leather chair behind Kiley's desk. Spread before us was the strangest collection of shit that I ever saw. I'd never had the pleasure to sit in Kiley's office and appreciate the true wonders it offered. Aside from the normal desk stuff like a phone, desk calendar, and your sundry office items, there were also many notable curios ranging from dusty bowling trophies, packs of golf balls, a Hustler magazine, two huge, overflowing ashtrays—the kind with the miniature rubber tires around them, and finally the open can of Planter's, where the ant had been living large.

Peck looked around him as if he just stepped in a pile of dog crap. This was so unlike his own desk that was polished to a high gloss each and every day by his devoted secretary.

Peck took a paper towel from a roll on Kiley's credenza and wiped the desktop in front of him so he wouldn't soil his suit. This ritual lasted for several moments as he nested and cleared away some debris. I knew his mind was working, planning.

I sat silently and waited. After a moment, he lifted his head and focused his stare on me, still not saying a word. Peck had assumed his favorite position with his hands folded carefully in front of him. He finally said in a controlled voice, "This is your chance, Nick, talk to me. Tell me why I shouldn't lock you up for attempted murder right now."

The old air conditioner in the wall behind him hummed; the office was cool and comfortable. I spied a pack of cigarettes on Kiley's desk, shook one out, and lit it. Peck shoved a brimming ashtray toward me with his usual look of disapproval. I'd already decided that I wasn't going to try to quit smoking today, so I could eliminate the usual guilt of certain failure. I felt light-headed as the nicotine coursed through my body. I closed my eyes and tried to gather my thoughts.

Peck sat and waited patiently with his huge paws

folded in front of him.

"It started this afternoon when I got home and found a message from Carla on my machine. I'm working on a new book about a psycho with multiple personalities. I spent most of the day talking to a couple of shrinks down in Hyannis."

"Names?" he asked, clicking his gold Cross pen and flipping open his pocket pad. I told him and Peck wrote them down in his little book.

"You still got your pistol permit?"

"Yeah, I'm legal, but Carla wasn't shot, was she? Hey, come on Captain, I don't even carry that thing. It scares me. I'd shoot my own foot off or something."

Peck shook his head and motioned for me to get on with my story. His probing stare made me squirm a tad.

"Not much to tell, really. When I got back to Carla she said she wanted to talk and asked me to drop by her office tonight after eight. We're in the middle of a wonderful lawsuit, you know. She's suing me for my book royalties. She's still into what's hers is hers and what's mine is hers. That's how Carla thinks, Captain."

"She say what she wanted; what her magic solution was?" he asked, inspecting his French cuffs.

"She didn't say much." I took a deep breath. "But I should've known something was up. She was nice to me. Carla was never nice to me, even when we were living together."

I looked at Peck with a small laugh. He didn't smile back, so I continued, "I told her I'd pop over after chow. When she called I was enjoying some serious Chinese food out on my deck watching the tide go out." Peck rolled his eyes.

"Another odd thing, now that I think about it, was that she stressed that I should come after eight."

Peck was quiet. He knew how to listen. I closed my eyes and tried to visualize each move that I had made as I sat there and savored that foul tasting, cigarette. Once I'd finished dinner, I put the top down on my old MGB and roared away from my little paradise by the bay to meet Medusa. I explained to Peck that I had pulled into the parking lot of CDI and saw her black Acura next to the front entrance. I parked the MG, shut off the lights, and got out, leaving my keys in the ignition. I looked up at Peck. He was leaning back in the chair with his eyes closed. He was filing every detail. I continued my story.

"I spotted something shiny leaning against the entrance door, a golf club—probably Shawn's. I knew he kept his clubs in the office in case he could sneak out and play when Carla took off somewhere. I picked up the club by the grip and tossed the damn thing in the bushes near the door. It was dirty so I wiped my hand on my jeans and proceeded into the warehouse. I called out her name, "Carla? You in here?" There was no response. I thought she was there because some of the overhead lights were on and I heard a radio playing. I saw the reflection of the computer screen on the wall, by her desk."

I remember feeling the hairs on the back of my neck stand up—something felt creepy, and I told Peck that.

I went on, "Carla?" I'd called out. But there was still no answer, so I walked around the small partition by her desk and stopped dead.

"There was Carla—face up on the concrete floor. Her mouth was open wide and her eyes were closed. There was a pool of blood around her head, and her chair had been knocked over, as if it had slid out from under her as she fell.

"I looked around to see if there was anyone else there. I saw and heard no one. I knew I had to check for a pulse, even though she looked dead, so I bent down and brushed her bloodied hair back from her neck and tried to find an artery. To my surprise, I found a faint throb under my fingertips, and it was then that I noticed the slight rise and fall of her chest. There was an ugly gash on the side of her head. I found a sweatshirt and wrapped it around her head.

"I straightened up, shaken, and used her desk for support. It was then that I noticed my hands smeared blood on the top of her desk. I remember just staring down at her body, then at my hands. I almost died myself when the phone on her desk rang. I didn't answer it. I just stood there in shock."

"I spun around, startled, as I heard the wail of approaching sirens. I hadn't called 911 yet, so I wondered who had called the police? If I was found here by the body with blood on my hands, I knew I'd have a damn hard time proving I didn't kill Carla."

Peck cleared his throat and broke the spell. I'd almost forgotten he was there. "That's quite a story, Nick. But you are going to have a hard time convincing anyone that you didn't do it. You never made a secret of how you felt about her. Even I know that. And a witness who called in and said you chased Carla into the building. Described your ass to a "T". They even told us what you were wearing."

"That's bull, Captain," I shouted, leaping out of my chair. "I never even talked to her except by phone tonight." I was hovering over the desk facing him in anger. "Who is this witness? I want to see his face."

Peck looked past me and shook his head. I turned and saw two cops watching me from outside the window with their hands on their weapons.

Sit," he commanded quietly. I looked back at the cops and decided that it was a good idea. The cops were still outside the dirty window watching and finally Peck waved them away.

I was in a rage because I knew he was right. Whoever tried to kill Carla must've known about our meeting and planned to pin it on me. It all pointed to me. If I were the cop, there'd be no question in my mind. I sat back in the chair and put my head in my hands.

I took a deep breath and looked up. "Peck, listen to me, please! Whomever made that call is a liar and probably the one behind this. You and I have had our battles in the past, but it was never anything as serious as this. I don't hurt people, and I certainly don't kill them. You know that. "

Peck just stared at me and made a point of looking at his watch.

"You know something, wise guy, I should hang onto you like a winning lottery ticket. But my gut says you're telling it to me straight." He paused to clear his throat and then jabbed a sausage-sized finger at me. "But let me tell you something, my friend, if your ex-wife dies and I don't have a warm body in a cell, I'm coming for you hard and fast. Do we understand each other?"

I was good at nodding by now. I couldn't believe he was letting me go. I got up to leave, but I saw he wasn't finished. "Thomas, I'm only going to say this once. I'll say it slowly so there won't be any remote chance of you misunderstanding me. OK?" He didn't wait for an answer and continued, "Do not, I repeat, do not go nosing around in my investigation or I will put you away for a very long time. Leave the detective work to us and be where we can find your sorry ass. Go, write another book or something, but stay out of my way."

I looked at him and smiled. We both knew there was little chance of that happening.

"You won't even know I'm alive, Captain."

Chapter 5

The afternoon sun washed over the rough-hewn floor of the loft and onto my king-sized bed where I was sprawled out with just a thin sheet over me in a meager attempt of self-imposed respectability. I pried my eyes open and shook my head a few times to clear away the cobwebs of sleep. Christ, I hurt. I've had better hangovers than this.

But it was a beautiful day and that was medicine in itself. A fresh spring breeze blew off the bay and a few circling gulls were crying outside. I heard the waves breaking on the shore, which meant the tide was in. It was either real early or very late afternoon. Through half open eyes, I decided it was a lot later than I wanted it to be and I'd better get up.

I hoped, with little optimism, that it was just a weird nightmare about Carla and Peck after me in some kind of big, jumbled mess. I remember Peck's big head right in my face like one of those odd shaped balloons with funny faces and grotesque smiles that you see at carnivals. But the memory lingered, as dreams do not. It was all very real, right down to the surreal image of Carla sprawled in a pool of bright red blood on the warehouse floor.

Every bone in my body seemed to scream in pain, as the fond memory of being in the back of that police car came back with vivid clarity. I crawled out of bed slowly, nursing an aching back and neck, and padded over to the bay window. No matter how many times I looked out over the water it never got old. I took a deep breath, and the fresh salt air filled my lungs and cleared my head like no other elixir.

Sailboarders crisscrossed a few hundred yards out, while a couple of old fishing trawlers headed toward Provincetown Pier. It was a clear, beautiful afternoon, and people were camped on the beach further down with sun block, kids, dogs, blankets, and Frisbees. That's what Cape Cod is all about.

My rustic little cottage was on an obscure dirt road that wound around through a nest of small hills, scrub pines, and sand on the bayside in North Truro. There was an interesting mix of very expensive summer homes, and a smattering of houses that fit into my category: small, cozy and old. My cottage was set on a small bluff with a great, unhindered view of Provincetown Bay. I had about fifty yards of sand between me and my beloved beach. I'd bought her for a song a couple of years ago from a friend who had had enough of New England's fickle weather and moved down to West Palm. That was the luckiest day of my life.

When I first took possession of Chez Thomas, it was a run-down mess unfit for habitation. The plumbing was old, nasty, and stubborn. It would make obscene noises and then grudgingly spit out rusty water when it felt like it. The wiring was ancient with large white ceramic knobs and switches that scared the hell out of me just looking at it, and there were more holes in the roof than I had pots and pans to catch the drips with. But she was mine, and I loved every rotten inch of her. I've fixed her up slowly and lovingly over time, and I can say proudly that it's comfortable and functional; the toilet works, the roof is new and I can sit at my kitchen table with my morning coffee and newspaper and look out over Provincetown Harbor. Beat that! In my world that's a home run.

I'd gutted the small interior and made it one open room with a stone fireplace on one wall with two worn leather couches in front of it. Upstairs, I'd built a spacious loft bedroom with skylights, huge windows on the side that faces the water, and a slider that led to my deck on the roof. Chris has tried to help me decorate, so there is some degree of taste, but there are some treasures that I'll never part with. For example, I found a ceramic bust of Ernest Hemmingway that I've grown quite fond of and talk to on occasion. He's one of my heroes. And what cottage would be complete without the dusty deer head mounted over the fireplace? Chris freaked when I came home with that treasure, whereupon she happily retreated to her own dwelling. She told me that I should be banned from yard sales. I think that's why we get along so well. She has her own space and her own identity and I have mine. Too many couples lose that when they get wound up with each other.

I showered until the hot water ran out, threw on some shorts and bounded downstairs. Well, maybe I didn't really bound. I'm not sure if I've ever bounded, but the shower did help rejuvenate me. I knew that it would be mere minutes before the first cup of coffee would explode gratefully in my system.

There's a friend of mine who sends me this special blend of coffee from San Francisco that makes your hair stand up and then eventually fall out. On my way down from the loft I decided to treat myself to a full, fat-laden breakfast with all the trimmings: 3 eggs fried Sunnyside up, and a good half pound of greasy bacon, with home fries and toast. I had a brief thought about having my cholesterol checked one of these days. I'd make a note.

The interior of my cottage is rough-hewn post and beam with lots of shelves and nooks packed with books, pictures, and doodads that represent the essence of my life. I've heard that one's home is a testimony of a person's character. I flipped the switch on my stereo on the way by and was rewarded with *In Memory of Elizabeth Reed*, an old Allman Brothers tune that I loved—an era I grew up in and refused to let go.

I froze halfway to the kitchen and saw that my rear slider to the deck was open. I was positive that I'd closed and locked it last night. I quickly scanned the room and called out, "Chris? You here?"

"Hello?" I tried again a little louder over the din of the stereo. Still nothing. Something was wrong. The hairs on the back of my neck stood up as I moved back toward my old roll top desk under the stairway, where I kept my trusty Colt Combat Commander .45 loaded with a full clip. Not a fancy weapon but extremely effective and very noisy, even if you miss. My mouth was dry and my chest pounded, as I slid open the desk drawer. I exhaled when I closed my hand around the cool metal grip. Easing the drawer shut, I crept toward the open sliding-glass door, hugging the wall. The screen was pulled shut and the drapes billowed slightly from the wind.

The stereo was loud enough to alert anyone out on the deck that I was awake. They knew where I was, but I couldn't say the same about them. I put my hand on the handle of the screen slider, when out of the corner of my eye I saw the heavy drape move. I whirled and dropped to one knee, bringing the gun level. There was a screech, and I almost fired when the drapes flew open and Bob, my overweight, perpetually pissed-off tomcat, flew past me in a blur.

I sat back flat on the floor facing the open screen door with my legs sprawled, resting on one arm behind me and breathing hard.

"Bob, don't do that!" I managed to whisper after a moment when my heart started again, and then watched his fat, gray ass disappear up into the loft. "Nice kitty. One of these days I will shoot you."

I scratched my head with the barrel of the .45 and looked outside. Whoever had come in was probably long gone by now. I think the door being left open was a message to let me know that I could be had. My defenses were down, and I didn't expect anything like this. Things were going great with the exception of last night. I didn't think I had done anything to anyone lately that would warrant trouble. I don't do journalism anymore, I write fiction.

Thinking back to last night, I was positive that I'd locked up after I fed Bob, and Chris wouldn't have come in and left the slider open. She's one of those people who checks the coffee pot three times before she leaves the house. So that left me with one option, I'd had an unwanted guest. The scary part was that someone could have been standing over me as I slept, and I wouldn't have known. I made a mental note to keep the .45 under my pillow. It wouldn't be the first time. I'd rig a few surprises in case he decided to come back and try his luck again. I can be creative if necessary.

It was when I went into my small kitchen to start my coffee that I saw the huge Rambo-style knife sticking straight up—dead center in my kitchen table slicing into a photo of Carla. I just stared at it. It was a photo from my album. I left the knife sticking out of the table and searched for the photo album on its usual shelf, found it and returned to the kitchen. I turned to the page and the photo was gone, and in its place were the words "You're next!" printed in precise block letters and underlined: I just stood there with my mouth open. Somebody was playing with me. Must be the same one who tried to kill Carla last night and left me there with my pants down. But, I thought, he can't be all that slick, because Carla was still alive.

I picked up the phone. It was time to take some action.

The man who delivered the food to the woman in the warehouse was scared. More than he had ever been in his whole life. After his delivery he had hidden down at the marshy shore by the marina and watched the cops come and go. He'd watched the helicopter land and then scream off into the night with what must've been the woman strapped to a wire stretcher. That meant that she was probably not dead, yet. She looked dead, that's for sure. He still saw the pool of blood by her head, and he thought he'd watched her long enough to see that she wasn't breathing.

He saw the police handcuff a big guy with dark hair and a mustache and stuff him into a cruiser. The guy looked familiar, but he wasn't sure. It was all so confusing. They would be looking for him soon enough. That much he did know.

Sometime during the hours that he waited, he fell victim to sleep and awoke, startled, as dawn peeled back the darkness and night turned to morning. It was chilly, he was wet from the dew, and he was really hungry. He looked at the parking lot and saw no one. He waited a minute and then made his way toward the road, skirting the parking lot and the marsh.

Chapter 6

I retreated with my cordless phone and a fresh mug of coffee to my favorite place in the whole world, my roof. People of Cape Cod had this great idea of building decks on their roofs so they could have an unobstructed view of the water. I built my deck facing the bay, and made it accessible through both a stairway inside the house and a retractable set of stairs off the side of the deck that led down to the beach. It was shielded on two sides by my roofline, so my kingdom was virtually secluded.

I pulled one of the oversized Adirondack chairs up to the railing and sat with my bare feet up on the rail and decided that it was time to call the hospital to check on Carla.

A snotty nurse in Special Care informed me that all she could divulge over the phone was that Mrs. Thomas was still in critical condition, and that if I wanted more information I would have to talk to 'Doctor'. She breathed the word 'Doctor' as if he were spawned from the great loins of Hypocrites himself. I told her I thought that was a great idea and asked if I could please speak to him. She informed me that

'Doctor' was not in the hospital. By then I was pissed and was not about to ask her when his Highness was due to return to us mere mortals, even though I knew she knew. I hung up more aggravated than relieved. The good news was that Carla was alive. The bad news was that there were people who thought I was the one who tried to kill her.

I dialed C.P.A.C. and asked for Peck. After a few minutes, I was told he was out and due back in an hour. Would I care to leave a message? No I didn't care to, but I knew I'd better, so I did just to let him know I wasn't fleeing the country.

Then I wondered about Chris. I hadn't heard from her all day, and I was beginning to worry. It wasn't like her not to call or show up, especially after what happened last night. I knew her boat was due in sometime after midnight and it was possible that she slept on board *Ulysses*. I dialed the Institute down in Woods Hole where I was told that the *Ulysses* ran late and had just docked about an hour ago. She asked if I wanted to leave a message for Dr. Todd, which was Chris, and I said, "No, that's quite all right." I dialed Chris' pager number and left her a message to call me with a 911 after it.

The phone rang several minutes later.

"Hi honey," I said into the phone.

"I'm not your honey!" It was my good friend, Captain Peck, exuding his usual warmth and good nature.

"What do you want, Thomas?" he growled over the phone.

What is it with people these days? "Nice to hear from you, too, Captain. Just wanted to touch base."

"Thomas, I'm a busy man, and I'm up to my ass explaining to a lot of pissed-off people why you're not behind bars. So what do you want?" There really was a nice man in there somewhere just dying to get out.

I told him about the intruder and Carla's picture with the knife sticking in it. He told me not to touch a thing and that a team would be out shortly, even though there would be little chance of any prints. I thanked him for his time and was rewarded by a loud click. He obviously was not in the mood to bond with me.

The phone rang again almost immediately and thankfully, it was Chris.

"Hi honey, I'm home," she teased. By the sound of her voice, she had not checked her messages.

I sighed and said quietly, "Hi baby. I'm sure glad to hear your voice. I've missed you."

She knew me all too well. "What's wrong, Nick?" she asked, her tone apprehensive, "Are you OK?"

"I'm not sure where to start, and I'd rather bring you up to date in person. Besides, I need a hug."

She hesitated a second and said, "I was going to stop home to freshen up and drop off my bag, but if you need me to come right up I will."

"I do. But go ahead and take the time to grab a few things. I would really appreciate your presence."

"I'll be there as soon as I can," she said. "You gonna be OK till then?"

"I'll be OK, baby. I just need to put my arms around you and tell you how much I love you. That's all."

"Liar," she replied and hung up.

I smiled at the phone and looked out over my domain. The day couldn't have been any clearer, and there was a soft, refreshing wind coming off the bay, so I decided that I was going to stay topside until

Chris arrived.

I needed time to think about what had happened and try to come up with a plan of attack. Chris was the master, though; she had a perceptive way of seeing things. It must be the scientist in her. And she loved to play armchair detective.

I went downstairs to my desk and got my notebook and pen. I need to see things in writing. I spent the next hour recounting last night's and today's events and made a list of suspects. That list had only one name on it. But even as I wrote it down, doubt began to shade my conviction. Shawn Kiley, Carla's not-so-esteemed business partner and whatever else he managed to be, was on the top of my hit parade.

Within the hour Peck's men arrived and tramped through my house, dusting for prints and asking me questions that I couldn't answer. They acted skeptical and almost annoyed at having to come out to my cottage. I asked the detective in charge if he ever awoke to a knife sticking out of his kitchen table? He ignored me, bagged the evidence and left. I retreated back up to my deck and waited for Chris.

I must have dozed off in the warm afternoon sun. I snapped my head up from the throaty sound of Chris's little Jeep as she navigated down my bumpy driveway. I went over to the far side of the deck and looked down just as she pulled in next to my MG.

I loved to watch her when she didn't know it. She had a confident but humble way about her, and she was the only person I ever knew who would stop whatever she was doing to watch a cloud pass or a wild sunset bloom. She always says that she's a student of life and it would be a sin to miss those things. I've come to agree. It's one of the many reasons I love her so much.

She still didn't see me watching her from above as she swung her long, tanned legs out of the jeep and hopped out. Chris was a slender 5'6" with bright green eyes and a happy smile. Her hair, a bouncy light brown, was tied back in a loose ponytail with a red ribbon, and she wore white shorts and a small red halter that accented her rich, deep tan. She worked days on end on the boat, which kept her in superb shape. I knew I was a lucky man indeed.

Chris reached into the back of the jeep and pulled out a grocery bag, and my hopes soared. She was going to cook for me tonight. Actually, we usually cook together and have a lot of fun when we do it. Sometimes we even manage to eat.

"Hey," I called down to her.

She looked up and smiled. "Hey yourself," she yelled back. "Don't move. I'll be right up. Need anything from down here?"

"Just you." It's possible that I might've leered a little.

"And that you shall have soon enough," she laughed, disappearing into the house.

After a long kiss and hug, I told her everything from the beginning. Together we went over the possibilities, again and again. It didn't make sense. Carla must've been mixed up in something shady to cause that attack, but as to why someone was messing with me was another story. The only logical conclusion was that someone was framing me to take the heat off of them.

"Well, what do you think?" I finally asked her.

"Kiley," she replied without hesitation. "It had to be him. He had the most to gain and, Nick honey, you and I both know that they were a little more than partners."

I kissed the top of her head. "I know, and it's not like I'm jealous. I'd be the best man at their wedding if they asked. It's just knowing that the slimy bastard has been laughing at me behind my back the whole time. Kiley thought he had to have her. Well, her got her all right and surprise! It'd be like opening a beautifully wrapped present with ribbons and bows on it and finding a big, nasty tarantula inside."

We both laughed at the thought, but sobered quickly. I continued, "I'll bet he finally had enough of Carla's crap and decided he'd better get rid of her before Karen found out." I felt myself getting hot. "When I get my hands on him he's gonna wish he was dead."

For the remainder of the afternoon, Chris curled up contentedly in my lap with her arms around my neck and head nestled on my shoulder. I looked down and buried my face in her hair. She smelled like apples and cinnamon and I thanked God once again for putting this woman in my life. I sat stroking her hair, gazing out over the bay. Every once in a while she would roll her head and look at me to make sure I was OK. I was.

The afternoon tide had come and gone and most of the beach people had packed it in. The few boats that were anchored nearby were resting on sand and seaweed.

Chris kissed my neck and put her lips to my ear. "Why don't we go down and take a little nap before dinner? What do you say, big boy? Seems like someone I know has some anxiety to burn off." She smiled at me slyly and ran her bare toes along my leg.

That was the best offer I'd had all day. I laughed

and gathered her up in my arms. "Nap time," I proclaimed and threw her over my shoulder.

"My hero," she giggled. "You're so strong."

"Yes I am," I answered, breathing hard, and then I carried her down the narrow stairway to my loft, bumping walls and laughing like a couple of kids.

My psycho cat, Bob, looked up at us in annoyance and padded over to a new warm spot in the fading afternoon sun.

Chapter 7

Much later, we feasted with sensual delight on Porterhouse steaks that were charbroiled pink to perfection, some nice, fat Portobello mushrooms, wild brown rice and oven-toasted French bread. Afterwards, we sat outside, barefoot in the cool evening sand with our mugs of coffee, and watched Mother Nature put the final brush strokes to yet another unique masterpiece.

Brilliant orange and red streaks of sunset burst over Provincetown Harbor in a bold but calming color, as we watched the black smoke from a large oceangoing tug curl up into the horizon. There was a cleansing absence of sound that didn't belong, just the soothing cadence of the waves lapping onto the shore as the evening tide began to creep in, and the echoing cries of a couple of gulls circling above looking for food.

It didn't matter how many times I sat there and watched the sun set, I always felt an incredible awe wash over me. I felt so small, so humble, yet so protected and centered. I think I finally understood my place, or at least a little part of it. My zodiac sign is water. Maybe that explains why I'm lulled and inspired so much by the sea. It had always been my dream to live here on Cape Cod, where I could feel the sea and breathe the air. My mother used to bring me here when I was a kid, and it was a part of my childhood that I never forgot.

I had everything that I needed: Chris, a perfect home, a lot of friends and most of all I had *me* back. And I got all that because I was sober. And now, for some unknown reason, someone was trying to stick me right in the middle of something very ugly and very serious. I felt rage begin to bubble up inside and it was then that I decided it would be a prudent idea to go to an AA meeting. When I shared my building anxiety with Chris she readily concurred.

Chris and I met almost two years ago. I'd gone down to Falmouth because I was working on a book that had a connection to the Oceanographic Institute at Woods Hole. Chris was the project manager of their research ship *Ulysses*, and at first I had a hard time believing that someone so young and attractive could be the project manager of an ocean research ship, but I discovered that she was more than capable, and much sought after in her field. Naturally, I was shocked when she sat down beside me at the AA meeting the next night. We connected easily and became fast friends and much more. It is a nice, small world we live in sometimes.

I closed my eyes and hugged her tighter. She snuggled back and murmured softly, "I love you, Nick. You know that. We'll get through this. We always have."

"I don't deserve you," I said.

"I know," she said, taking a sip from her mug.

I called the hospital before we left for the meeting and was told that there was still no change in Carla's condition. I got the feeling that everyone I talked to over there became guarded once they found out who they were talking with. My curiosity was peaked. What weren't they telling me?

I decided I'd drive down in the morning and stop at Cape Cod Hospital to check on Carla before I saw Peck. It was only a few miles from the C.P.A.C. headquarters in South Yarmouth.

We cleaned up the dishes and headed down to the meeting in Wellfleet in Chris's jeep. The night air was cool and refreshing, and we both were looking forward to the meeting. That night neither of us knew the woman speaking in that church cellar and it really didn't matter much. It just felt good to be there and among friends, although my mind was racing. While the woman told of her climb back from hell and demon rum, I thought of Carla.

Forty-five minutes later Chris nudged me with her elbow, "Hey Sherlock, it's break-time. Do you want to leave?"

I came back blinking, "No. No. I need to be here. Was I that obvious?" I'd been miles away.

"Just to me. I know you," she stroked my hair, which I love. I was a Golden Retriever in my last life.

I leaned over and kissed her. "Come on, let's get some coffee," I said.

I started to get up, but felt a hand clamp like a vise on my shoulder and almost pluck me from my seat. I knew without looking who it was.

"Mac. Am I glad to see you!" I stood and hugged my dearest friend. I was so out of it that I didn't see him come into the meeting. Mac was a fellow drunk, the man who helped me learn how to be me again. He was also a retired state cop who knew and had worked with Peck.

Mac smiled down at me and took a sip of steaming coffee from a Styrofoam cup. He was a tall man, fit, both mentally and physically, with sharp gray eyes, short steel-colored hair and deep brown leather laugh lines around his eyes. He was dressed as always, in L.L. Bean casual, with creased khaki pants and a white polo shirt.

Mac was the guy people talked to when their marriage was crashing, their children sick, or when the bank was calling. He knew how to listen, and he knew how not to judge. That's what made him such a good cop. Mac helped me find my lost humility and faded self-esteem when I surrendered from booze. I have two people in my life that I trust completely and Mac is one of them. Chris is the other.

He wasn't smiling now though. "Peck called me today, Partner," he said quietly to me as he hugged Chris. She pecked his cheek and wandered off.

Mac looked at me and said, "Word has it that you are a heartbeat away from jail, my friend. Peck wants answers, and he thinks you have them." His intelligent eyes searched mine and his expression softened, "You OK, Partner?"

I shook my head, "No, I'm not OK. This whole thing stinks, Mac. It was a setup. Somebody knew I was meeting Carla last night and somebody also knew that we were not on the best of terms. I've been thinking. It's got to be Kiley, Mac. Who else would have anything to gain by killing Carla?"

"Besides you?" he asked me directly.

I stared at him with my mouth open. "Mac, not

you, too?"

Mac put his arm around my shoulders and said, "I had to ask. I know you wouldn't lie to me." He looked around the room before he spoke again, "She was pregnant, Nick. Did you know that? Carla was pregnant."

My mouth was open to say something and it stayed that way. I couldn't form any words.

"Say it ain't so," I managed to say. "That's not funny, Mac. Carla was pregnant? Serious?"

"As a heart attack, my friend, and you're not supposed to know yet. My ass will be Peck's breakfast if he finds out I told you. She aborted the fetus this morning. They figured it was about three months old."

"Jesus Christ, it wasn't mine Mac. Honest. I'd rather sleep with a rattlesnake. I didn't have a clue, and it's not something Carla would share with me over a cup of coffee."

"Didn't think it was, but Peck doesn't share my faith in your character. That man has a long memory and you've painted him into a corner with some of your pre-sober stunts. He's still inclined to haul you in, so don't be surprised if they come knocking."

"Come on, Mac. It's all bull. I wouldn't hurt Carla. I know I'd be the first person they'd look for. I really don't have any burning desire to be someone named Bubba's Valentine in jail. Not over her, that's for sure. Besides I got Chris. Do you think I would ever screw that up? No way, my friend."

Mac's eyes crinkled in a small smile and he squeezed my shoulder. "OK, just so you know what end's up and where it's coming from. Now, what can I do to help, Nick? You need me to do some nosing around, I will. You know that."

"I know, Mac. And I'll probably take you up on that. But first, how about trying to keep Peck off my butt for a few days?"

"I'm retired, Nick, remember? He only called me because he knew you and I are friends and thought I'd talk some sense into your stubborn head. Peck figures you're if you did try to kill Carla you're dangerous. He also figures you're even more dangerous if you're innocent and are trying to run your own little investigation. Don't get in his way, Nick. You know better."

"That I do. But I still think it's that slime Kiley. He's been playing hide the salami with Carla and they weren't exactly discreet about it. Maybe his wife, Karen, finally got wind of that around the same time Carla told Kiley that he was about to become a daddy, and he snapped. It fits, Mac. I wouldn't put much past him."

Mac was back to the no-smile mode, which I didn't like. It meant that he was worried, and Mac didn't usually worry about a whole lot. "It appears that Kiley's got a good alibi, Nick. Peck's checking it out, but from what I heard it's solid."

"I'll bet. What did he come up with? A car full of nuns or maybe his church's whole bowling team? Come on, Mac, with him there's got to be some holes, big holes. I know it. I can feel it." I also felt a knot forming in the pit of my stomach. The reality of it all washed over me as I stood there looking at Mac. I sat back down hard on the metal folding chair and let out a deep breath.

"Christ, Mac, they could hang my ass out to dry if I can't prove someone else was there. You know that?" Of course he did. Mac looked over my shoulder and said with a chuckle, "Don't look now,

Partner, but here comes a perfect example of how small the world can be."

I turned in my chair to see a smiling, freckle-faced Ian Kiley, Shawn's son, making his way over to us. He was fairly new to AA, and I'd spoken with him a few times. I'd even given him my number in case he needed to talk. We alcoholics have to stick together. That's how we stayed sober.

He was tall and sinewy, with neat red-brown hair, hazel eyes and a shy smile. He had the look of a runner. He was about twenty-five, and ironically, I met him through Shawn Kiley. They had come to despise each other so I figured the kid couldn't be all that bad. He was a cop, too. He worked at the Truro Police Dept. up on Rt. 6, and from what I'd heard, he'd been given a choice between unemployment or rehab. He chose AA. He annoyed me for some reason that I couldn't put my finger on. He was too nice, and he smiled way too much. I have a hard time trusting anyone that smiles all the time.

Ian Kiley extended a strong hand and gripped mine, "Hello Nick. It's good to see you. Heard about Carla. Sorry," he murmured, looking like he was going to cry. What the hell was he so sad about? Sometimes he was a little too sincere.

"Yeah, I'm OK. What's doing, Ian? Seen your Old Man around?"

"No, I haven't seen or heard from the son-of-a-bitch," he said with his eyes flashing in anger. I winked at Mac and put my hand on Ian's shoulder, "Relax Kid. You got to work on that anger. Let it go. That stuff's no good for you," I said lightly. "Now in my case, I have a different type of anxiety directed at your old man. All I need is to locate him and I would work through that anger in a different way."

Ian shrugged, looking uncomfortable and distracted, and said, "More than likely you'll find him down at Ray's. He sure as hell wouldn't be home on a Friday night. If you guys only knew the crap he's put my mom through. Well, good luck, Nick, I gotta go." He gave us a small salute and headed off in the direction of the door.

I looked at Mac. "Strange boy, but harmless enough, I think. Hey, I need take a ride over to Ray's. What do you think? Wanna come?"

Mac shook his head and answered with less enthusiasm, "I think you should keep as far away from this whole thing as you can. But I know you better. Just be easy on Kiley and remember Peck's watching you real close."

The chairperson banged the gavel which meant that break was over, so we all sat back down.

⋺⫘⫘⫘ϐ

The old house was finally quiet. He'd finally made it home after hiding under an old boat in the marsh all night and the next day after the woman was found. When the cops and all their people finally left late in the afternoon he crept out of his hiding place and made his way quickly home.

Shit he didn't do nothing to that woman. Just tried to deliver her dinner and there she was. Dead or so he had thought. So he dropped the food and ran out of the warehouse and hid watching while the whole circus went on last night. Pete knew they were gonna blame him—they always did. He never did go back to work.

Now he was home and had to deal with Momma. The old bag must've gone to bed, he thought, with relief. Pete knew that she knew he was down there, but she would never dare follow him. It was the one line she never dared to cross. He told her once that if she ever went down there he'd kill her and they'd never find her body, and she believed him. He hated her, the woman who had given him life.

Tonight, over dried up pork chops and pasty instant potatoes, she'd questioned him about the girl. She saw it on the news and just knew he had something to do with it. She had screamed at him with her foul breath and called him a pervert, called him sick. She didn't know shit. He thought about creeping upstairs and killing her. He was keyed up. His palms were sweaty and his throat was dry. Soon, he thought. Real soon. He would wrap a lamp cord around her wrinkled turkey neck and watch her die slowly. Yes, he would. But he also knew it was just a matter of time before they came after him.

His head hurt. As he took a long pull from the near-empty bottle, the cheap vodka burned with familiarity on its way down ending with its warmth filling his stomach. He loved that feeling and, with it, he felt that familiar stirring in his groin.

He leaned back with his feet up on the battered metal desk that he'd salvaged from work. A dirty bulb hung from a chain over the desk. This was his spot. He opened the bottom drawer almost reverently, knowing that they were in there waiting for him. Nobody else! No one could take them away. He opened one of the well-worn glossy magazines and found the photo that he stuck in the center. It was a dog-eared 8 x 10 color shot of a woman lying on the hood of a slinky black sports car. She had long dark curly hair and wore a white bikini bottom and sexy high-heeled sandals with ankle straps. Her huge brown nipples were erect as she cupped a full breast with one hand and pinched its swollen nipple between her thumb and forefinger. She had her full red lips parted and was blowing him a wet, open-mouthed kiss. She wanted him now! There was some faded writing on the bottom of the picture that was unreadable now but he knew what she had written there for him by heart. He grew hard as he always did when he thought of her.

His breathing quickened as he found himself and called out to her in a hoarse voice, "I'm here, Baby. I'm here for you."

Chapter 8

The next morning, I was ready to rock and roll. Chris had left early to go back down to Falmouth to water her plants, do laundry, and whatever else a woman does.

The first thing I did was to put in my obligatory call to the hospital. This time I was told by a different snotty nurse that there had been no change in Carla's condition. Now, I knew something was up. There was no mention of her being pregnant and no mention of her losing the baby.

I dragged my thermos-sized cup of coffee and the newspaper up to the deck about eight o'clock, which was still a bit late for me. Usually, I was showered, dressed, and fed by seven. I enjoyed the early part of the day.

This part of the Cape came alive slowly, starting with the fishermen stirring on the docks making ready to cast off at dawn, and then as if orchestrated, came the crews who combed the streets, cleaning up the debris left by the stampede of tourists the day and night before. Next was the flurry of workmen and delivery people in vans, trucks, and bicycles.

By eight you could smell the coffee brewing, bacon frying, and eggs cooking.

I sat perched on the wooden railing and sipped my coffee. It was another perfect day. The bay had a nice even chop of white and silver against a brilliant blue sky, looking like thousands of sparkling diamonds spread out on a plush, blue velvet blanket.

But all was not so wonderful in the world of Nick Thomas. I was in deep shit, and I had a lot to do with little time to do it. I just had to figure out where to start. I raised my coffee mug in a silent salute toward the bay and it exploded in my hand. The impact sent me reeling back off the railing and I hit my head on one of the Adirondack chairs, scalding my hands and arms with hot coffee. Dazed, I heard the crack of the second bullet as it splintered the wood railing above my head. I stayed down and tried to see where the shots came from. I felt for blood but found none. I wasn't hit, so I lay flat and waited, my heart pounding in fear. I listened carefully and heard no more shots. Maybe he thought he got me. I went down fast, and it would be hard to see me from the ground.

I raised my head a fraction and looked around in both directions down the beach. Not a soul. I sat up slowly and, out of the corner of my eye, saw a trail of dust about two hundred yards to my left, but I couldn't make out the vehicle on the dirt access road that led away from a small private boat launch. This area is riddled with small hills and bluffs hidden by scrub pines and tall grass, so it would've been easy for someone to climb up on a small hill and wait for me to appear. Whoever it was had a clear shot, with me sitting up on the deck railing like a carnival turkey.

I rolled to my right and flattened my body against

the side of the house, straining to hear any sound. I heard none and prayed the danger was over. I stood and checked myself for damage and saw that I was none the worse for wear. The plastic handle from the coffee mug was still in my hand. I guessed that it was some sort of high-powered rifle with a scope. He shouldn't have missed that shot.

First the knife buried in Carla's picture on my kitchen table and now this. By all rights I should've been dead twice already today.

I looked closely at the railing where the bullet hit and dug the slug out with my pocketknife and dropped it in my pocket. I'd give it to Peck to chew on. Maybe now he'd start believing me. I gave one last look around and went down to call him. I knew Peck'd be thrilled to hear from me, but I wanted answers and he was as good as place as any to start. If I didn't move fast I'd be behind bars before the day was out.

I have two voices that talk to me on a regular basis, neither of which I would admit to in the presence of anybody who possessed the power to put me in a place with all the other people who hear little voices. I have a good voice and a bad voice, both of which I've gone to the extreme of naming and giving personalities. Nichole talks to me constantly. She is beautiful and sexy with a soft seductive whisper that caresses my ears with hot breath and exciting white lies. She even tells me I can drink. All men have a Nichole, just as women have some version of a shirtless, unshaven, sexy bad-boy swimming around inside their heads.

Then there is Nicholas. Nicholas is my practical side, my Superego; Freud calls him our inner policeman who I secretly think works in conjunction with Chris. Nicholas is the one who knows I can't have that one drink, he keeps me sane, honest, and tells me not to listen to Nichole. Right now, Nicholas was telling me to book a seat on the next space shuttle, and I had the feeling he was right on the money!

I dressed casually in my faded jeans, black tee-shirt, and my Miami Vice white-linen sport jacket with the sleeves pushed up. Chris told me that I looked like I was trying to be Don Johnson in that outfit. I happily agreed. I checked myself in the mirror by the door and smiled despite my grim circumstances. I thought I looked pretty good for forty. Chris says that men age better than women. That always makes me feel better. I'm a little under six feet tall, 200 lbs, brown sun-bleached hair with lots gray on the sides, and blue eyes that still have a sparkle most of the time. I studied the man in the mirror and met his gaze evenly. I told him that I wouldn't give up what I have for anything. I'd get through this somehow. I'd been in tighter spots and stayed sober. He agreed.

I grabbed my punch list for the day and headed out to my MG. She was parked in the overhang carport with the ragtop down next to my old Harley Police Special that I'd been restoring for years. I like old stuff. Hell, I am old stuff.

I slid in behind the wheel, and my blood ran cold!

Propped up neatly by the stick shift was a photo of Chris getting out of her Jeep hugging a couple of bags of groceries. The photo was grainy, which told me it had to have been taken by a long lens. This guy was beginning to spook me, and I felt violated. I held up the photo and looked at it closely. I recognized the outfit. It was the same one Chris had on yesterday.

There was a heavy black X over her face and printed across the bottom was, *"Are we having fun yet, Thomas?"*

In frustration I slammed the MG into reverse and spun dirt in all directions. When I got my hands on this guy, he'd be dead meat. Now he's messing with Chris. I sped past Rudy Kemp's place and turned down the boat launch road. I really didn't expect to find much, but I had to look. Parking off to the side, I walked, scanning both sides of the road and saw a single knobby tire track that looked fresh. A few yards further, up on the right; I noticed indentations in the sand leading to a small bluff that was hidden from the road. This must be where he had been. I could feel it. I scaled the small hill, slipping and sinking in the heavy sand, and when I got to the top, I saw a clear, unobstructed view of my deck about seventy-five yards away. The sand was smoothed out and a gleaming rifle cartridge was stuck on a small sprig of scrub brush for all to see. This was one cool customer. I broke off the branch and dropped the shell casing into my pocket along with the slug that I dug out of my deck. Somehow, I knew there'd be no prints.

OK wiseguy, it's my turn now. I'm mad.

The first thing I was going to do was to try to sneak in and poke around Carla's office. I figured Kiley would be blissfully absent on a weekend, without Carla there to ride his butt. I knew there was a key hidden in the rain gutter over the door. I saw Carla use it once, when she misplaced her keys. I hoped it was still there.

Chapter 9

It was a beautiful, clear morning as I roared down Route 6 toward Wellfleet with the top down. I drove in unusual silence for me. Usually, I had the tunes cranking, but I needed the quiet to think. I knew that I was fighting against time on all sides. The mysterious adversary, who was clearly playing a bizarre game of cat mouse with me would only play so long. What did he want me to do? If he wanted to kill me, he'd had at least two easy chances. More than likely, he'd been watching me and getting to know my habits. I surmised he needed me for something else. I also figured that he would soon get restless and want to finish the job. I didn't know the who, what, or why, but I knew he was there. It was really quite simple, him or me. Being a writer, I can put myself inside someone's head and I become that persecuted one or visit that self-justifying sociopath's mind long enough to figure out what he might do next. I prayed this one would make a mistake before anybody else got hurt. And when he did that, I'd be there to nail his ass.

What puzzled me the most was that I couldn't

figure out the motive. Why was Carla attacked, and what in God's name did this guy want with me? I could see Kiley involved in the attempt on Carla, but he sure wasn't smart enough to play this dangerous game. There had to be someone else involved and possibly the two were not even connected. But, I'm not a big believer in coincidences. I'm sure that Carla's secret pregnancy is part of the equation and my money was on Kiley as the proud father.

On the other front was Peck, stoking a slow fire with fantasies of roasting me over it. If Carla died before she could identify her assailant and I couldn't provide a viable alternative, I'd be residing in some jail for a very long time. I didn't find either of these scenarios pleasant.

I turned off Route 6 and slowed through the quaint shop-riddled center of Wellfleet. Art is the heart of this neat little town that has over twenty galleries, each with its own distinct personality and charm. The large houses along Main Street were all well maintained with manicured lawns, lush gardens, and window boxes brimming with brightly colored wildflowers. Even at this hour, small herds of camera-toting, baby-pushing families began to flow steadily, itching to burn up their plastic. People sat cross-legged on the grass outside the coffee shop sipping their French vanilla and munching on huge, warm poppy seed bagels slathered with cream cheese. It was a normal summer morning on Cape Cod.

I downshifted and powered the MG down Bank Street toward the town pier where CDI was located. I loved the throaty roar of the old sports car. When she wanted to run, there was none better. The British made some interesting cars in the fifties and sixties and if maintained lovingly, they gave a lot back. My MGB was tooled in Britain in the vintage year of 1965. She had four strong cylinders, twin side-draft Stromberg carburetors, dual, tuned free-flow Abarth exhaust, and a four-speed transmission with electric overdrive. Over the years, I'd restored her in detail and perfection from her original British Racing Green, all the way down to her chromed wire wheels with bullet shaped knockoffs. The cockpit was all leather and steel with chrome-rimmed Smith gages, wooden shift knob, and the original, mahogany MG steering wheel. She was clothed in black leather seats and rag-top, which was rarely up in good weather.

The dirt parking lot was empty, with the exception of an old Ford van parked in front of the art co-op, so I pulled my MG around the side of the building and parked on the far side of the loading dock, where it would be hidden from the road. Peck would have my testicles mounted on a nice lacquered plaque on his office wall if I got caught doing this, but I figured I had little to lose.

I reached up into the rain gutter for the key and came up empty. The key was gone. I surveyed the door and decided it wouldn't take too much to breech. It took all of fifteen seconds to feed a coat hanger that I'd found in a handy pile of garbage by the dumpster through the old metal door and open it, by hooking onto the crash bar and pulling. I grinned at the warning sign by the door, telling tales of silent alarms, Dobermans, and a high-tech security system. I knew better. The only thing they had here that would bite was Carla, and I knew where she was.

The warehouse was dark, except for hazy shafts of light that spilled onto the dusty floor from the high casement windows. The place was stone cold quiet, almost eerie. I stopped to let my eyes adjust and then made my way toward the office area, where I'd found Carla Thursday night.

The mess of take-out food that had been on the floor by the entrance had been cleaned up and the crime tape was gone. Something nagged at the back of my brain, but I couldn't put my finger on it just yet. The place wasn't bottled up tight because the crime was assault and attempted murder. If Carla had died, or does have the poor taste to die, the cops would be back tearing this place apart. I told myself that I'd be in and out in ten minutes, no more.

I made my way with care, making sure that I didn't impale myself on some of Shawn's junk. When I reached Carla's desk, bare with the exception of her terminal and keyboard, I flicked on the polished brass banker's lamp and sat down. I figured her files were protected so Shawn couldn't snoop around. Carla was into computers before they were cool, and she knew her stuff. But I had a slight advantage. I'd overheard her on the phone one night telling someone that I was so stupid I'd never figure she'd use my name as her pass code.

I turned on the monitor. An immediate prompt asked me for my password. I sat hunched forward over the keyboard and typed in *Nick Thomas*. The screen told me No! I tried again.

Hmmm, I thought. OK Carla, let's try just plain *Nick*. I tried only to be rejected again. Maybe she did fool me after all. I stared at the blinking cursor and then in a moment of divine inspiration typed in *Dickhead* as a joke and hit Enter. That's what she usually called me lately. The screen before me smiled, made little trumpet sounds, and graciously admitted me into OZ.

As smart as Carla liked to think she was, she was very predictable. And I happened to be very lucky. I clicked into MS Word and pulled up her file list. It was a while later, after sorting through dozens of letters to prospective clients, freight carriers and the like, that I found something peculiar.

I found a letter Carla wrote to the Wellfleet Police Department back in April thanking them for rectifying her predicament. What predicament was that? What the hell was this all about? I brought the police letter back up and hit print. The printer hummed and spit out a nice copy that I folded and stuck in my pocket. After I shut her computer down and was poking around in the file cabinets, I found what I had been looking for, the company insurance policy. The two-inch think manila file folder was nothing I had the time to digest here, so I tucked it under my arm, slammed the drawer shut, turned off Carla's desk lamp and left the building.

Some forty minutes later I pulled into the drab, red brick hospital in Hyannis and parked the MG in the shade. I had this ominous feeling of impending doom, as I pushed my way through the circular doors and into the air-conditioned lobby. I should have come down sooner, but I couldn't bring myself to do it, especially once I found out she had been pregnant. I wasn't self-righteous, because we'd been separated for a long time. She went her way and I went mine. But Carla had said, many times, that she never wanted kids. Maybe she didn't know; she couldn't have been far along. I thought back, as I rose in the ancient elevator, to when I saw her last. The best I could figure was a month, maybe more. I avoided her like the plague whenever possible. She didn't look pregnant then.

The doors opened at the third floor, and I stepped out. At the nurse's station directly in front of me, two nurses were looking at one of those metal patient charts. A stern-looking older woman, with hair dyed the color of warm mud, sporting half glasses perched on the tip of her sharp nose and a dark blue sweater draped over her broad shoulders like a cape, was seated behind the counter. She had that special look of intolerance reserved for outsiders, insects, and men. She looked up at me with a scowl.

"Yes?" she scowled. The two nurses stared at me as if I caught them bathing. I flashed my best Nick smile, leaned on the edge of the counter, and asked sweetly, "Is this the Intensive Care Unit?"

The head nurse looked at my arms resting on the counter and up at me with obvious disapproval. I decided that I would stay as is.

"Who might you be, and why are you here leaning on my counter?" she asked me, thumping a pencil on her blotter. I had a problem with rude people and recognized her voice as one of those bitchy nurses I had spoken to yesterday. Maybe she needed a hug. I tried my smile again. "My name is Nick Thomas, and Carla Thomas is the reason I'm leaning on your counter. I'm her husband, and I'd like to see her."

The warden stared at me with a small flicker of fear. You could've cut the tension with a knife. One nurse left abruptly while the other came up and stood behind the head nurse, looking nervous. Did they think I had a machine gun under my coat?

"Ex-husband. And that's just not possible, Sir." Her voice was cold and her stare venomous, pencil still thumping. "The police said you were not to see Ms. Thomas."

I'd had enough of this, so I leaned over and plucked that damn pencil from her hand and snapped it in half, while staring down at her. She didn't flinch. Her eyes locked with mine. I took a deep breath. "OK, I'm her ex-husband, but I will see her one way or another. Do you get my drift?" I was done being nice.

This made her day. What more could she have asked for than a direct confrontation that could turn ugly? "We have orders from the police that nobody is to see her. Do you have a problem understanding that? It is out of our control."

"Nobody," she repeated with a small victory smile. The second nurse returned with a pudgy uniformed security guard who looked scared. I got the impression he was going to draw his flashlight any second. I tried not to smile.

"What's going on here, Mrs. Day? Is this guy giving you trouble?" His voice quivered and he didn't make eye contact with me. I wanted to slap the little toad, but self-control won out. I took a deep breath and tried again.

In a voice that I reserved for small children and the mentally challenged, I said, "Look, my friend, all I want to do is see my wife, excuse me, ex-wife. I'm not here to cause a row. But, you are almost crossing the line. She was brought in here the other night and nobody seems to want to give me any information. Now wouldn't you be concerned if the tables were turned?" I directed the last bit to the trio of nurses standing behind the counter, much like the offensive line of the Green Bay Packers.

The older nurse spoke. "Mr. Thomas, as I have said we have our orders. We were instructed to keep Mrs. Thomas completely isolated and to inform the police when anyone tries to see her or asks about her, which, by the way, we've already done." She looked with satisfaction in the direction of the nurse who had disappeared and then turned back to me with raised eyebrows. She might as well have stuck her tongue out at me. It had the same effect.

"OK, who do I have to talk to? I'm sure we can straighten this out."

"The best thing you can do is to sit tight and wait." A strong young voice said behind me. "Someone will be here directly to answer your questions."

"Directly?" I said, turning. Who the hell says 'Directly', I thought.

I faced a tall officer dressed in a crisp State Police uniform, his hand resting lightly on his holstered gun. He could've been the poster child for the Marine Corps recruiting office. He was young, slim, and alert, with that look of conviction the new young breed of cops have. Trooper Boggs, as his gold name plate above his left pocket stated, had on a razor sharp gray shirt with dark blue accents and piping, with the fierce-looking C.P.A.C. emblem patch on each shoulder. He had the expected aviator sunglasses worn outside of the pocket, and dark blue uniform pants with a gray stripe that were perfectly creased, along with black Cordovans with a mirror finish. I noticed he had unsnapped the polished leather flap of his holster, and I knew he would draw and fire if he felt the situation warranted it. He had that look. Nothing personal. Just business. I also had the feeling that deep down he would really love to shoot somebody.

I had no desire to antagonize this guy so I said to him calmly, "Yes, Sir. Can I assume Captain Peck will be here shortly?"

His eyes didn't flicker as he said, "Please follow me to the waiting area, Sir."

I shrugged and nodded. The nurses snickered as I followed him down the hall. I didn't like the smell of this, but I went in and sat down.

I really wanted a cigarette and looked hopefully over at the trooper who stood by the door of the waiting room. I saw that it was useless. He never smoked a day in his life, and I shouldn't either. I know I promised Chris, but this was different . . . "Are you guarding my wife?" I asked him in an agitated voice. He didn't even look at me. "Come on, I just want to find out what's going on here. I think I have that right."

"You're lucky you're not in jail! Never mind your rights." A voice boomed in the doorway, and I knew my day had just turned to shit in a hurry. In walked Captain Artus Q. Peck in a dark blue pinstripe suit, white shirt and powder blue tie. He stooped as he cleared the doorway and his massive bulk seemed to fill the room. He reminded me of a James Earl Jones type with extreme attitude.

"Trooper, please leave us," Peck commanded, and Boggs left without a word. Imagine a whole army of those guys? I wondered where they put his batteries. I know where I would've put them.

"Morning Captain Peck. I was planning to stop by and to see you."

"How nice for me."

"I came in to see Carla. What the hell is going on? No one will tell me squat."

He eyed me carefully before he spoke, "Not good. They don't expect her to regain consciousness. The head trauma was serious."

"Where's that leave me?"

"With your fly down, my friend. If she dies and I don't have any other suspects, you know who I'm going to look at real hard, don't you?"

I looked at him. He had deep creases that looked like laugh lines at the corners of his eyes making him appear almost kindly. He wasn't as tough as he wanted everybody to think.

I gambled and volunteered, "I heard she was pregnant, Captain. That true?"

He studied me closely and then grabbed a straight-backed chair, pulled it over close to me and sat.

I stayed quiet and waited.

"You didn't know?" He asked, his probing eyes not leaving mine.

"Come on. I swear. I haven't seen Carla in over a month. I haven't even talked with her except the other night when she called me and said she needed to talk. I just assumed that it was about the lawsuit. And, I really don't think I'd be the first one she'd share the joy of her pregnancy with."

Peck stared out the window and then said, "They want me to bring you in now. With the baby in the equation, there's a manslaughter charge hanging."

I jumped out of the chair in frustration and anger and walked to the window. I turned and faced him, "Captain, I swear on all that's holy that I had nothing to do with any of this. I had no reason to attack Carla. Don't get me wrong, there were times I would've loved to strangle her, but I didn't, and wouldn't. Yeah, I walk on the edge sometimes and stick my nose where it doesn't belong, but it's always for the right reasons. I don't go around hurting people."

Peck held up his huge paw and leaned in my

direction. He motioned for me to come back over and sit, which I did. "What have you found out?" he asked me with a sigh. "I know you been sniffing around even though I told you not to."

I outlined the incidents at the beach house, leaving nothing out. I had little to gain by being cryptic with Peck. He wasn't my enemy. I gave him the slugs and shell casings. He was none too happy that I didn't call in the attempt on me up on the deck.

He listened carefully and, when I finished, sat back to collect his thoughts.

"Nick, listen to me carefully. I tend to believe you. It looks as if someone is going to a lot of trouble to spook you. But, the next time something happens, I want you to call it in. I want this all on the record, and I don't want you playing Batman out there. If you find something out, I want to know about it before it reaches your subconscious. Do we understand each other?"

I nodded and smiled. I knew, then, that I was still a free man.

"Captain, I don't mean to tell you your business, but has anyone talked further with that dirtball, Kiley?"

Peck rolled his eyes and said wearily, "Oh yes, our respectable and eager-to-help Mr. Kiley. It seems he's got a solid alibi and he is convinced that you are behind this. But, he and I will talk again. I'm not sure all that spews from his mouth is laden with truth. Just remember, stay out of my way and be where I can find you."

"Thanks, I will. Can I still pop in and see Carla. I feel that I should."

"Yeah, I'll clear it with the desk."

"Please do, that nurse out there is part Doberman."

He chuckled, but then held up a large finger and said in a serious tone, "Remember Thomas, if Carla dies all bets are off. Then you have to come in."

I nodded, thanked him, and scooted out the door while I still could.

❦❦❦❦❦

I stood at the doorway to Carla's private room in semi-darkness. The curtains were closed, so the green glow from the bedside monitor cast an eerie light over her face. I heard it beep intermittently, and I followed the sensor wires to the bed, where they were taped to Carla's head and chest. A green oxygen mask covered most of her face and she wore a white cotton Johnny. Her thick, raven hair was splayed out over her pillow and an IV tube ran to her left arm. Her eyes were closed, and I could see the ever-so-slight rise and fall of her chest. Her breathing was irregular and jagged. The side of her head, where she had been hit, had been shaved and the wound had been bandaged with a generous patch of gauze, secured by white tape.

I stared down at her for the longest time, not knowing what to say. I felt sad. There was a time when we loved each other, and then life happened and we couldn't cope. We just grew apart. She couldn't understand about me being an alcoholic, and her values were far away from mine.

"What did you get yourself into this time, Carla?" I asked her in a soft voice.

I wished that she had answered. It might've made things a whole lot simpler.

Chapter 10

For the remainder of the day I had two priorities, to find and squeeze Carla's slimeball partner, Shawn Kiley, and to have lunch at Rays. I deserved some reward for my troubles and was hoping to combine my quests, because I knew Kiley liked to hang around there. He had delusions of being something of a ladies' man, and I looked forward to finding him for some intimate conversation.

With the top down on the MG, my linen sport coat off, sunglasses on, and some Bob Marley cranking on the stereo, I roared toward P-Town and my friend Ray's club on the bay.

Montego Ray's was a great little place located where the town ends and pier begins in Provincetown. Ray and his wife, Jazz, built a place on the water that had a righteous mix of Key West, Montego Bay, and Cape Cod. They brought the colorful club to life with great Caribbean cooking, a lot of hot Island Reggae and a bunch of good people. I loved Ray and Jazz. They were family.

They ran a tight ship and didn't tolerate any trouble in their place. Ray stood about six foot three with a great, shiny bald-head; sharp raven eyes, and arms the size of Cleveland. He sported a large, gold hoop earring in his left ear and had a gleaming gold tooth smack dab in the middle of his puss. He liked to smile a lot and said the gold tooth gave him character. No one felt the need to argue.

There was very little that went on at the Cape that Ray was not privy to. He always had his ear to the ground and had sort of a tongue-in-cheek, one-hand-washes-the-other relationship with the police. They tended to look the other way about his backroom poker games, and he'd throw them a piece of helpful information occasionally. There was a rumor that Ray was distantly related to Peck, but neither would give any credence to that allegation.

I downshifted and slid the MG onto Route 6A in Truro, which wound along the bay toward Provincetown. I always took this way on my way to Provincetown. It was longer, but it always put me in a good mood. It was crowded with scores of small bright cottages and motels adorned with wild flowers and artsy flags of sunflowers and sailboats, Adirondack chairs, and barbecue grills. It was alive with people walking and riding bikes to and from town or the beaches.

As I tooled along 6A, I thought back to when I first met Ray. It was a few years back when I was a major contributor to Ray's liquor sales. We became fast friends and mortal enemies on the Backgammon board, and in some respects he was a big help in keeping me sober. It was simple. He told me once that if I ever picked up another drink, I wouldn't have to worry about the booze killing me. He'd do it for me, quick and sure. And I believed him with every bone in my body.

The low, open-aired, gray clapboard building was set back on the left at the end of Commercial Street, right on the water by the town Pier. The club was marked by a bright orange neon sign that said: MONTEGO RAY'S ISLAND RETREAT. The catchy sign was flanked "tastefully" on both sides by fluorescent art deco palm trees crowned by a red and green neon parrot perched on top of the "M." The canopied entrance had several hefty potted palm trees on either side that gave the place what Ray proudly called "Island Flavor." Many a drunk had been found tangled up in those palm trees. And yes, I speak from firsthand experience. I pulled in and parked in the reserved area next to Ray's gleaming red '72 Corvette and went in.

The inside of Ray's was more of the same, with lots of bamboo, slow moving ceiling fans, and straw covered booths. There were two live parrots and a couple of white cockatoos in big brass cages behind the bar that talked to you if you were drunk enough to listen. Sweet, jazzy Reggae and the melody of steel drums floated from the Bose sound system at a comfortable level. Ray's had atmosphere with the low lights, Panama fans, ocean smells, and soft music. I paused to let my eyes adjust and spied Ray at the end of the bar chewing on a pencil and studying the sports page with intense concentration. He looked up and rolled his eyes at me.

"Been reading 'bout your ass in the paper, mon," he smiled, showing off plenty of gold. He patted the paper on the bar in front of him.

"Yeah, I'm famous," I answered, hoisting myself up onto the stool next to him. "Get me a tall seltzer with lime, will you? I'm dying." My hand zeroed in on a fresh bowl of beer nuts all on its own. I think they're considered a protein food. Chris told me I had to balance my diet better.   I told you I could justify just almost anything.

The club was quiet, and there were only a few people scattered down the length of the bar getting a head start on a fine liquid lunch. It was a little too early for the legitimate noon crowd. Ray put my seltzer down on a red napkin with palm trees and slid it in front of me.

I studied the napkin. "Ray, be honest with me. Have you ever seen a palm tree on Cape Cod?" I asked. He pointed behind me solemnly. So, I turned and followed his finger to the entrance where the six potted palms sprouted majestically in the sun, and we both burst out laughing.

Ray put down his paper and said, "Couple of cops in here yesterday asking 'bout you. I told them to fuck off. Hope you don't mind. They were pushy, mon. you know me, I don't like cops anyways."

I would have paid to see it. Most people, even cops, were scared of Ray.

"Peck's boys?" I asked.

He got up and popped open an icy bottle of Corona and, with a practiced ceremony, squeezed a fresh lime into it and said, "Sure. Didn't bother to look at their shields. That pissed them off, too. Young studs thought they was TV cops. They lucky I was busy. But you know me, mon. I still found a little time to fuck with 'em. They went away mad. Made my day." He smiled with genuine pleasure.

We both laughed. "What a shame. They say what they wanted?"

Ray shrugged and took a long pull from the Corona that started to look real good. He caught me eyeing the beer and said, "I'll break your arm first.

Don't you even be thinking 'bout any booze now, mon. You behave yourself. He looked at me for a long moment and asked, "You OK?"

"Yeah, just scared. Somebody has gone to a lot of trouble to put me in the middle of this and I have no idea why. And on top of that, he's playing some kind of cat and mouse game with me." I told him about the incidents at the beach house.

He sat and listened. "Want me to poke around, mon?" Ray knew people who knew people. "Guy sounds crazy to me."

I stared at my reflection in the mirror behind the bar and ran a hand through my hair. "He is, Ray, this guy could've killed me at least twice that I know of. It gives me the creeps. The worst part of it was that I never sensed his presence. Ask around quietly, though, Peck doesn't want me near this. He told me that he'd cut my balls off if I got in his way." I laughed and continued, "The problem is, my friend, that if Carla has the bad taste and timing to die before I find out who attacked her and why, Peck's going to bring me in and charge me with two counts of murder one."

"Two counts? What you talking 'bout, mon?"

"She was pregnant."

"What?!! Who was pregnant? I missed something, mon." Ray almost choked on his Corona.

"Carla, Ray. She miscarried in the hospital. Mac told me. He said she was only a few months along. If that."

"Yours?" he asked.

"Don't even joke, man." I said quickly.

Ray looked thoughtful for a moment. "What you think is going down? There gotta be reasons, mon. Too much shit happenin' to be coincidence."

I shrugged my shoulders. "Could be Kiley, that scumbag partner of hers. He could have had a few motives. If Carla was pregnant and he was the proud father, it would make things a little sticky for him at home. Karen would cut his nuts off. Maybe Carla started squeezing him or maybe he was after some kind of insurance payoff from the business. Who knows, man. Speaking of Kiley, you seen him? I think he and I need to have a little talk."

Ray laughed, "Dickhead was in here last night spreading cash around like he won the lotto, mon. Left with some lady I never seen before 'bout midnight. Want me to shake him a bit, Nick, and see what falls out?" He gave me a wicked smile with his gold tooth gleaming. "It'd be my pleasure."

I pictured Ray holding Shawn Kiley by his heels upside down. That would be a sight, but I answered, "No. I'll handle Kiley. I think he's the one behind this, but I don't think he's the shooter. He's not that smart, and his balls aren't big enough. No, I think the shooter was hired help to send me a message. See if you can find anything on that end."

People were starting to filter in from the morning's shopping. The harried husbands headed straight for the bar, while the wives and their miserable kids crammed into booths with their bags of treasure and paired off for the bathrooms. I smelled a sweet aroma from Jazz's kitchen and remembered I was starving.

Ray stood and put his hand on my shoulder. He bent down and said in my ear, "Follow the money, mon. It's always 'bout the money! Even when there be women involved its still 'bout the money. I'll be in touch. Stay safe, mon."

"Thanks Ray. Now how about a menu?"

Ray left me to my thoughts as Jazz served me a lunch fit for a king, or in this case a very tired, confused writer. Ray's wife, Jazz, was quite the character in her own right, animated and larger than life. She usually could be heard either booming with laughter or screaming with rage at one of her employees, all within seconds of each other. She was both loved and feared by all that knew her, especially Ray.

Jazz was an imposing figure carved in deep ebony, with long, black dreadlocks that grew like wild snakes from her head and she carried her bulk of well over two-hundred pounds with the grace of a dancer and the spunk of a teenager. She wore large gold rings on each of her plump fingers, including her thumbs, along with dozens of gold bangle bracelets on each wrist. Jazz always wore a muumuu with a brightly flowered pattern, even in the winter. It was her trademark. This afternoon she was lit up in a sea blue muumuu with loud red and white flowers and fluorescent green sandals on her tiny feet. On her it was poetry.

Jazz did her best to cheer me up with a bowl of her own special lobster bisque followed, with ceremony, by a platter of fresh bay scallops in a light white sauce served over a bed of wild rice and herbs. Lost in my own thoughts, I didn't notice that the place had filled up for the lunch hour. I was swimming in my own maze of daydreams as I ate. Ray put on some old Jimmy Buffett which got quite a cheer from the over-thirty crowd. I never liked Jimmy Buffett, and I never got that "Parrot Head" thing. I laughed to myself and wondered if Jimmy Buffett would give a shit what I thought. Somehow, I doubted it. He was a lot richer than me.

Thinking back on my plight, I couldn't help but feel that I was missing the obvious. There had to be a clue right in front of me, but I was too close to see it. Ray said follow the money. OK. Who would benefit the most from Carla dying? It was a short list, Shawn Kiley and me. I didn't like those odds and for some reason Kiley wasn't acting guilty about anything. That made me a little more than curious.

"Shit!" I said aloud in frustration as I finished my seltzer with lime and pushed back my stool to leave.

"Shit!" Someone echoed back from behind the bar. I snapped my head back around and found the source. Staring back at me from behind the bar, in his huge brass cage was Walter, one of Ray's South American Parrots. "Shit! Awwwwkkkkk!" he screeched again, waiting for a reply from me. "Awwwwkkkk!" He cocked his head to one side waiting for my answer, but I wasn't biting. I was in no mood to banter with a bird. I waved for Ray to bring my check, which I knew, and he knew would be none.

He waved me off, "Later, mon."

The parrot cocked his head again and eyed me suspiciously. He wasn't used to being ignored. I obliged and stuck my tongue out at him as I left.

I swore he called out, "Jerk!" When I pushed through the door. I guess I haven't lost my touch.

I walked out into the bright afternoon and headed toward my MG when I spotted trouble in high heels leaning against the rear fender of my car. It was none other than Katlin Ross. I looked around and spotted her News 3 car across the street by the pier. It was empty, and she appeared to be alone.

But I was careful, nonetheless. I put nothing past her. Hidden cameras and mikes were in the realm of possibility when it came to Katlin Ross.

She was a stunning woman, if you went for the soap opera type, a woman who would never be seen without makeup and her hair done. She had on a peach colored suit, white silk blouse, and open-toed peach pumps that accented her bare tanned legs. The little guy on my left shoulder was saying bad things in my ear. I thought of Chris, and it quickly put things into perspective.

"Hello Nick. Could we please talk?" she asked in her husky voice, straightening up and smoothing her skirt.

"Hello Kate. What a surprise." She could always smell blood, like any good shark.

There was a slight breeze tousling her rich auburn hair. She had an intoxicating aura of perfume, scarves, high heels and sensuality that almost sucked me in a few years back, until I realized that she had a hidden agenda. Katlin thought she could attach herself to some of my success and I here I thought it was my charm and sparkling personality.

Somewhere deep in the recesses of my conscience was a small shred of common sense and intuition that reached up and smacked me in the head just in time.

She met my gaze with a dazzling smile and put her French manicured hand on my arm, "Still a little bitter I see, but I'm not as bad as you like to think, Nicky. I never did anything to hurt you on purpose. Come on, give me your side and I'll tell it like you want it. Please." Katlin paused for effect. "I'm not here to screw you." She looked up at me with a small smile and added, "At least not like that." She ran the tip of her tongue around the outside of her full red lips not taking her eyes from mine.

I swallowed and tried to ignore the obvious. "OK, Kate, listen. There really isn't much to tell. But I'd rather have you hear it from me. Where's your crew?"

She plucked a cell phone from mid air and said, "Give me five minutes."

Chapter 11

What else could I do? I was brief and honest in my interview with Katlin. I told her and a million viewers that I had gone to the warehouse that night to meet with Carla at her request, and found her on the floor bleeding to death. I also told Katlin that some good citizen called the cops, who conveniently found me on the scene with blood on my hands—literally! End of story. No, I had no idea who might've done it, and I didn't know who could've called the police that night. Well, that's not entirely true but I didn't want to scare anyone off just yet. I had my theories.

I thought, as I drove home, about how Katlin left me virtually unscathed. The interview went as promised; unbiased, straightforward, and brief. I wasn't big news anymore, but I had a creepy feeling that wasn't going to last. And I didn't trust Katlin Ross as far as I could throw her.

It felt good to get home, and I looked forward to enjoying rest of the day up at my deck. I changed into shorts, popped in a vintage Neil Young CD, and hauled the thick insurance file I'd found at CDI up to my haven on the roof. I had a feeling some answers lay between the heavy manila covers of the file. I needed some direction, and I really needed to know who was messing with me. When that thought crossed my mind, all of a sudden the roof didn't feel that safe anymore. I looked around and felt a chill. He could be out there watching me right now. "Damn him!" I swore aloud. Now, I wasn't comfortable in my own home.

The cat was sunning his royal keister in the corner and looked over at me with annoyance. I must've woke him up, poor thing. I patted my knee and called, "Come on, Bob. Come on over here. I need a friend right about now."

He stared at me as if I were some sort of insect and then closed his eyes and resumed his laborious task of relaxing. He had it rough.

"Yeah, same to you fella. I'll remember that when you're rubbing your fat ass against my leg for your dinner." He didn't even bother looking up.

I called Chris, filled her in on my day, and told her that I was hunting Kiley tonight. I asked her if she wanted to join me, but she declined. She had a class and needed to catch up on some paperwork, so we agreed to hook up on Saturday for dinner. Chris got a little edgy when I mentioned Katlin Ross. We had no secrets, and I assured her that I loved her, and only her, with all my heart. She grunted, unconvinced, and hung up. Women have this radar thing that men don't.

Next, I dialed the hospital and was informed that there was no change in Mrs. Thomas' condition, and would I like to leave a message for her doctor? I told the woman I did and left my number. I felt helpless and a little guilty for not being more upset about

Carla.

I opened the insurance file and began to sort through a solid ream of legal-ease mumbo jumbo. I've never read an insurance policy in my life. It's just one of those things we all pretend to do but don't have a clue about what the hell it's saying. That's why I wanted Chris to have a look. She was the exception to the pretend-to-read rule. She doesn't even sign a birthday card without reading it thoroughly.

There was a dog-eared business card stapled to the outside cover of the jacket boldly announcing that a Ms. Maxine Gill was a Senior Account Manager for Bay State Life & Casualty. The card listed the main number in Hyannis, but scribbled across the bottom in Carla's open script was a phone number with the word "Cell" in parentheses. That worked for me. I began to feel like a real detective. The P.I. from my novels, Eddie Kane, was stirring in my gut.

I'd learned a long time ago that I didn't have to know everything. All I had to do was find those who did know and play stupid. Most people will tell you anything you need to know if you know how to ask. Hell, when people find out I'm a writer, they tell me their life story complete with graphic details of marriages, sex lives, and any other little nasties without me even prying. I promptly dialed Maxine Gill's cell phone and left my number.

The result was immediate. The young woman who called me back was all sweetness until I told her who I was and asked her about Carla and Shawn's policy. She chilled instantly and informed me that she had told the police everything she knew about the policy and if I wanted to know anything I'd have to ask them. She then told me that she was a very busy woman and didn't appreciate the intrusion. It seemed as if I only attracted people with attitude problems lately.

Through clenched teeth, I managed to ask, "Who is your supervisor, Miss Gill?"

No answer.

I continued, raising my voice a tad for effect, "Know what, lady? I find you rude, offensive, and quite frankly, you're pissing me off. I happen to know a few people down at Bay State. Now how do you want to play this? You really want to find out who I know?" It was sort of true. I knew this guy, Gus, who worked in the mailroom. He was in AA.

There was a marked silence on the line.

"Ms. Gill? You there?"

"I'm here." The voice was smaller.

Now, I almost felt bad. "Look Maxine, could we please meet just for a few minutes? I only need to know a few things, and I promise that I'll never bother you again. OK?"

"I don't seem to have much choice," she answered in a beaten voice.

"No. No, you don't." I continued the bluff.

I suggested a drink at Ray's, but she quickly told me that she didn't frequent bars. Lucky for them. But she did agree to meet me in P-town for coffee after her dinner. She had an appointment, but she would see me punctually at seven.

I hung up the phone and sat back admiring the late afternoon sky and my newly found detective skills when my neighbor, Rudy Kemp, shouted up at me from the beach below.

"Thomas. Hello? Thomas are you up there?" He always sounded irritated, and I loved to feed his fire. I leaned over the railing and smiled down at one of the strangest people I'd ever met.

"Rudy, what a nice surprise. Come on up." He hated to be called Rudy. I lowered the retractable external stairway that was on the side of the house. It operated with a series of pulleys and ropes and I usually kept it up to prevent unwanted guests. Rudy waited with his hands on hips and a scowl on his red face.

I had two neighbors within shouting distance, both of whom I'd become quite fond of in their own respects. Rudy, or Rudolph as he insisted on being called, lived to my right about a hundred yards away in a large weather-beaten house that had been in his family for generations. He was a retired English professor who had been working on the great American novel for at least 10 years, which he admits he'll never finish. He felt the public wasn't educated enough to appreciate his work. He never missed an opportunity to let me know that the type of fiction I wrote was a heinous crime against the English language, and that I should be ashamed to accept money for my labors. That told me he'd read my books.

Rudy was a character of undeterminable age. He was tall and lean, with a perpetually red face, and the whitest shock of hair and eyebrows I had ever seen. He was a strange old bird who had never trusted me because I didn't drink, and he'd said as much many times.

When I bought the cottage, he sent me a formal invitation requesting that I join him for an afternoon of backgammon and cocktails aboard his boat, The *Dickens*. Delighted and curious, I went over expecting an afternoon at sea relaxing aboard a gleaming motor yacht playing backgammon and being served lemonade by a white-coated steward. Let's just say

I was a little surprised when I got to his house. *The Dickens* was an old, rotted, wooden cruiser resting with finality in the sand a few hundred yards from the water, where he'd set up lawn chairs and a card table on its rickety deck. Cocktails consisted of a battered, red cooler that held a couple of six packs of *Coors Lite*. The luncheon fare was in the same vein—a bag of chips, clam dip and a couple of tuna sandwiches with pickle. Actually, it wasn't bad—not what I expected, mind you, but not bad.

I guess it was all in the eye of the beholder. I didn't drink his beer, and I beat the pants off him at backgammon. Consequently, he didn't speak to me for a year, and as I left that day he told me it was un-American not to drink, and that he'd be watching me real close.

On the other side of me was a whole different story. Her name is Regina Lambert. She 's about fifty years old, although you would never guess it by looking at her, with blonde hair, and a body most twenty-year olds would kill for. I wasn't sure where her money came from, but she lived alone, drove an older Mercedes and seldom went anywhere.

I'd spied her running on the beach one morning after I first moved in and hastily ran out to meet her, pretending to be jogging myself. She stopped that morning not even breathing hard, and smiled at me in a way that made me feel naked and fourteen-years-old. WOW! I still remember her standing there, barefoot, with her ash blonde hair in a ponytail, a white tank top exposing a beautifully flat, tanned stomach and white Nike shorts that accented the most perfect set of legs I'd ever laid eyes on. She was a true goddess indeed.

We became good friends and share coffee on her

terrace on occasion. She discretely informed me once, that after two horrendous marriages, she no longer had any interest in men, period-if you get my drift. The standing joke between us was that someday she was going to give me a chance to convert her back. I told her all she had to do was whistle. She laughed and told me she saw that movie, too! But she and Chris became fast friends, so I had to behave myself.

Anyway, Rudy huffed and puffed his way up my stairs and plopped into one of the green Adirondack chairs next to me. He grudgingly accepted some ice tea from the small refrigerator.

"You know, you could keep some beer up here for normal people."

"Don't need the temptation, Rudy. What's up." He never came to visit. Rudy's pure white hair stood straight up from the wind and he reminded me of a tall white chicken. I tactfully kept this observation to myself.

"Something's going on around here, Thomas, and I don't like it. Don't like it at all."

He had my interest. "What do you mean, Rudy?"

"I saw the paper and read about your little incident the other night."

He watched for my reaction, but I remained stoic. "And?"

"Suppose you tell me what's going on, Thomas. I have a right to know if you're a violent sort. We are neighbors. First I read that you are a suspect in attacking that crazy ex-wife of yours and then I hear shooting out here. I heard shooting, Thomas, don't deny it. I called the police, you know." I couldn't see where any of my troubles had anything to do with him, but I humored him.

"Rudy, it's a long story, but the short of it is that I was framed. I did not under any circumstances try to kill Carla and I have no idea who is trying to kill me, if that's what they are trying to do. Yes, someone took some pot shots at me and missed. I don't know who it is and I certainly don't know why."

"Paper says you're the prime suspect," he persisted, drilling me with his red-rimmed eyes. He was like a pit bull.

"Yeah, Yeah." I waved my hand in frustration. "Of course they're going to say that. They don't have anybody else, Rudy. Not yet anyway. But, believe me as I stand here before God, I didn't try to kill Carla."

Rudy had met Carla on several occasions and was quick to pass judgment. "She's no good, Thomas. She probably rubbed somebody the wrong way. God knows she was good at that. I never liked that woman. Fact is I've never liked most women. That's why I 'm not married."

I laughed at his reasoning and then prodded him gently, "Rudy, have you noticed anything unusual around here in the past few days?"

"That's why I'm here," he snapped. "Friday morning as I was going for my paper, I saw a man walking down your driveway. He had a white van with a ladder strapped to it. It was your typical work truck with some sort of lettering on the side. It could've been a cable truck or something like that. At first, I thought you were having some work done. But something about him bothered me. He was dressed all in black like one of them S.W.A.T. fellows you see on TV. Never seen a cable guy dressed like that. A bit odd for August, don't you think?"

I sat up quickly. He had my attention now.

"What did he look like, Rudy? Did you get a good look at him?" I tried to hide my excitement.

"I saw him from behind the first time."

I interrupted him, "The what? Did you see him around here more than once?"

"Twice, so far. Once that morning walking down your driveway and again yesterday down by the boat launch on a motorbike."

"How do you know it was the same man, Rudy? Did you get a good look at his face?"

Rudy held up his bony hand and said, "He had light hair, and he was young. I didn't see his face, but I know people. I could tell that he was young by the way he walked. He seemed quick and strong."

"Christ Rudy, a lot of people have light hair. What's light, Rudy, blond, brown, red?"

"Couldn't say for sure. But it was the same guy, Thomas. I don't care if you believe me or not. Just thought I'd pass it along." He popped out of his chair, finished his tea and slammed the can down on the table. "Got to go. Get some beer, Thomas. Wouldn't kill you."

"Look Rudy," I said getting up with him. "Please let me know if you see this guy or anybody where they don't belong. I've got somebody playing some serious games with me."

He nodded and stormed down the stairs.

CHHB

The cops had come and gone several times in the past few days. Pete knew Momma had called them. He'd listened at the door carefully when they questioned her that afternoon. What she didn't know was that he was close, real close; killing close. He'd hidden his van in the garage next door during the night and slipped in quietly when she was sleeping. The neighbors lived in Florida and wouldn't be back until spring, so he picked the lock on their garage door and parked inside.

He'd heard the cops tell Momma that if she heard from him to give them a call. There were a few questions they'd like to ask. She told them that he was no damn good and never was. Pete controlled his rage when he heard her say these things. He'd kill her soon enough. Yes indeed. Soon!

Pete slugged down some vodka from a fresh bottle and tried to think. As the vodka spread through his body, he felt himself get aroused, but knew there was no time for that. He had to get out of there. It would be just a matter of time before he was found, and he couldn't spend his life in the cellar. He'd just go up and get it over with now. The vodka took the place of reason.

The old woman was in the kitchen making herself dinner with the familiar clattering of pots and pans as she stomped back and forth. He climbed the rickety stairs slowly and tried to turn the doorknob. It wouldn't budge. He tried again. Still wouldn't move. The old bitch locked the door. Did she know he was down there? The kitchen was quiet all of a sudden. He pressed his ear to the door and heard her breathing on the other side.

"Momma? Momma you there? Come on, open up the door, please. It's me," he said. "Open up."

"I'm gonna call the cops. I knew you'd turn up down there, you sick bastard. Just like a rat. You're no good," she screeched through the door. "I'm calling them now."

Pete put his shoulder to the old door and hit it hard. The rotten frame splintered and the door flew open, knocking her backward onto the floor. He cleared the door and stood over her not knowing what to do. She lay there cowering. Her watery eyes softened and she asked him in a small voice, "Don't hurt me. Help me up, please, son. Maybe I can help you." She held a hand out to him.

He stared down at her, confused. What was she saying? She was never nice to him before.

"Please, Petey," she pleaded. "Help me up."

He reached down, took the old woman's withered hand and pulled to her feet.

"Have you eaten?" she asked.

He shook his head and replied, "No, I'm starved."

"Come on, sit down and eat. Then we'll figure out what to do."

Still confused, he sat at the table and noticed that she'd already set two places. She'd known that he was down there the whole time.

Pete ate cautiously and was glad dinner was almost over. He wanted to stuff one of those dried out pork chops down her throat. Momma started in on him as soon as he sat. All she ever did was nag him, and tonight was no exception, grilling him about the girl. He'd expected nothing less. Momma was convinced he had something to do with it, and she was going to stop at nothing short of a confession.

Pete gulped down the last of his milk and got ready to leave the table when Momma clutched his sleeve and pulled him back down to the table. He smelled the stench from her foul breath. "They're going to come back, you know," she hissed, looking him dead in the eyes. "And this time I'm going to tell them the truth about you."

He pulled away, repulsed from the sight and smell of her, "Momma, you're fucking crazy. I didn't do a thing to that woman. I didn't even know her. Leave me alone, will you?" He just wanted to get out of the house. He needed a drink and to be with alone with his girls. It had been a rough day. At least they didn't ask questions. He liked that.

"You think I don't know how sick you are?" she screamed, still holding onto his sleeve.

"I found those magazines, and I know what you do with them. You're a pervert!"

Pete stared at her with his mouth open. She'd never gotten this crazy before, and she wouldn't let go of his arm. Someone would hear her screaming. That was all he needed.

"Momma, let me go! You're wrong. I have to go," he pleaded, ripping his arm away from her. But she was lightning fast for her age and condition, and he was stunned when she bolted up from her chair and came after him. He raised his arms to protect his face as she clawed wildly at him. He felt a warm trickle of blood on his cheek where her first swipe struck him.

"You son of a bitch!" she screamed. "I'll kill you first before you hurt someone else."

She was wild and out of control. He backed up as she lunged at him again, but she caught her leg and fell over one of the kitchen chairs, tipping the table and everything on it on top of him. She scrambled up and came at him with renewed insanity. He felt around him for something to defend himself with and his hand closed around a long bread knife. He tried to push the heavy table away so he could stand but Momma kept coming, and she stumbled again over the leg of a fallen chair, landing on top of him. He could smell her sour breath on his face. He opened his eyes and saw a look of horror in her eyes. Her mouth opened to scream, but thick, crimson blood bubbled out as she slumped on top of him.

Oh my God. He rolled her off of him in horror; the bread knife was buried to the handle in her heavy chest.

No, this couldn't be! His mind screamed. He got up frantically and looked around the kitchen. There was blood all over everything including himself. What to do? She looked dead. He had to think.

Pete moved cautiously to the kitchen window, stepping over Mama's body and looked outside. Nothing out there looked unusual, maybe nobody heard anything. Pete looked back at his mother realizing that he didn't have to hurry. They never had any visitors, and if no one heard the ruckus, he was safe. He needed a drink and happily realized that he could have one right here in the kitchen if he wanted to. The old bag couldn't yell at him now! Pete ran downstairs and retrieved his bottle.

He would wrap Momma in a tarp, clean up the kitchen, and put her downstairs in the cellar until he could figure out what to do. She was heavy, but he carried her down the old stairs to the cellar and put her in the hatchway where it was cooler and she would be out of sight. She'd keep there for a while, he thought. Pete then cleaned up the kitchen as best he could, making extra sure to get the blood off of everything. He even washed the dishes.

He hummed a crazy little tune as he showered and changed his clothes to go out. God, he felt good. He was finally free.

Chapter 12

I whipped up a quick cheeseburger complete with onion and fresh tomato before I ventured into town. Chris suspected how I tortured my body when she wasn't around, but I didn't make it obvious, and she chooses not to pry. I eat healthy when we're together, so she probably figures that's better than nothing.

I put in a quick call to Mac and left a message telling him I was OK and where I'd be if something came up and also called Ray's and talked to Jazz. Ray was off somewhere on one of his "missions" as she called them and wasn't sure when he'd be back. I told her I'd be by later and to keep an eye out for Kiley. She assured me that she'd sit on him, if necessary—and there was no doubt in my mind that she would do exactly that if she had to.

I walked into the small bagel and coffee shop off Commercial St. to meet the apprehensive Ms. Maxine Gill at precisely 6:15 p.m. She'd informed me over the phone that her time was precious. I didn't like this anal-retentive little yuppie already.

I wasn't prepared for the woman who awaited me. A striking brunette with shoulder length hair and gold rimmed glasses gave me a small wave and gestured me over to the corner where she was seated. There were only three small tables in the place so it'd be hard to miss anybody. I wondered how she knew it was I.

I'd seen her somewhere before, but I just couldn't put my finger on it. She was dressed in stone-washed jeans, pumps and a maroon Martha's Vineyard sweatshirt and wore a minimal amount of makeup. She had deep dimples, nice skin. She was a cool package to say the least.

I flashed her my best Nick smile, pulled out one of the white cafe chairs and sat.

"Hi Maxine. Thanks for meeting me. I . . . "

She cut me off, obviously not impressed, "Mr. Thomas . . . "

"Nick! Please, call me Nick," I persisted, still smiling. "Have we met before? You look real familiar." She took an annoyed breath and continued, "Mr. Thomas, let's get to the point, shall we?" She closed her daybook and folded her perfect hands in front of her. I wondered if her nails were real. I wanted to ask but thought better of it. Small talk with this one would be a waste.

"Coffee?" I asked her, undaunted. "Are you sure we've never met?"

"Thank you," she said giving me a level stare. "And no, we've never met. That would be something I'd not forget easily-like eating a bad clam."

I thought it best to leave that alone, so I gestured to the girl behind the counter. The girl was about nineteen, with a masculine haircut, men's shoes and surprisingly enough, a man's voice.

I tried my smile again. "Hi, could we have some coffee?" I looked at my companion and asked her, "Would you like a pastry, or bagel, or something?"

"Just coffee with cream and sugar, and please hurry," she added, looking at the girl and then her gold watch. I got the feeling this woman woke up upset that the day wasn't longer.

I gave up. "Same here. Black."

"Stuff's on the table," our devoted waitress informed me between pops of her gum, and shuffled off.

I must've wasted eight whole seconds while the charming Ms. Gill cleared her throat. She was irritated about being here and did her best to let me know it.

"Don't you ever relax?" I asked, trying to find some thread of humanity under her hard veneer. She took a deep breath and looked at me like I was a child. "Mr. Thomas, you are the one who called me. Now what is it that I can do for you?" I noticed she didn't have a wedding ring on. What a shame.

"In a nutshell, Ms. Gill, I'd like to find out who would benefit the most from my wife's death. Specifically, who would get the money? I know Bay State wrote the policy and that there is some sort of survivorship clause naming her partner the beneficiary. But who else gets a piece of the action? I'm not really insurance savvy."

She looked down at her hands and said, "Ethically it's wrong to discuss this with you."

"But you will."

She continued, "In the event of Mrs. Thomas' death, Mr. Kiley would receive a sum of one million dollars to purchase the deceased's stock in the company. There is also a personal rider naming you as a contingent and also Mr. Kiley's wife, Karen, in case something happens to him."

For a moment she seemed almost human. She picked up her gold pen and tapped it across her full rose-colored lips.

I broke the spell. "So let me get this straight. If Carla dies, Kiley gets a mil?"

"That's correct, Mr. Thomas."

"What would I get?"

"One hundred thousand dollars."

"No shit? Uh, sorry about that." I whistled and sat back trying to digest this. Needless to say, I was shocked. What I couldn't figure out is why Carla had left me anything. Hell, she didn't even like me.

Our waitress thumped the coffee down and disappeared before we could ask her for anything else. I sipped stone cold coffee while I digested this information. Ms. Gill left her coffee untouched. She had culture.

"There's no mistake?" I asked her incredulously.

"No mistake, Mr. Thomas, and Mrs. Kiley would receive the same in the event of her husband's death. It's a standard rider that adds very little to the cost of the policy. Carla even has you insured. Did you know that, Mr. Thomas?"

"No, no I didn't." I thought about this. "OK what happens if I die, too?"

"Mr. Kiley's survivors would collect."

It was complicated, and I could see that she was just about finished when she gathered her daybook and rose to leave.

"Thank you for your time, Ms. Gill."

With a level stare she said, "Don't bother me again, Mr. Thomas. That who-you-know bullshit won't work twice." And with that, she stalked out the door, slamming it behind her. I stared after her. What a bitch. It bothered me that I couldn't place her. I knew we'd met before.

"Must be your smile," said a voice behind me.

I spun around to see our waitress leaning on the counter with a smirk on her face.

I stuck my tongue out at her, swallowed the rest of my cold coffee, and dug in my pocket, unearthing a shiny penny that I placed neatly beside my cup.

I walked the few blocks to Ray's lost in thought. I couldn't, for the life of me, figure why Carla named me as a beneficiary. The only thing I could think of was that she'd done it while we were still married and forgot to change it. She had no other family that I knew of. I had asked a few times and was cut off at the knees. All she told me was that her parents died when she was five or six years old. It was sad to think that I was the only one she had had. But also, in the same stroke of bizarre behavior, she took out a policy on me. That I could understand knowing the way I used to live.

I wanted to go over all this with Chris. She always helped me put things in perspective. But in the meantime, I still wanted to find Kiley to hear his side of this situation. I was going to bait the son-of-a-bitch to see how good he was glued together.

Friday nights in August were hot times at Ray's, and the place was packed. There was a young Reggae band jamming in the corner doing real justice to an old Jimmy Cliff tune, over an ambient roar of loud conversation, laughter, and glasses clinking. If you closed your eyes, the sounds blended, and it almost sounded like the ocean.

I said a few hellos to some of the regulars as I made my way to the back. Ray's corner of the bar by the register was sacred ground that had a certain status involved. Regulars knew not to sit in there and those who didn't know were politely told not to.

Ray loved to brag that he was my personal friend and bodyguard and I was a famous writer. Famous was maybe stretching it a bit, but I kind of liked the bodyguard idea. Ray's "PR" probably sold more books than my publisher's.

Ray's throne in the corner near Jazz's kitchen and the phone, had an unhindered view of the cash register, the front door, and his big screen TV. I usually sat on one of the other two stools with the heavy, wooden arms and crushed velvet seat pads. Jazz was hustling behind the bar screaming at one of the young bar boys who was trying to stock a cooler with beer. Stuff had to be done her way or no way. When Jazz screamed they scurried in fear of their lives. Most of the help they had were Jamaicans, sent by friends and relatives for Ray and Jazz to keep an eye on.

"Hi honey," she blew me a wet kiss and gestured to the stool. "Sit. Ray be here somewhere. He'll be 'roun soon. You hongry? Yes?"

I love Jazz. That day she wore a neon-pink muumuu with green palm trees and brown natives dancing around a fire. On her feet were electric blue sandals with white plastic flowers and her dreadlocks were pulled back with a yellow daisy on each side. Few could pull that outfit off like Jazz did.

"Jazz, you're what dreams are made of," I teased.

She laughed deep and loud and squeezed my arm, "You know it, Nicky baby. Someday, I'll get a hold of your cute little butt and teach you 'bout dreams. You be screamin' my name in your pillow the rest of yo' life. Spoiled for any other woman."

We laughed together, and she put my seltzer with lime on a palm tree and slid it in front of me.

"Your frien' be here, mon. The one you be lookin' for." She pointed to the middle of the long bar, and there, lo and behold, sat Mr. Shawn Kiley in the throws of bullshitting the striking redhead seated beside him. I wanted to wash my hands every time I saw him. He didn't see me and, from the looks of him, he didn't see much, except that poor woman who had the misfortune of choosing that particular barstool. Kiley's white hair was disheveled from combing it back with his beefy hands the way drunks do, and his face was puffy red and sweaty. He had on a black golf shirt that was stretched tight over his ample stomach and over it he wore a rumpled, khaki-colored sport coat. There was a pile of swizzle sticks, crumpled up napkins, and an ashtray stuffed full of butts in front of him, while the rest of the bar was gleaming. I guess Jazz refused to clean up his mess, and he'd sit in it all night. I've seen her do it before to people she didn't like.

Strangely enough, the woman next to Kiley seemed to be listening. Their heads were close together, and his mouth was moving like a guppie trying to eat. I figured it was time to spoil his day, so I got up and pushed my way through the crowd to where he was beached. He didn't see me as I approached, but I picked up his voice several feet away. It was like a hoarse fog horn.

". . . and I've been looking for investment opportunities in the area for some time," he was saying, taking a slurp from his drink and spilling some down the front of his shirt. He looked down and dabbed at it with a bar napkin, grinning like an idiot.

I patted him on the shoulder and said with a wide smile, "Well hello Shawn. Fancy meeting you here. How's the wife? What's her name again? Karen, isn't it?" He opened and closed his mouth a few times without sound. *And I thought he looked like a fish before.*

I turned to his companion and held out my hand, "Hello. My name is Nick. Nick Thomas. I don't believe we've met." Her green eyes twinkled as she looked me over. I felt naked. She was a stunning redhead, on the tall and slender side, somewhere in her forties, I guessed. She was dressed in a white, low-cut tank top, a short denim skirt that rode high up on her tanned thighs, and her feet were bare with perfectly painted toenails. Her short red hair was brushed back in a stylish bob that was carefree and sexy.

She held out a thin hand with beautifully sculptured nails and a single ruby ring on one finger. Her watch was a gold Rolex clone. "My name's Trish." She looked me up and down again purposely. "Nice to meet you, Nick."

Her grip was warm and firm, and her eyes twinkled as she added, "And I don't care if he's married or not. I'm not looking for love." She drilled me with those eyes and said, "At least I wasn't when I came in." She puckered her lips and raised her chin slightly for effect. She was brushing her bare toes along my leg under the bar where Kiley couldn't see. It was real warm in there all of a sudden, and it was hard to breathe. I smiled back at her and nodded. Kiley let out a large belch, and I remembered why I was there.

I cleared my throat and broke the spell, "I just

need a minute of our friend's time here, and then he's all yours. God only knows why." My voice sounded a bit high to me. Jesus, what a woman! She was dangerous. I quickly thought of Chris and it strengthened my resolve.

"What a shame," she said with more than one meaning.

I held her gaze for a moment and then turned my attention back to Kiley. He put a sweaty hand on my arm and hissed in my ear, "What the hell you doing, Thomas?" I smelled a nice bouquet of cigarettes and whiskey on his sour breath. "I got a shot here, and you're trying to screw it up. What gives?"

I had a special smile for people like Kiley. The unaware saw only teeth, the wise watched the eyes. I love that line. I used it in one of my Eddie Kane books. I reached over, still smiling, and peeled his fat thumb off my jacket and back in the direction of his wrist while firmly holding his elbow. Kiley slid off the barstool and onto his knees in about half a second. The sound that escaped his lips was none that I'd ever heard before. Mac had been a cop for many years and a Marine before that, and he'd showed me some of the moves when I was researching one of my earlier books. I was pleasantly surprised that it actually worked.

"Ow...Ow...Shit!   Thomas...Nick, please," he cried. "Come on, man, I was just kidding. Let go of my damn thumb! Will you?"

"Let go! Let go!" screamed the cockatoo in front of us. "Ow, let go."

The people who were standing around us at the bar disappeared in various directions and the crowd got quiet. I glanced down the bar and gave Ray a nod. He turned and resumed making drinks for the waitress in front of him. I let Kiley go and helped him back onto his barstool. Trish caught my eye and hid a giggle behind her hand. Her eyes danced in amusement. I turned back to Kiley.

"OK Shawn, listen up. I'm only going to ask these questions once and if I don't like your answers I'm going to break your fingers one at a time." I moved closer and looked him dead in his bloodshot eyes. What I saw in them was fear and a lot of alcohol. "Are we clear, Shawn. I'm past mad. Somebody, and you better hope to God it's not you, is messing with me big time, and I've lost my sense of humor." He backed up as far as he could against the bar and I was right in his face.

The bar resumed the normal roar and people were thick around us. Trish tapped me on the shoulder and breathed into my ear, "Have a seat, Tiger, I gotta go powder my nose." I nodded and took her stool, and Ray appeared with my seltzer. He looked down disapprovingly at the mess in front of Kiley and then over at me. I was breathing heavy. I wasn't a tough guy. But I was sick of getting jerked around.

"Thought you was gonna need some back up, mon." Ray smiled at Kiley, with his gold tooth gleaming. "But looks like you got things well in hand." With that, he moved off down the bar.

I turned back to Shawn. "So what's it going to be? We gonna play with each other or are you going to come clean with me? I've got a lot of time."

He looked like he was going to be sick. "What you want from me, Thomas? I got rights you know."

I reached over and grabbed the lapel of his greasy sport coat and pulled him toward me. He held up his hands in front of him. "OK. OK. Look, I had nothing to do with Carla getting beat up. I thought it was you. Honest, Nick. The cops know I got an alibi. I'm clean. Honest!"

"You know she was pregnant, Shawn?"

He looked at me in shock for a long moment and then managed to stutter, "Wa...wa...wawait a mi...mi...minute, Thomas. You're not saying it was me. I haven't touched her for a long time. Honest. I swear to God, Nick. I didn't know nothing about no baby!"

His red, florid face was coated in a sheen of sweat and his chalk-white hair was plastered to his head on the sides and sticking up in front. His bloodshot eyes searched mine and then darted back to the bar. He tugged open his shirt some more and reached for his drink. I clamped my hand on his arm and leaned toward him. I'm not a violent guy by any means. I'm a writer, not a fighter, but my adrenaline level was peaked as a result of all that was going on. I just knew Kiley had his slimy hands in this somehow. That I'd bet on, and I wanted to rattle him a bit.

I squeezed his arm and growled in a low voice, "Kiley, listen to me and listen carefully. Someone is shooting at me at my home, and someone is trying to frame me for the assault on Carla. If I find out you have anything to do with any of it, I will personally cut your fat little dick off and feed it to the sharks out on the race. Do you understand?"

He groped himself at the thought. His big sweaty head bobbed back and forth like one of those rear window bobble heads. "Thomas, I swear. Listen man, I'm not gonna lie and say I'll miss the little bitch if she dies. Cause I won't, and neither will you. But, I didn't attack her, and I didn't know she was knocked up." His red face was all contorted and sagging as if he were going to cry.

I felt sick just looking at this flaccid lump of humanity. I saw Trish approaching out of the corner of my eye, so I slid off the barstool. I'd had enough of Kiley for the moment, and besides, he was half shit-faced. I doubted he'd remember our little conversation at all. I pointed my finger at him and pulled the trigger. "Kiley, you be sure and have a nice evening. Remember I'll be around."

Trish gave me a wistful smile and took her stool next to Kiley.

"Leaving us so soon, Nick?" she asked putting her hand on my arm.

"It was really nice meeting you, Trish, but I've got miles to go before I sleep."

Pete needed desperately to think. His life had turned into a royal mess in a hurry. Everything was just fine until that woman had to go and almost get herself killed. Now Momma was dead, and he was sure that he was the prime suspect in the attempted murder of Carla what's-her-name. There was only one smart thing to do, as far as Pete was concerned, and that was to get out of there and fast! If he were lucky, nobody would miss Momma for quite some time. She didn't have any friends, and Pete was the only family she had left. He'd found himself smiling at the thought of the old witch bundled up like a taco in the hatchway of their cellar. Served her right.

Pete knew it was just a matter of time before the cops would be looking for him, to try to pin the attack of that woman on him. Just for convenience sake. All he did was bring over the food that she ordered. That's when he found her laying on the floor all bloody. He panicked, dropped the tray of food, and took off. He didn't go back to work either. It wasn't safe there anymore.

He rubbed his eyes with the back of his hand. Yeah, it was time to move on. But where? And most of all, how? He took what little money he had stashed in the cellar and found another sixty dollars in Momma's secret hiding place. His total fortune amounted to two hundred twenty-six dollars and whatever was in his change jar, which he threw into his bag along with a few odds and ends of clothing. He forgot his most valued possessions in the bottom drawer of the old metal desk in the cellar. He toyed with the idea of going back for them, but his little voice told him it would be too dangerous. He could never go back there. He knew the cops would find the magazines and would think he was a real sick character. The old familiar anger swelled up inside him. He was sick of being made fun of and decided that would not happen again . . . ever! He'd make them pay-all of them.

Pete sat inside his van with his trusty bottle of Popov between his legs, parked in the rear lot of Montego Ray's. He'd only been inside once; the big Jamaican who owned the place scared him. He kept watching Pete as if he were some kind of cockroach.

So, Pete resigned himself to sitting outside in his van in back by the beach, because no one really noticed him there, and he could watch a pretty girl come out the back and walk on the beach now and then. Once, he watched a couple screw right there on the beach behind the bar. He climbed up on the small crest of dune and watched them screw their brains out, not ten feet away, as he lay on his stomach. He saw everything that night, and they saw nothing.

Pete took a long pull on the vodka and felt the warmth spread through his body. God, how he loved that feeling, he thought to himself, as he closed his eyes and leaned his head back on the seat. Maybe this was all a bad dream.

A woman's laughter from the rear exit of the bar brought him back to the present. He looked up and saw a man and a woman walking unsteadily toward a silver van that was parked in the opposite corner of the lot, about sixty feet away from him. The man was leaning heavily on the woman and appeared to be very drunk. Pete laughed quietly to himself. That guy ain't getting much tonight, and then he slumped down a little in his seat so they wouldn't see him watching. The van looked vaguely familiar, and then

Pete put it together. It was the big silver-haired guy from downstairs, the murdered woman's partner. Now, this was interesting.

As the couple neared the van, the big man stumbled and fell, and the woman went crashing down with him, cursing up a storm. "You stupid fuck!" she screamed, as she scrambled to her feet. Then to Pete's surprise, she kicked the man viciously in the head several times. The man on the ground did not move. Pete saw the woman turn back towards the building and raise her hand as if she were motioning someone.

Out of the shadows, a tall thin man strode quickly to where she was standing. Pete could not see either of their features clearly, but what he could see froze him in his seat. Pete slumped further down in his seat to make sure he was not seen and watched in horror. The tall man bent down over the prone figure, rolled him over, and pulled him up by his lapels. Pete saw the Irishman's head loll over to one side as if his neck was broken. The tall man let go of the Irishman and let him fall back onto the gravel. Then, he straightened up quickly and grabbed the woman's arm. Pete heard them talking in hushed urgent tones as they turned and walked quickly around the corner of the building, out of sight. Pete knew there was something wrong here. Shit, he thought, this is all I need. He took another long pull from the bottle, emptying it, and tossed the bottle out of the window into the bushes next to the van.

He looked over and saw that the big Irishman still had not moved. Against his better judgment, he opened the door of his van and climbed out slowly, watching the rear entrance of Montego's with a wary eye. He did not want to be seen. He could feel his heart pounding. He looked around quickly in the direction that the couple had disappeared. Nobody was in sight, so he trotted slowly towards the prone figure. The hairs on the back of his neck were standing up and his mouth was dry as he neared the body. Something told him that he was looking at a dead man, and he should turn around and get the hell out of there. But Pete was never one to listen to that little voice, unless it suited his purpose. He figured alive or dead, the guy probably had a wad of cash and possibly even some credit cards on him that would help him in his escape. Pete's immediate dilemma outweighed any semblance of common sense that he might have had.

The lone spotlight on the back of the building illuminated the back lot just enough so he could see the blood flowing down the Irishman's face and the spreading pool around his head. Pete felt faint and fell to his knees a few feet from the body, fighting the urge to throw up. The man was most certainly dead, with a neat red hole in the center of his forehead. Pete thought that the tall man had cut the Irishman's throat, but the fat man was shot. He didn't hear a shot, and it didn't look like the tall man shot the Irishman. So, who did?

Pete scrambled to his feet and stumbled backward in horror, as he realized he just witnessed a murder, and the killer could be watching him right now. Forgetting all about the dead man's wallet, he turned and ran back to his van. Shit, he thought, if anyone sees me here they'll lock me up and throw away the key, not to mention dear old Momma chilling out in the hatchway.

This has been a day from hell, and it's all that woman's fault. Pete never hurt anyone before. Now he could be wanted for three murders, only one of which he actually committed. It would be the chair for sure.

"Hey you!" Someone yelled. Pete's heart stopped and he glanced over his shoulder as he ran. Two men came out of the bar's rear entrance.

"Nooo." moaned Pete, as he sprinted the last few yards to his van. The men stopped by the prone figure in the parking lot and then looked in his direction, yelling for help. They started to run towards Pete, who reached his van, yanked open the door and scrambled inside. The two men were about twenty feet from him as he gunned the old van to life and slammed it into gear. One of the men reached his door and tried to grab the handle as Pete gave the van gas and fishtailed towards the side driveway, spraying loose rocks, and dirt behind him. He saw the man's face drop out of sight and fall as he swerved away and sped out of the lot. He heard a sickening thud against the side of the van as he accelerated.

Pete didn't see the dark colored Lincoln parked in the driveway until a second before impact. He screamed and threw up his hands to cover his face. There was a blinding light and a terrific explosion as darkness settled over him like a warm blanket on a cold night.

Chapter 13

I saw Carla several fuzzy yards away, her eyes wide, her thick, dark hair splayed like Medusa. She was reaching out toward me—pleading. A harsh stream of bubbles spewed from her mouth, and her face was contorted, as if she were trying to yell something to me underwater. I used all of my energy to swim toward her, but it seemed like the harder I tried, the slower I went. It felt like something held me from behind, an unseen grip pulling me in the opposite direction. It was all so bizarre. She was supposed to be in the hospital in a coma, not out here in the bay. I strained against the heavy current and reached out to her, but she moved further away still, and the cold, murky water made it hard to see her.

My body was numb from the cold, and my lungs screamed for air. I felt myself begin to fade. The little voice in my head told me to swim toward the surface to get air and that I'd have to come back down for her. She was still alive, that much I knew. I looked up and saw the dim light of the surface far above and swam furiously toward it, knowing that I didn't have much time. I looked down to where I had last seen Carla. She had vanished. The water was too dark and cloudy. No matter, I would go back. I had to.

The alarm kept echoing in my head louder and more insistently, so I swam harder, but the surface seemed no closer. I felt panic. My arms and legs wouldn't move anymore, and my chest was about to explode from lack of air. I screamed in desperation and closed my eyes knowing I was about to die. From a place deep within, I found a primal strength. Pushing with all I had, I felt myself break the surface and rise up out of the water with a crash. I was light headed as I gulped the clean sea air, but I was free, and I could breathe.

It was dark, and I was bathed in sweat, gasping for air. I looked around me, confused and disoriented. It was then that I realized that I was sitting up in my bed, and it was the telephone ringing loudly on the nightstand that brought me out of my nightmare. I groped blindly for the cordless phone and picked it up. "Hello?" I whispered hoarsely. I still wasn't completely sure where I was. I saw the moon out over the water through the bay window, so I knew it was still night.

"Thomas? Thomas, wake your ass up. We need to talk, now!" The low, quiet voice chilled me. I was awake now. It was Peck, and my eyes traveled to my clock. The red LED display told me that it was 4:50 a.m.

"Peck, what's wrong with you? It's 4 o'clock in the morning. Don't you have a life?"

"It's almost five. Now shut up, and listen to me."

I did, and what I heard next left me cold and wide-awake.

"Kiley was murdered last night outside of Ray's. We found him in the back parking lot with a nice little hole in his forehead. "

I turned on the light next to the bed, sat up fully, and felt a chill run down my spine. "I just saw him tonight," I said. "He was at Ray's when I left, talking to some red head. Trish was her name, I think."

"That we know, and I also have a whole bunch of people who say you got physical with him at the bar and threatened him. It don't . . ."

"Now wait a damn minute, Peck," I yelled into the phone. "You can't pin that on me! I don't even own a rifle."

"Who said anything about a rifle?"

"OK. Come on, Captain, whoever shot at me used a rifle. Please! I didn't do anything to hurt that son-of-a-bitch. You got to believe that," I pleaded with him. This was getting bad. There went my number one suspect.

I continued, "He was drunk and breathing when I left the club about eight o'clock. Ray will tell you that."

"He did, but I've got to bring you in. I'm getting pressure, and this makes two dead bodies with nobody to answer, and you seem to be in the middle of it all. Not a situation I like. Especially in the middle of tourist season."

"Come on, Peck. I'm being framed here from all directions. I didn't even know about any baby until yesterday, and I sure as hell wouldn't want to kill the main suspect."

"So you say," he said quietly. "Right now you're my main suspect." The line was silent and my head was spinning. I paced the loft in my underwear, frustrated, and not knowing what to say. "Captain, you've known me a long time. Do you really think I'd pull something like this and stick around for the posse? Hell, I'm a writer, not a hit man."

"Don't matter what I think, son, you're now an official suspect in one case of manslaughter and one homicide, and the law says that I got to bring your ass in. Now do you want me to send a car, or will you drive down on your own in the morning?"

"It is morning," I grumbled. "I'll come in. You don't need to send anybody to get me. I'm innocent for Christ's sake! You believe that, don't you?"

The line was quiet for a long second. "Be here by nine," he said and hung up abruptly.

I stood there with the cordless in my hand and looked out my side window down at the road. In the early, gray light of dawn I saw a dark Ford sedan with a whip antenna parked off to the side of the road about a hundred yards away. Artus Peck never took chances.

I sat up on the roof, bundled up in my old sweats and slippers, with my mug of coffee, and watched the sun come up over the bay. It was 6 a.m., and I was trying to find a reason not to disappear off the face of the Earth, and get roaring drunk. Whatever was going on had me completely baffled, conclusively implicated, and totally frustrated.

I thought back to a few weekends ago when life was good, and I remembered a perfect Saturday when Chris and I took our small sailboat, *Serenity*, out for the day. The water was calm, the wind steady, and we'd packed a bountiful lunch of cold chicken, potato salad, French bread, and love. It was a beautiful August day; we made love in the sun, fed each other a sensual and messy lunch, and then fell asleep in each other's arms anchored in a small cove south of Wellfleet. It didn't get any better than that. It was that day that Chris helped me rough out the plot line for my new book, In the Eyes of Madness. It seemed to be shaping up as a psycho-suspense thriller in which Eddie Kane stumbles over a very nasty character that has a full-blown case of Multiple Personality Disorder. Chris loved to help me with the books and admittedly, she has great insight and imagination when it comes to weaving unusual plots. I always tell her she has a suppressed dark side. She tells me to stick to writing and leave the psychoanalysis to the qualified eggheads. And as usual, I nobly concur.

I didn't revel in my paradise long before going back to the insanity of the present. I wasn't sure what was happening to me, but one thing I did know was that whoever was behind the curtain pulling the strings was damn good at it. It was as if he knew every move I was going to make, and he had the stage already set for his next episode of skillful deception. And I seemed to be playing right into his hands. I almost admired him, but I remembered vividly Carla lying in a coma and Kiley chilling nicely in rigor down at the morgue. No, whoever this guy was, he wasn't nice, and I think I know now why he hasn't killed me yet. The son-of-a-bitch is setting me up to take the fall for this whole mess. So, whoever was behind this had something to gain. OK, it made sense so far. Now what do most people lust for besides sex? It had to be the money. I needed to know the "why", and then I'd be able to work backward.

"Follow the money," Ray had told me. That made sense.

I've always wanted to know how the criminal mind worked to make my writing more credible, so I dug around and found that the majority of master criminals were people of extreme focus and determination. Now I was dealing with someone who lived on that higher level, and it looked like I was smack dab in the middle of one of my own mysteries. A mastermind, of the type that I'd create from the bowels of my own personality, was pulling the strings from behind some elaborate stage. What would Eddie Kane do? Eddie was a hard-ass with the luck of an Irishman and the insight of a good woman. He could always manage to separate himself from the eye of the storm and see the whole picture. Eddie's philosophy was that all crime was simple if you could sift through all the smoke and find the real motivation. And from there it was easy to see who would benefit the most. Where would Eddie look in this case? My first thought was Kiley, but now he had the bad timing to wind up dead. So, who was next? Ray said follow the money. Ray had the primal simplicity to see things without a lot of complication.

My heart pumped pure adrenaline as I realized just how real this was and that it was up to me to figure it out so I wouldn't go to jail. There was a degree of excitement from the danger. I'll get you whoever you are, I promised myself. Oh yes, I will!

I stood up, paced the deck, and leaned against the rail facing the morning tide. The wind was soft and cool on my face as I took a deep breath and closed my eyes. I heard the surf lapping on the sand below and the echoing cries of a couple of hungry gulls.

I loved this place more than anywhere on this Earth. Now, some son-of-a-bitch was trying to destroy it for me. I paced some more and looked around the side of the house toward the road. I saw that the blue Crown Victoria was still there. I couldn't see if there was anyone in the car or not, but I assumed there was. They were waiting for me to fire up the MG and head down to South Yarmouth to turn myself in. I don't think so fellas. All of a sudden, that seemed like a poor option to me. I was the one who had to find the motive before they locked me up and threw away the key.

I slammed my empty mug down on the spool table next to my chair in anxiety. I had to do I something, and I needed to do it fast. I figured whoever was behind this was smart enough to wrap me up in a nice package complete with a ribbon, for the cops to put me away for a long, long time. Especially now that I knew about the insurance Carla had set up for me. I'd bet my last dollar that Peck knew all about the insurance. That would be the first place he'd look to for motive, money, and maybe jealousy or revenge! It was no state secret how I felt about Carla and her wicked ways. The only thing I was counting on was that Peck knew me well enough to know I'm not money driven and I really didn't care about what Carla did. I was happy. I had decent income from the Eddie Kane series, so I had no burning need for Carla's insurance money, and I had the woman of my dreams in Chris. There wasn't much in this world that would motivate me to throw all that away.

I went back to what Ray had told me about following the money trail. It made sense. But who here was to gain beside myself? I had to admit that if I were on the outside looking in, I'd be the prime suspect, with more than one motive.

I tossed this around in my head as I showered

and from the far recesses of my mind the beginnings of a plan formed. It was at that moment that I made one of the bolder decisions of my life. Notice that I didn't say smarter.

Chapter 14

I think when most of us were young, each of us felt that we were destined for great things, whether it be riches, fame, glory, or something else that drove us on. We all needed dreams, otherwise what would be the sense of getting up each morning to take the daily pounding that life gives us?

I had my dream, and I still do. My vision is to become a great writer—one of literary importance. The Eddie Kane books have paid the bills, and they've also helped me to become a better writer. We have to believe in ourselves, and we have to keep walking toward the light. These things drive me forward. I resolved that I would not let this insane situation, or any other like it, run me off the road. It's all in the perception of the problem and the real trick is in how well you deal with it. I've come too far to dive back into the bottle, and I sure as hell wasn't going to jail for something I didn't do.

I figured that since I wasn't going down to turn myself in just yet, I'd better make good use of what time I did have. I knew I couldn't elude Peck for very long, especially when he's as mad as he's going to be when he learns that I gave his men the slip. I made a note to call him a little later and try to explain. Maybe some flowers would do the trick, I thought with a chuckle.

I dressed quickly in my standard faded blue jeans, black polo shirt, and topsiders without socks. I briefly thought of the .45 downstairs in the desk, but I put that thought out of my head completely. All Peck would need is to find me running around with a gun.

An absurd vision came to me with shocking clarity, of Artus Peck in a loincloth, dancing around a fire, and chanting my name as he stoked the flames to the sound of thundering drums and screaming natives. And there I was, bound, gagged, and naked on a huge wooden spit, waiting to be roasted for dinner. I shook this unpleasant thought from my head and got ready to leave the cottage. If a shrink ever got into my head, I'd be in deep shit. There are things that pop into my mind that I can't even tell Chris. This thing about Peck and the chanting natives would certainly raise some questions regarding my sanity.

My plan was to slip out the back and go down the beach toward P-Town where I figured I could get a set of wheels from Ray. Then I could solve this caper on my own, restore my sterling reputation, and live happily ever after. To be quite honest I wasn't that optimistic about any of it. More than likely, I'd either get arrested, shot, or possibly both.

It was almost 7:30 a.m. I knew I'd best be on my way before Peck's men started getting antsy and charged up to the cottage to get me. I grabbed a windbreaker, my leather briefcase, and my cell phone. I figured I'd need that stuff if I was going underground. I smiled to myself. This was it! I <u>was</u> Eddie Kane, private investigator, solver of heinous crimes; and we had a plan.

It was time to pay the widow Kiley a visit.

Let me tell you what I do know about Karen Kiley. She was born and raised in a small town in upstate New York where she met Shawn in high school, pledged her undying love, and married him when she turned eighteen. She was deflowered in the back of a 1949 Buick Roadmaster that Shawn had borrowed from his uncle one Saturday, and she has never been with another man to this day. This last piece of intelligence was from Shawn, who was shooting off his fat mouth down at Ray's one day. I happen to know a whole different side to Mrs. Karen Kiley that Shawn Kiley will never know in his present refrigerated condition. I realized that I liked him a whole lot better now.

The first part about Karen was true. They did meet in high school somewhere up in the far reaches of the Adirondacks. They fell in lust and were married at the wise age of eighteen. Shawn then decided to leave New York and set out for fame and fortune with poor, innocent, and a very pregnant Karen in tow. I'm not sure how he ended up on Cape Cod or why. The relevant part was that they came into my life a few years after Carla and I married. Somehow he slithered under the door and convinced Carla they would make a good team in a business venture. I didn't realize what was going on because I was still functioning in altered states. Most of the time back then everything was a painful blur. To make a long, complicated story short, he ended up screwing Carla in more ways than one and left poor Karen home by her lonesome self most of the time. Rumor had it that Karen took to entertaining anything that would come near her house, and she did it well and quite often, from what I'd heard.

When I first met Karen Kiley, she was a quiet, demure brunette with straight shoulder-length hair, huge doe eyes, and penny loafers. And I would've bet my 401k that she had a poodle skirt somewhere in her closet. She was the kind of woman you feel guilty swearing around. After a few years of neglect from her betrothed and a secret emancipation after the kids had grown up and set out on their own, she'd managed to transform herself gradually right in front of Shawn's unobservant eyes. He never noticed because he was so wrapped up in Carla that he couldn't see straight. By that time, I'd already left, gotten sober and was writing my first Eddie Kane novel. And the next time I saw her was at Ray's, and I almost fell off my stool.

I remember that day as if it were yesterday. It was a lazy Saturday afternoon. Ray and I were locked in mortal combat over the backgammon board and in strolls this doll that stopped everything including the clocks. This babe strutted into the bar wearing skin tight jeans, black leather knee-high boots with spike heels, and a billowy, white, almost completely transparent blouse that accented the biggest, hardest nipples I'd ever seen. She had wild brown hair that curled around her face and down her back, and she strutted in with the swagger of a porn star. Even the damn birds behind the bar whistled at her. She came straight down the bar toward us with a wide smile and a look of total recognition that puzzled the hell out of me. I looked at Ray and he shrugged. He didn't know her. She walked right up to me. And when I finally pried my eyes up to her face, I just stared.

Holy shit! I knew that face. It was none other than Karen Kiley-Shawn's mousy wife. Well let me tell you there was nothing mousy about this lady! She looked like a band of renegade Frederick's models had kidnapped her for a weekend and performed a major overhaul. And I never would've dreamed she had a body like that.

She stood in front of me with a hand on her hip and two fully erect nipples. My attention was hers.

"Buy a girl a drink, Sailor?" she cooed with a sly smile.

"Karen. How...Hi...I mean...Wow! You look great!" I stammered. "I didn't recognize you." I occasionally had some trouble speaking English.

"Hi, Nick," she breathed in a huskier voice than I remembered. "What ever do you mean?" She put her arm around me and kissed me on the cheek. Her heavy breasts with those swollen nipples brushed up against me through the thin fabric of her blouse as she spoke. Her breath was hot and sweet. I opened my mouth a few times, but no sound came out. Why was I always being tested?

Ray saved me. "Wan sometin' to drink sexy lady?"

She circled her lips with her tongue while still looking at me and said to Ray, "Surprise me. Something tall and cool with an umbrella and maybe a cherry."

"Yo Jus sit tight. Comin' right up, Darlin. I put two cherries in just for you." Ray chuckled and disappeared down the bar to make her cocktail. The white Cockatoo in the gilded cage whistled again.

"Awwwkkk. Sexy lady. Awwwkkk!" and he hid his head under his wing.

"Well Karen, what brings you down here?

Where's Shawn?"

Her eyes locked into mine and said casually, "Oh, he's probably somewhere with your wife, and you know what? I couldn't care less, Nicky."

"With your wife, awwwkkk. Sexy lady. awwwkkk!" I shot the bird a murderous look, and he prudently retreated back under his wing. I remember the way Karen said it—cool, calm, and matter of fact. I could still smell the musky scent of her perfume and see the raw animal in her mannerisms.

"How nice," I'd said with the same irony. "I've always said it's good to know where your spouse is. Don't you agree?" I think she tried to shock me. Hell, I knew that Shawn and Carla were playing hide the salami a long time ago. It was no surprise, and it was I who couldn't have cared less.

That was the way Karen was: hot, horny, and very direct. As a matter of fact, she mentioned she would welcome some company that afternoon if I were available. I gallantly declined and called Chris as soon as I was able to stand and dial a phone. That chance meeting was a couple of years ago, and I've bumped into Karen on occasion, usually with some different young guy in tow. She always gave me that flirty smile as if to say, "You don't know what you missed!"

It took me the better part of an hour to walk the beach into P-Town from my cottage. I kept looking back, expecting to see Peck come screaming down the beach in his shiny, new Bell-Ranger helicopter, but I guess I didn't rate that level of intensity just yet. I figured he must have had his men go up to my house and check on me by now, and he must've been one pissed-off dude when he found out I was gone. I fingered the cell phone in my jacket and decided to wait to call him. I wasn't ready for the lesson in profanity that I knew I'd hear. And it was possible that he didn't know I had given his boys the slip yet. I thought about that a minute and laughed to myself. If I were those guys, I don't think I'd call him right away. I'd try to find me first. Calling Captain Artus Peck would be my last option.

When I finally reached *Montego's*, I managed to commandeer the old Jeep Cherokee that Ray kept at the club for utility purposes from Jazz. She knew not to ask a lot of questions and told me that Ray was off doing some "bidness" somewhere and wouldn't be back till later in the afternoon. I gave Jazz a note for Ray explaining what I needed him to check out for me, and I told her I'd call later and explain what I was up to. She patted me on the ass and told me to be careful. If she only knew what I had in mind . . . .

I played back the tapes in my head from the last several days over and over as I drove out toward the Kiley's modest house in Wellfleet. Now that Shawn was dead, my original theory was shot to hell. Or was it? The possibility did exist that he was the one who tried to kill Carla for reasons only I could understand. It sure was a sloppy attempt and would certainly fit his character. But, it also could be someone who'd calculated the layers of confusion and possible motives by involving me and, the now properly chilled, Shawn Kiley. The one thing I was sure of was that Kiley wasn't smart enough or brave enough to be behind those little encounters at my cottage. Someone else had to be involved and was pulling the strings.

I reached over and flipped on the radio. I wanted to hear some news, but it never fails; when you want music, every channel on the dial has some stupid commercial or news. I found Michael Bolton wailing in chronic abdominal pain, then some consistently nauseating Hootie and the Blowhards, and then on to some primal screaming that scared even me. To my relief, I finally found a station out of Hyannis that had on some news. And guess what? I was the news!

An excited news jockey reported that Mr. Shawn Kiley of Wellfleet was found shot to death outside a fashionable Provincetown nightclub (Ray is going to love that one). Nick Thomas, a local mystery writer who lived in Truro, was the prime suspect in the shooting, as well as being connected to a felonious assault on his estranged wife a few days ago. The announcer went on to say that a high caliber hunting rifle, believed to be of the same type used in the Kiley murder, was found in a cursory search of the suspect's home earlier this morning. So far, the suspect had eluded police and was considered armed and dangerous. The lad was then kind enough to give a fairly good description of me and happily recited the emergency number at C.P.A.C. if someone spotted me.

Midway through the news spot, I pulled Ray's jeep off the road onto a sandy spot with some overhanging trees and just sat staring at my hands on the steering wheel, stunned with disbelief. Stick a fork in me; I was done! Armed and dangerous with what? My cell phone? I didn't even own a rifle. My head was spinning. Christ, three days ago I had a life second to none. Now, it seemed that I was a fugitive wanted for murder, and I didn't feel like the crime-busting and dauntless Eddie Kane any longer. My short-lived bravado had vanished.

I banged my fist on the steering wheel and swore. What was I going to do now? It wouldn't take the cops long to figure out that I'd headed into town and probably went to Ray's, but I knew Jazz wouldn't give them the time of day; she hated cops. So, I thought that I was probably safe in the Jeep for the time being and after serious deliberation I decided to visit Karen Kiley just the same. What did I have to lose?

Something kept nagging at the back of my mind, but I couldn't put my finger on it. My little voice told me I had all the answers. I just didn't know it yet. I slammed the Jeep into gear and got back onto Rt. 6 heading toward Wellfleet. I shut the radio off, having decided I'd had enough cheer for awhile.

I was lucky enough to have been a guest at the Kiley estate several times when Carla and I still functioned as a married couple, so I knew exactly where it was. I pulled off Route 6 onto a series of small hilly lanes that led out toward the bay, and I recognized the Kiley's small, ramshackle cape immediately by the overgrown condition of the lawn and Shawn's dirty, silver van parked next to the garage. The driveway was dirt and deeply rutted with patches of spotty brown grass. The lawn looked exactly the same. The house was a faded and peeling coral blue with black shutters and dirty windows. The front screen door stood ajar minus the screen and any semblance of paint; a domicile certain to be noted in some future issue of Better Homes and Gardens. I parked the jeep up close to the van and sat for a moment to collect my thoughts. What was I going to say to Karen? Would she call the cops on me? That I doubted, but you never knew.

I took a deep breath and got out. I thought I'd start by offering my condolences and hoped she believed my sincerity. I navigated my way up the crumbling brick walkway, elbowed open the screen door and rang the doorbell several times. It never occurred to me that she wouldn't be home, but the house was silent and no one answered the bell. I knocked loudly and waited. Still nothing. Oh well, I'd come back later if I weren't in jail.

As I turned to leave, I heard a horn honk and a sleek, black Mustang 5.0 convertible roared into the driveway with Karen Kiley behind the wheel. She parked, shut off the powerful motor, and looked over at me with a wide smile. The top was down, so her hair was windblown and wild.

"Well, well, look who's come knocking," she said, leaning back in her seat, stretching like a cat and taking off her sunglasses.

Said the spider to the fly, I thought to myself. "Hey, Karen, how you doing?" I called from the walk.

"Nicky come to console the poor widow?" she mocked puckering her lips a bit.

"Please, Karen, I need to talk to you." I tried to appeal to any sympathetic side she might have hidden under that slick, barracuda skin.

She smiled, opened her door, and got slowly out of the Mustang, showing plenty of well-shaped leg, sans stockings, with a short denim skirt, black high-heel pumps, and a white tank top that accented those famous nipples I mentioned before. She was a breed of cat that was very aware of her sexuality. She made me very uncomfortable, and I knew that I had to set some boundaries with this woman if I was going to get anywhere besides in deeper trouble.

I took her hand and as I helped her out of the car, she leaned into me and gave me a warm, wet kiss on the lips. "I'm glad you're here, Nicky. I need a friend," she breathed and held me close. I smelled booze on her breath. It was warm and thick smelling. Nick Jr. immediately responded, to my dismay.

Why am I always being tested? I pulled away and managed to say in a fairly controlled voice, "Karen we need to talk. It's important."

She looked into my eyes for a long moment and then grabbed my hand. "Come on, Nicky. We need a drink."

I started to protest, but thought better of it as she led me up the brick walk to the house. I'd deal with the drink thing inside.

She pulled me into a small and cluttered living room and showed me the couch. "Sit. I'll be back in a sec. Gotta go powder my nose and get a cocktail. Want one?" She asked me with a mocking smile. She knew I didn't drink.

I shook my head and sank into the couch. I was tired and emotionally drained. "I'll be here. Take your time."

After she disappeared down the hall, I closed my eyes and tried to stop my head from spinning. I was thinking hard about that drink. It would be easy to slip back there now. Just one. Yeah, right! There's never just one for an alcoholic. That old saying rings true. 'One's too many and a thousand is not enough.' I knew all too well that a drink was always but an arm's length away—just a slight raise of my hand or a quick nod at the waiting bartender, and my troubles would fade for that moment. Whenever my mind went there, I could feel the fire of tequila gold spreading in my gut and the warm glow it would bring. But I also knew what else lay inside that serpentine package. Alcoholism, the only disease that tells you that you don't have a disease, it waits with the patience of death and the seductiveness of a woman for those of us who have dared to defect.

I've pictured the showdown a thousand times over the past five years. I'd slip into some dark, smoky, pub where I knew no one and stare across the bar at those gleaming rows of colored poison. But, I'd see that man peaking back at me in the mirror behind those bottles. I knew I could never look him in the eye again if I picked up that drink.

I don't know what it would take for me to lose that battle, but I pray hard and often for strength when that moment might arrive. And if I lost that battle, I could simply hand the knowing barkeep the keys to my car, the deed to my cottage and whatever else I hold of value, because I know alcohol would take it back from me quick enough if I lost that battle of wills. Sadly, I also knew that Chris would be gone, too! That was not an option.

I opened my eyes and was startled when I saw Karen leaning in the doorway sipping a drink, watching me. I hadn't heard her come back. Her eyes danced at me from over the rim of the glass.

"Let me guess why you're here, Nicky. You want to tell me how sorry you are about Shawn. Right?" She took another huge swallow of her drink. The heavy ice cubes never had a chance to melt as they clinked at the bottom of the empty tumbler. "You know the cops say you did it, Nicky. Know that?"

I shook my head. "Karen listen . . . I didn't have anything to do with Shawn getting killed or Carla being attacked for that matter. I was set up."

"Who cares," she said as she kicked off her pumps and curled up on the couch next to me, her head resting on my shoulder. I smelled her musky scent, mixed with the sweet smell of whiskey on her breath. It was intoxicating. She slid her hand behind my head and began to rub my neck lightly and slowly. Her fingers glided softly under my hair; they felt like feathers on my neck. I closed my eyes and almost slipped away. It would be fun, but . . .

I shuddered and grabbed her hand in mine and held it. I didn't want her wrath from rejection, especially when she'd been drinking, but I didn't want the situation to get out of hand. I was not going to get tangled up with Karen Kiley.

"Karen, let's talk first, OK?" I asked her. "I need your help."

She was quiet for a minute. Her head was still resting on my shoulder with her long dark curls splayed across my chest, and then she pulled herself upright. She passed her hand through her thick hair and looked at me. Her eyes were shinning and watery.

She sniffled and then said, "OK, Nicky, let's do cut to the chase. Shawn was an ass. We both know that. But, honey, he was much, much more than just your garden-variety ass. He was a low-life, a lying, cheating slob who got his jollies by slapping me around for eighteen long years. You know that? Oh yes, but I still cooked his damn dinners every night, whether he bothered to show up or not. I waited and I cried many nights for the son-of a-bitch when he didn't bother to come home or call. But I started getting real tired of his shit. It only took me almost twenty years, but I got real tired, Nicky—real tired." She took a deep breath and went on, "You know that sometimes, Nicky, the bastard would have the balls to come home smelling like someone else and want to know where his dinner was."

"Karen, I . . ."

She came close and was inches from my face and hissed, "Shut up, Nicky. You wanted the story. You want the story? Well, here's the real story. And you're gonna listen. You owe me that, Nicky. OK?"

I nodded and picked up her hand. I did feel for her.

And so for the next hour she opened the floodgates of hell, painting a very ugly picture of what her life had become; the abuse, both verbal and physical; the other women; my wife, Carla, his so called business partner. Karen's voice had become detached and low, almost guttural.

"You knew, Nicky, didn't you?" she looked up into my eyes, her voice trembling. "You knew they were screwing, didn't you?" I felt the rage building up in her. Her eyes were watery and wide and her expression was tense. She gripped my hand tighter and was inches from my face. Her eyes were probing mine, looking for something, validation maybe, I didn't know.

"I guess I didn't want to know," I said quietly.

"You knew."

I closed my eyes. "Yes, Karen, I knew. I guess I knew all along. All I wanted was out," I said. "I just wanted to get away from that woman, and I wanted to get on with my life. End of chapter.

"Me too, Nicky. I wanted out so bad I could taste it. Living with that fat slob, looking at that pig when he ate or pissed on the floor when he was drunk. Oh, Nicky, you have no idea."

She sat up and extended her arm outward and around the shabby living room, palm up.

The furniture was cheap and worn and the clutter was shabby.

"He gave me this. Shangri-La. This is my nightmare. This is what it all ended up to be. I'm forty-five, Nicky, where do I go from here? Where?" She demanded, gripping my shoulder hard and sobbed, "this sure ain't what he promised me when I was eighteen while he was screwing me in the back of that Buick."

I didn't have any words. I sat and rubbed her hand, looking down at the floor.

She took a deep breath and continued, "I lived with that son-of-a-bitch for twenty years and put up with more bullshit than any one person should ever have to endure." She got closer, and I felt her breath. I met her wide-eyed stare.

"And you know what, Nicky? I'm glad he's dead. I don't give a flying shit if you killed him or not. At least now I have a little bit of my miserable life left. The only decent thing he did for me was to die!"

I needed to get out of there all of a sudden. It might've been that stifling little house or maybe her pathetic story or just simply good instincts. I stood, held her hands in mine, and met her glassy eyes. "The one thing that I want you to know is that I didn't kill anybody, Karen, but somebody is going to a lot of trouble to make it look like I did. If you can think of anything that might help me, please try to get in touch. Talk to Ray. Ray always knows how to get in touch with me. OK?"

She nodded numbly, and I left her sitting there in her own hell.

Pete was aware of a beeping sound somewhere off in the distance; part of a dream maybe. It persisted, as he slowly became conscious. He was afraid to move. His whole body was numb, but he was warm and in bed. He felt tightness in his skull and a throbbing at his temples that snapped him to the present. Still afraid to open his eyes, Pete sensed that he was alone. He felt like he was under water and fighting to break the surface when loud voices nearby startled him. As his head cleared, the beeping noise grew with intensity.

"When can I talk to him, Doctor?" a deep voice asked somewhere outside Pete's room.

Another male voice replied, "Hard to tell. He is in rough shape from the accident, and he's been out since he's been here. The man's got a fractured skull and multiple contusions on his head, face and neck. It's a question of waiting, Captain, he could regain consciousness at any time. Actually, he's damn lucky to be alive. The x-rays also show that he has two broken ribs, a lot of cartilage damage, and a punctured lung. But he'll make it. He's a young, strong guy. Looks like he has some problem with alcohol, though. His blood alcohol level was .38, which as you know, is almost comatose, and I suspect some early signs of liver disease."

"When he wakes up I'll need to talk to him. He's a suspect in my murder investigation, and I'll also need to put an officer outside this door. I don't want this bird to fly."

Pete did not recognize either of the voices, but he knew that one of them had to be a cop who was just dying to talk to him. Pete pretended he was still out. Slowly, the previous night started to come back. He remembered the Irishman being killed, running to his van, and then crashing into something. He remembered looking up and seeing that big black car fill his windshield. That was it. That was why he was here, and this was a hospital; more than likely it was Cape Cod Hospital in Hyannis. He ran into a parked car outside *Montego Ray's* and he didn't die. Son-of-a-bitch.

He opened his eyes slowly, blinking to adjust to the harsh light in the room. He was in a hospital and he saw that there were tubes and wires all over him. His arms and legs were strapped in, preventing him from any movement. He tried to turn his head toward the voices but was rewarded with shooting pains down his neck and at the side of his head.

"Oh shit!" Pete bit his tongue to keep from crying out from the blinding pain. He didn't want them to know he was conscious. Not yet. He knew he was not going far any time soon. He promised himself, though, that he'd never go to jail—never!

Chapter 15

I called Ray's and Jazz told me I was in a whole bunch of trouble. I thanked her for the news flash and asked where Ray was. She told me that Ray wanted me to call him at eight tonight, and that I should eat something. Jazz was one of those women who figured food could fix anything. Most times I tended to agree with her.

As I drove down Route 6 back toward Wellfleet, I prayed with all my heart that the good guy, who happened to be me in this case, would win out in the end like in my novels. But I had a feeling that my old adversary, the shit fairy, wasn't quite done with me. I weighed my options for the one-hundredth time. It was really simple. I only had two options: drive down and turn myself in or continue this idiotic fantasy of being a detective on my own. Playing Eddie Kane was fun for a while, but in fiction I could always put him back in the book or just turn off the computer. This situation was the real deal; I was scared, and the fact suddenly sunk in that I might possibly get shot at by some over-zealous cop. Maybe, I should trust them to do their job. But, I guess the real problem I had was my festering lack of honest-to-goodness faith in our legal system. I was innocent. I knew that, but it sure as hell looked like I wasn't. The thought hit me that whoever this person was, he was smart, maybe even smarter than me. Imagine that!

I headed down to a burger joint on Rt. 6 in Wellfleet that was famous for its roadside cuisine. I salivated like a dog at the thought of one of their juicy, fat-laden cheeseburgers, with a basket of golden french-fries smothered in ketchup and salt and about a quart of good, strong coffee to wash my impending heart attack down. Jazz was right. Food did make things better for a while, at least. I'd abandoned any pretense of eating healthy through this ordeal. Just like the smoking. It proved to be a great excuse for falling back into old, dangerous habits. I'd already bought a pack of cigarettes and was savoring each one as though they were spun from the heavens. If Chris knew she would kill me before the cigarettes and bad food would.

I was either getting brave or reckless by going back down Rt. 6, but I figured the cops would not expect me to be so brazen. They were probably combing the woods and already had my house and my boat staked out. They might even assume that I was already off the Cape. I thought about phoning in an anonymous tip that I spotted me driving over the Bourne Bridge. I liked that one a lot. They'd have to revive Peck from a shit hemorrhage if he thought I'd slipped away. And God help me if he caught up with me before I proved that I was innocent.

I stopped the Jeep by a roadside paper box and grabbed a Times. When I opened the paper in the car, I lost my appetite instantly as I stared at the headline above my favorite book jacket photo, front page center. Chris took that picture to go on the back of my first novel. It was of me on the beach, framed in blue sky and white clouds, with my Cape Cod ball cap on, T-shirt, sunglasses, full moustache, and a killer tan. I loved that snapshot. That was until I saw it on the front page of the Cape Cod Times in that context.

The headline jumped out at me. It took me a minute to really grasp what it said.

"Murdered Woman's Partner Found Dead in Provincetown. Local Mystery Writer Sought for Questioning.   Considered Armed and Dangerous!"

The lead story went on to say that Shawn Kiley was murdered outside of Montego Ray's last night. His partner, Carla Thomas, died early this morning from injuries received from a vicious assault several days ago. There was another suspect in custody who was involved to some degree, and whose name was being withheld at this point. The article described the massive manhunt taking place for me, and that they were closing in on me fast.

I sat feeling numb and just stared out the windshield—not seeing anything. Carla had died, and I didn't know what to feel or how. I was sad for her. I didn't love her anymore, but I still had a heavy heart. We did love each other for a brief period of time, and it was real, the way all new love is. Then when the lust wore thin, we found that we really didn't like each other much at all. Especially after I got sober, and we saw that we wanted different things out of life.

I closed my eyes and said a silent prayer for her.

I never wanted her harmed. I would've liked to see her enjoy life for what she had instead of what she thought she wanted so badly. But the reality was that the police were now looking for me. And who was this suspect they had in custody? Maybe I'm already off the hook. But the paper didn't say that. It said that I was a fugitive. I decided that I'd wait and talk to Ray before I made any bold moves. Actually, I was leaning toward turning myself in, but my little voice told me to push on. I listened this time.

The strange thing was that I hadn't seen a cop all day. It sounded as if they had roadblocks, helicopters, and S.W.A.T. teams with bullhorns swarming over the countryside with wild-eyed, drooling Dobermans, looking for me. Hot shit! I wondered where they were hunting and I was suddenly really glad that they were apparently looking somewhere else.

Then that I decided to have a little fun. I was already in trouble. I found a pay phone, dialed C.P.A.C., and told the duty officer, whose voice I didn't recognize, that I was a friend, and that I saw Nick Thomas driving a black, late-model, Cadillac Seville over the Bourne Bridge in the direction of Boston, earlier that morning. A black Seville had just passed me going in the right direction with a guy roughly my age with a mustache driving. He'd be in for a surprise if they caught up with him. Sorry, guy!

I hung up quickly, before he could ask any questions. Short and to the point through a wad of napkins that I'd put over the receiver. I spoke low and fast. I knew they recorded every call that came in, and I'd bet my last dollar that Captain Artus Peck was listening to the tape that very moment as I drove off in the direction of Provincetown.

I must've subconsciously slipped into Eddie Kane again, deciding that the whole persona might be bizarre enough to work in this case. After all, it works in my books. Eddie pokes around and finally comes across what's really going on. The motive is usually money, and more often than not, sex is involved. What the hell. If the cops catch up with me, I'll just lie down, spread-eagle, and pray as loud as I can. I'd give my ass up in a heartbeat if I thought for a minute that they were going to shoot me. But in the meantime, I might as well see what I could find out. After all, I created Eddie Kane, and he always finds the bad guy. Why couldn't I do it in real life?

I looked again at the picture of me on the front page of the Times and decided that if I wanted to pull this off, I'd better change the way I look. Anybody who saw the picture in the Times would recognize me. I have the kind of face people remember. So, I pulled the jeep off in Truro at Pamet Road and stopped at a small convenience store/gas station. I laughed when I saw its name, *EarthMart*. And earthy it was. It was a long ramshackle clapboard building that looked like it could've been a converted garage with two antiquated gas pumps in front and an old, red soda cooler by the door on the cluttered porch. There was an assortment of rafts, umbrellas, and beach junk tied to the wooden railings and the stairs were adorned by an assortment of sunflower and sailboat flags that people hang on their houses. Even the signs looked old. It's funny; I never paid this place any notice before and here was Rockwell's Americana at its finest right under my nose.

I just knew that some old hippies, long-haired, wire-rimmed products of the sixties, owned the place. It would shatter everything I believed sacred if I found out that *Shell* or *Sunoco* owned the *EarthMart*. It would be like finding out that the Arabs really owned *Yankee Stadium*, which they probably do.

I looked up in the rear view mirror and caught my own eye. My face looked hard, and the lines around my eyes were tanned and deep. The moustache I loved so was thick and speckled with gray and white. I felt old and tired, but I told myself I had to believe I could make this work, and I had to believe that I could find whatever the police couldn't. I needed to talk to Ray. He was my friend, and he was the only one, besides Chris and Mac, that I trusted. I didn't want to involve Chris, and Mac was still a cop at heart. Even though he was retired; he was still a cop and would feel torn between our friendship and his instincts and sworn duty.

I sat in the Jeep for a minute and rested. I reached in the pocket of my jacket and fished out the crumpled pack of cigarettes. I had one left. This would not do. I remembered the vow I made this morning about not quitting smoking today, so I shook out the last one happily and guilt free. I punched the lighter on the dash of the old Jeep, hoping that it worked. Thankfully it did.

I'd parked on the far side of the building and looked around carefully before I got out. Nobody seemed to be paying any attention to me. A few cars passed by, but the coast seemed clear, or at least as clear as it was going to get. No cops yet, which was all I really was concerned with. I got out of the Jeep and headed around to the front of the store. I pushed open the old door and was announced to all within by a leather strap with reindeer bells on it that was tacked to the inside. So far, EarthMart was right on target. I strained my ears for a little Jefferson

Airplane or Allman Brothers. Sadly, I heard none.

I guess I expected an earthy looking exotic woman named Jasmine, with long dark hair, in an Indian print skirt, with a white peasant blouse, sandals, and silver bangles on her wrists. Instead, my vision was shattered by a young kid with more pimples than even God could love, behind the counter, talking on the phone, picking his nose, and looking real cerebral. I literally stopped for a moment and stared. I was crushed. And to add insult to injury, he had a black and chrome boom-box that was spewing forth something that sounded like a cat that got its tail caught in a lawnmower.

The kid turned and looked at me, with the phone still to his ear and his right index finger buried up to the first joint in his nose. He raised one pierced eyebrow at me in question. I shook my head and quickly moved to the back of the store. Dismissing me, he went back to his conversation. I found what I needed in a large display of personal and medical items against the back wall. I grabbed a pack of disposable razors, shaving cream and a pair of scissors. I also had the foresight to pick up a toothbrush and toothpaste, a bar of soap and a Spiderman beach towel that I've lusted over for so long. I might be a fugitive, but I still needed to feel somewhat clean.

As I walked toward the front of the store, a large bag of chips leaped right off the shelf and stuck to my hand. I made a note to speak to the management about that. I had no choice but to buy them and some soda to wash them down with. But the crown jewel, the belle of the ball, lay in an old glass and chrome ice cream cooler. It was like a cool, tropical oasis in a sweltering desert. She sat there proudly and lit majestically. Inside was an artery-clogging collection of Mexican burritos, microwave soy cheeseburgers, green hot dogs, and some questionably fresh-looking deli sandwiches that would make any American proud. Happily, I found a couple of small ham and cheese subs. If I were to guess, they were made sometime this week. It was good enough. And yes, I did buy another pack of cigarettes, knowing all along that I'd be better off with Peck, if Chris ever caught me with them.

I proceeded to the register and dropped my stuff onto the cluttered counter with a thud. The kid was still talking on the phone, ignoring me, as I stood there waiting with waning patience. I cleared my throat politely as I looked over his shoulder out the dirty window. No cops yet, maybe my luck would hold out a bit longer. Pizza Face gave me a look of annoyance and said good-bye to whomever.

"That it, man?" asked the kid.

I hate that word 'man'. "Yeah." I managed to say between clenched teeth. "Oh, by the way, where can I find a pay phone close to here?"

He seemed to ponder this for a moment, fingering one of the zits on his cheek.

"Round the side, by the restrooms. It's a quarter now, you know," he said smiling proudly as though he just informed me of something profound. I didn't think we'd see this one on Jeopardy any time soon. I paid for my loot and grabbed the bag that he managed to jam everything into. The chips were at the bottom of course. It was a good thing for him that I've had a lot of therapy. I really wanted to strangle him. Slowly.

"Thanks kid, you've been a great help." I said grabbing the bag and heading out the front of the store.

Once outside, I looked around the parking lot and then scanned the road. I saw nothing unusual or suspicious, so I headed 'round' the side to where my young friend said the pay phone was located. It was there next to the restroom, which was really stretching syntax, but the need was there, and I wanted to wash up and regroup. I held my breath as I used the facilities and made myself a bit more presentable and much less noticeable. I took off my jacket and shirt to keep them clean and hung them on a nail on the back of the door. Then, painfully and regrettably, I shaved my beloved mustache and cut my hair to within an inch of my scalp before I had second thoughts. It was a crude but effective makeover. I washed the hair off me, scrubbed my face and neck, and dried off using my new Spiderman towel.

I looked up into the filthy mirror in shock. I didn't know the man looking back at me. I looked like a poster child for the Marine Corps Reserve. My face was clean-shaven for the first time I could remember in my adult life, and my hair was butch-short. I looked nothing like the Nick Thomas they were looking for. It wasn't pretty, but it would work for a little while anyway. I felt better with my face shaved and hair washed. If this were a movie I'd be singing some stupid little song. Thank God, it's not! I have not yet elevated to the mind set of song here today.

I exited the less-than-sanitary facility and saw the phone on the wall. I realized at once that it was in a great spot, because it couldn't be seen from the road. This was both good and bad because I couldn't see the road either. The hell with it. I dropped a quarter in the slot and punched Chris's number, praying she was at home.

She picked up the phone on the second ring. "Hello?"

"Honey, it's me, Nick." I whispered as I kept my eyes on the corner of the building. There was a stunned silence.

"Nick where are you?" she whispered. "The cops just left here looking for you. They're not going to go away. Nick, I'm scared."

"Honey, I can't talk. I'm OK so far and please believe that none of what they say is true. Please believe that, honey."

"I know. I want to see you. We need to be together," her voice sounded small. I wanted to be with her so bad. But I knew the clock was ticking and they were probably trying to trace the number.

"I love you, Chris. I'll call you tomorrow. You know where. Remember Kane's Law." And with that I hung up. It tore my heart apart to hang up, but I couldn't involve her in this. It was too dangerous. People were dying. Somebody was shooting at me with annoying persistence, and I was probably going to get arrested and thrown in jail any minute now. I prayed she would figure out that there was no prearranged "where" that I would call in an emergency and remember to carry her cell phone. She hated that thing, but it was the "where" that I meant, because the "where" would change as she moved. It was a passage from one of my earlier Eddie Kane books, Kane's Law, which she'd helped me plot and would remember it. Eddie kept in touch with his girlfriend, Sandy, by cell phone. They were harder to trace.

I moved to the front corner of the old station

and nonchalantly tried to peer around the corner. There were several cars in the parking lot, but none looked to be out of the ordinary and traffic on the road was still light. So, I went back around the side and behind the building to where the old Jeep was parked. I noted that there were no cars parked near it. Everything was good, so far. I had one more call to make, so I doubled back to the phone.

I dropped a quarter in the slot and punched Mac's number, praying that he would be at home. Mac picked up the phone on the second ring. There is a God. "Hello?"

"Mac, it's me, Nick." I kept my eyes on the corner of the building.

There was a stunned silence.

"Partner you're in a lot of trouble, but you already know that. What the hell is going on Nick? The cops just left here looking for you and they said they would be keeping an eye on this place. They're not going to go away. First of all where are you?"

"Mac, listen, I didn't do it. I was set up. I need help, and fast. The only way I'm going to get out of this is to find out who did it, and I have some pretty good ideas."

The line was quiet for a second and then he said, "OK, relax Nick, we'll figure this out. First, tell me where you are."

"Close. Can we meet?"

Mac's voice sounded calm and reassuring, but he always sounded like that. I guess being a cop for twenty odd years made him ready for anything.

"Not right now partner. If I were them, I'd be waiting around the corner to see if you showed up here."

"I know Mac, but it's a long story and I need to

talk to you to try to sort out what has happened." I could see him standing there in his kitchen, where we had shared many sober hours talking about how we can change our lives, gazing out the back window. I had helped Mac build that house four years ago when I first got sober. He said it was good therapy to get involved in something and help others-not to mention the free labor.

"Look Nick, just where are you now?" Mac asked me. I told him.

"OK , first of all you have to get rid of the Jeep. They know you have it. There's a dirt road about a mile west of that store that leads down to the old boat launching area. Not many people know about it. Do you know where I mean? You passed it on the way to that store."

"Yeah, I think so, Mac. I'll find it." I sighed. It was good to have someone else think for awhile. My overworked brain was tired and undoubtedly confused.

"Good. Take that Jeep down there and pull it off the road into the woods as much as possible and then hide yourself and watch for me. I'll take my time and make sure I'm not being followed. Just stay put. I'll be there."

"Hey Mac?" I asked before he could hang up. "Bring me some fresh clothes, you know, some old jeans and a sweatshirt or something. OK? I'm dirty and tired."

"Sure Partner. Just relax. I'll help you out of this somehow. Try not to worry. I'll be there as soon as I can." Mac said quickly and hung up the phone.

I felt better already, but I was getting madder by the minute. I had to keep affirming to myself that I was not guilty of a damn thing except maybe evading the police. And that was really up for interpretation as well. Eddie Kane lives! I would find this psycho and deliver him to Peck wrapped up like a Christmas present. I'd really love to know who was in custody and what he, or she, was charged with. And why were they still looking for me?

I jumped in, started the Jeep, and pulled back on the main road going back the way I came. I saw the kid from the store standing on the porch smoking a cigarette, watching me as I left. I put him out of my mind. If ever there was a poster child for retroactive birth control, he was it.

Mac said the dirt road was just a little way up on the left, which was good because I noticed for the first time that the Jeep was on empty. Please don't run out of gas now, I prayed once again. I figured that I'd keep an open line to God going today. Did you ever notice how most people get real religious when the shit hits the fan? What is the first thing someone says something really bad is happening? Please God help me out of this one, and I'll never do it again! Words that do tend to come back and haunt you. Because, we all seem to do 'it' again. Whatever the 'it' may be at the time. That was my creed as an active alcoholic.

I rounded a long, lazy bend in the tree-lined road and there it was, just like Mac said it would, a small opening in the woods with a dirt road leading down towards the boat launch. There was a short wooden sign that had a white boat painted on a chipped green background with an arrow pointing into the woods. I turned down the darkened path, praying that no one saw me. And no one did as far as I could tell.

My heart almost stopped as I heard sirens screaming behind me on the main road. I nailed

the Jeep out of instinct and sped down the bumpy
dirt road and rounded a sharp bend. I skidded to
a stop and rolled down the window to listen. The
sirens kept going and it sounded as though they
were headed towards the store I just left. That kid
probably recognized me and called the police. And
now I was trapped down this small dirt road with
nowhere to go. Thinking fast, I realized I had to
hide the Jeep off the road and quickly. There were
bound to be cars using this road. Up on the right,
I saw a smaller dirt road, which was actually more
like a path, which branched off into thicker woods.
I took it, not really caring where it led. I plowed
the old Jeep through overgrown branches and ruts,
bouncing painfully as I went. I drove through about
50 yards of scraping branches and potholes when I
came out into a long field. There was a burned out
barn up ahead with all sorts of debris and several,
old rusted out cars around it. It was perfect. I drove
around the far side of the barn and saw that if I were
careful, I could pull the Jeep inside under the part of
the roof that was still standing. I managed to bounce
the Jeep over the old tires and fallen timbers and got
it inside the old structure.

My heart was still pounding and I just sat and
listened. The only noise I could hear was the ticking
of a tired engine and a low hiss from the radiator. I'd
already mentally bought Ray a new Jeep so I didn't
care. He would be cool with it.

I tore open the bag, opened a soda, and attacked
one of my flattened sandwiches. I think it took all
of about 30 seconds to finish the first sandwich, and
I ripped into the second one immediately. They
actually weren't bad, but dry as a piece of Styrofoam
without even a drop of mayo. The kid could've told

me. They were edible just the same.

I knew I didn't have the luxury of time. The hounds were close. I had to get near the other road fast in case Mac showed up, so I stuffed what was left of my lunch, soda, and the carton of cigarettes in the paper bag and made my way carefully out of the old barn. I couldn't hear the sirens anymore, but I wasn't sure if that was a good or a bad thing. The cops were probably questioning the kid back at the store. They ought to get a treat out of that encounter. Hopefully he'll send them in the wrong direction. It wouldn't seem out of character for him.

I ran out to the dirt road from the barn and stayed close to the woods in case someone came by. As I neared the small road, I heard something up ahead. I stopped in my tracks and crouched next to a tree at the side of the path. From where I was crouched, I saw the small dirt road that probably led down to the boat launch. I strained my ears and distinctly heard the slow crunching of tires on gravel. A large car was making its way slowly down the road. I held my breath and waited. If it was the cops I was going to lie down in the middle of the road and give up. Hopefully, they wouldn't shoot me. I looked carefully through the trees and saw the nose of a blue Bonneville come around the corner. The front license plate read SOBER-1. It was Mac, so I jumped out of the bushes and ran over to the car.

When he spotted me, he buzzed his window down, did a double take at my new appearance, and barked, "Get in the trunk, now!" He popped his trunk from inside the car. I didn't say a word. I raced around to the back of the Bonneville and climbed in, closing the trunk behind me. Mac didn't seem to want to have a conversation, so I followed his lead. We'd have time to talk soon enough.

I felt the car move forward and then turn around on the narrow road. I heard Mac swear as the branches from the overgrown trees and brush scraped against his new car. You have to understand, Mac got annoyed when it rained on his car. Never mind branches scraping the paint off of it. I knew he was already planning how he'd have me compounding out the scratches, and it would bug him until I did.

"Mac?" I yelled through the trunk hoping he could hear me.

"Nick, whatever you do, keep quiet. Don't talk, don't breathe and we'll try to get the hell out of here in one piece," he yelled. Then I heard him turn on the radio. It was out of my hands now, I thought, and believe it or not, I think I fell asleep.

I had been in a lot more comfortable places than the trunk of Mac's car, but at the time I could think of no place safer. By the sound of the road, Mac had gotten on the highway and was going at an even speed. I knew I'd dozed off for a few minutes or longer; it was hard to tell. The even hum of the tires and the faint sound of music from the radio were mesmerizing. The events of the last eighteen hours were still kind of blurred. I wonder why.

"Mac?" I yelled though the rear seats, "Where the hell we headed?"

"Relax , it's just a few more miles and we'll be safe." His voice was barely audible over the hum of the highway. I wasn't sure where Mac was headed, but I trusted this man, and if he were headed to the police station with me in his trunk, I'd have to believe it would be the right move. Although, I sincerely hoped he wasn't. I'd come too far today to just turn myself in. I needed to get to the bottom of this. It was personal.

I felt the big Bonneville slow down, as if he were getting off the highway and then come to a stop. Wherever we were headed, I knew we'd be there soon. I could sense we were in a more populated area as we stopped for a traffic light. I heard the sounds of cars and a few large trucks around me. If my guess was right, by the time we had traveled, we were back in Wellfleet. I prayed Mac knew what he was doing.

After about ten minutes of stop and go, I felt the car pull into a gravel driveway, go for about twenty feet and then stop. My heart was pounding, not knowing what to expect, as I heard Mac get out of the car and shut his door. He banged twice on the trunk lid and said, just loud enough for me to hear, "Sit tight a minute, Nick, I want to see if the coast is clear." What was I going to say? I really was in no position to argue. After all, I was locked in his trunk.

It seemed like he was gone for an eternity, when it was probably only a couple of minutes, and finally I heard a door slam and quick footsteps coming around the back of the car. Someone fumbled with keys and the trunk popped open and I was looking at Mac's un-smiling face.

"Better get used to being locked up, my boy," said Mac, looking down at me with raised eyebrows and a faint bemused look. I was in the basic fetal position with my hands up under my chin and my cramped legs drawn up in front of me. "Thanks buddy, I needed that." I grumbled as I tried to climb out. My bones and sore muscles said no. Mac reached in and grabbed me with his powerful grip and literally lifted my hurting carcass out of his trunk. I hugged him on the spot, hoping no one was around to see this strange sight.

"Come on partner, let's get you inside. You are a sorry sight to say the least."

I reached back in and retrieved what was left of my lunch and cigarettes. I followed him around the back of an old two-story colonial, which was set off from the road sufficiently so no one could see us. I recognized the house as Father Tom's, another brother alcoholic. We called him Father Tom affectionately because he was always helping those newcomers who just couldn't grasp the idea of sobriety. He would patiently take them under his wing, feed them, take them to meetings, and even try to get those who needed one, a job. He was known and respected by many. Mac and I had spent more than a few nights in Tom's kitchen drinking coffee, smoking cigarettes, and solving world hunger. AA worked for those who wanted it to. I was one of the lucky ones so far. It felt like being home, and I knew I was safe here, at least for the time being.

It had been a long day. All I wanted was a hot shower, clean clothes, and a good, hot meal. Then I knew we could figure out some sort of a solution to my dilemma.

When I finally came downstairs to the large country kitchen, Mac and Tom were huddled at the thick, oak kitchen table, talking in hushed, animated tones. They both looked up at me as I came in and plopped down on one of the heavy wooden Captain's chairs. I had on some gray sweat pants, heavy, white socks, and a blue New York Yankees T-shirt that I had found on the bed when I got out of the shower. At least I felt clean, and Tom saw to it that

I had fresh clothes. Being clean gives one a whole new perspective on things. The next important and extremely necessary ingredient is food.

I looked at each one of them as I poured coffee from a stainless steel carafe into a heavy mug. Alcoholics take their coffee very seriously, probably as serious as they took their booze before sobriety. I know that was true for me; I loved my coffee. It bordered on religion.

Coffee or no coffee, I could tell by their expressions that I was in deep shit.

Tom always looked neatly disheveled if that's possible. He was probably somewhere in his early sixties, tall and thin, with thick, unruly gray hair, half-glasses perched on the end of his nose and a low, gentle voice. He always wore a flannel shirt and dungarees, winter or summer, and he usually had on a faded, blue ball cap that had Cape Cod stitched on the front. And he always had a cup of coffee and a cigarette going somewhere close by.

Mac was the same way with his coffee, but completely opposite in his dress. Mac always looked neat, tanned and pressed. His white-gray hair was expensively cut, and he usually wore a classy polo or golf shirt with precisely creased khaki Dockers and handsome leather Top-Sider shoes. And his socks always matched his shirt. I enjoy busting his stones about that and he'd laugh and tell me I was jealous. And he was right. You know how some people just naturally look good in any type of clothes. They stand out even when they are casual, and they could wear old jeans and make them look stylish. That was Mac to a "T".

There was a plate of ham and cheese sandwiches on the table that I attacked immediately as I sat down. Between bites, I managed to mumble, "It's not good guys, huh?" The answer I knew already.

For the next few hours I recapped the events of the past day and a half the best I could. Mac, ever the cop, would interrupt and ask questions, then prod me to continue.

"Mac," I pleaded. "I'm exhausted. I have to get some sleep." Now that I was clean and my tummy full all I needed was Chris to tuck me in. I thought about calling her, but decided it would be too dangerous from where I was. I'd call her in the morning from a pay phone. I knew she was probably going crazy, but I couldn't help that.

"Go on up Nick," said Tom, "you know where the guest room is. We'll see you in the morning. We'll work it out." I could tell by his expression that he was less than confident in his own words. They were worried. Well folks, here is a news flash; so was I.

I got up to go and Mac put his hand on my arm. "Nick we're with you all the way, old buddy. You're not alone on this one." Tom winked at me and gave me the thumbs up.

However, relief was not the feeling I had as I trudged upstairs. I fell into bed and sleep came over me quickly and mercifully.

Chapter 16

The next morning, I awoke slowly, almost afraid to open my eyes. I heard sounds of life outside and felt the chill of morning through the open window next to the bed, and I could smell the salt air from the nearby ocean. I lay there and listened to the distant ringing of a channel buoy somewhere out in the harbor. Tom's house was across a small country road from the beach-front and you could see the bay from his top floor windows. Paradise!

It only took me a moment to snap back to reality and remember what I was doing here in Tom's guest bedroom. That desperate, sick feeling returned immediately. OK, what was I going to do? I needed a game plan. I knew I could not endure another day like yesterday, and I was no closer to finding a solution. As always, I felt that I was the only one who could control my fate. Not that I didn't have any confidence in the police, but it seemed they were convinced I was guilty. Or let's at least say they really wanted to have a nice long conversation with me.

I knew I had to call Peck. This whole charade, my growing delusion that I was the invincible and intuitive Eddie Kane, Private Investigator, was total insanity. I mean, if you think about it, they really had a good reason to think I was nuts; actually several good reasons. I'm not Thomas Magnum, I don't drive a Ferrari, I don't have a buddy named TJ who owns a shiny helicopter to come and rescue me, and this sure as hell isn't Hawaii. I put my hands behind my head on the soft, cool pillow and stared out the window. The sky was a deep, chilly blue with big patches of cotton-white clouds. It was a gorgeous, breezy Cape Cod morning, I thought, in spite of my predicament.

There is no place like this on earth. I truly am blessed to live here. There are those who hate The Cape, and I'm glad there are those, too. I didn't want a lot of people liking it here. It was crowded enough!

I stretched my aching muscles under the heavy covers. It was nice and warm in there, and I was wanted for murder, or several murders, by some very irate and motivated police. It was a contest between the old glass is half-full or half-empty thing. Yes, it was a nice day, but the real problem was that I was in the worst predicament of my life. The bravado I had yesterday was gone.

I decided I'd call Peck and pray he'd listen to me. He was a good guy at times and he would listen, maybe. But, on the other hand, he could be real pissed off at me for making his police force look foolish and put me away for a long time. I wasn't sure how tight this frame was or what they had that pointed in my direction. I knew there were the obvious facts: I was at the scene when Carla was attacked, and I did have blood on my hands and clothes. But, the most damaging thing was that they believed I had a strong motive. Yeah, I didn't love the idea that she was always coming after me for money and trying to cash in on my success as a writer. It was always something. Believe me, Carla was the biggest pain in the ass I've ever had. That gave the police a motive along with some damaging physical evidence. The only thing I had was that, just maybe, Peck believed my story, or at least part of it, and believed that there actually is someone out there playing a dangerous game of cat and mouse and murder! I didn't know what to expect.

I concluded, that if I had any prayer of getting out of this mess in one piece and not incarcerated, I'd have to find this trickster first. If they were convinced it was me, they wouldn't be looking for anyone else. Hell, I'd be looking for me, too! I knew one thing: whatever had to happen would have to happen today and fast! My time was running out. But maybe I could be Eddie just a little while longer.

A dog barking across the street brought me back to the present. First, I'd better get out of bed and see what Tom and Mac are up to. I'm an advocate of trying to start the day with a positive attitude and see how long it takes for someone to mess it up.

The house seemed still and deserted as I fought the urge to burrow under the covers and go back to sleep. Where were Mac and Tom? I wondered. They were both early risers if they even slept at all. I always wondered about that. They were like bats. I got out of bed and crouched down beside the open window and peered out, half-expecting to see the block cordoned off by police with dogs and bullhorns- Alice's Restaurant all over again, in three part harmony. I took a deep breath of the morning with my eyes closed, crouched by the windowsill. I leaned my elbows on the sill and looked out.

I watched a quiet Cape Cod neighborhood slowly come to life. A man across the street was putting out his trash, and a few people were walking toward the beach for a morning stroll. I heard a car start up nearby but couldn't pinpoint where it came from. I looked down the gravel driveway leading towards the back of Tom's house. It was empty. Mac's Buick was gone and the door to Tom's garage was closed, so I couldn't see if his car was there or not. I had this eerie feeling that I was alone in the house.

I straightened up slowly, wincing in pain. And I became vividly aware of the abuse I had put my body through in the past twenty-four hours. Yesterday morning I woke up a wanted man and I've been running from the law ever since. Talk about a reality check, this was the big wazoo. I pulled on the old flannel robe that Tom had laid out for me and headed for the bathroom. To my delight I found a set of fresh clothes on the hamper beside the shower. At this point I really didn't care if there were S.W.A.T. teams in the trees outside. I needed a shower first and then, hopefully, breakfast for twelve.

I took one last look out the window in the bathroom and crawled into the shower. I wasn't in the mood or condition to hop, as they say, into the shower. Life always looks a little better after a nice hot shower and shave. With a little luck, they'd have a hot breakfast waiting for me downstairs.

However, I discovered I really was alone in the big house when I ventured downstairs to the kitchen, clad in fresh blue jeans and an old flannel shirt, almost feeling human again. The large kitchen was deserted, as was the rest of the house. I looked around the kitchen and found that they left fresh coffee in the pot and a note on the counter. It read;

NICK,
WE'VE GONE OUT FOR A WHILE TO
TRY TO FIND OUT WHAT IS GOING ON.
DON'T ANSWER THE PHONE OR LEAVE
THE HOUSE. PLEASE! WE'LL BE BACK
IN A FEW HOURS. DON'T BE A HERO.
TRUST US PAL, IT'LL BE OK.

MAC

I sat down at the kitchen table with my mug of coffee and a fresh onion bagel smeared with cream cheese and chives that they had left for me and stared at the note. So much for a nice, hot breakfast. Where the hell did they think I was going to go? I know these guys were doing their best to help me. I just hoped it would be enough, and I hoped it would be quick. Unless the real killer has turned up, or I can find him before they find me, I'd be going away for a long time. It was a good frame. My prints were on the murder weapon and near the body, and they think I had a motive.

I was lost in that happy thought when I heard a loud pounding at the front door. I knocked over my coffee as I dove to the floor. I lay there for a few seconds, waiting, and then I raised my head to peak over the windowsill next to the table. I saw two cops coming around the side of the house toward the back door. I'm dead, I thought, but I rolled quickly out of sight, and then crawled down the dark hall towards the cellar door. My heart was pounding so loud I couldn't hear them knocking. I could not think of anything brilliant to do except hide. I guess I wasn't ready for a confrontation with the police. I just followed my instinct, or was it Eddie's? For some unknown reason I didn't panic. If I decided to turn myself in, I would to do it on my own terms and not be dragged away in cuffs. That would be humiliating, to say the least.

I heard the cops outside knocking on the back door, and I assumed there were at least a couple of them around the front. How the hell did they know I was here? Or did they? They might just be trying to run down all the people I was known to associate with. It's what Eddie would have done, if the scenario were reversed. There really was no escape and no immediate alternative. So, I figured I'd hide in the cellar and if they were persistent and found me, I would go as peaceably as possible.

I fumbled with the latch on the door that I hoped would lead to the basement and found, thankfully, that it did. I opened the old door as quietly as I could, held my breath, and descended the dark stairway, closing the door softly behind me. I no longer could hear anyone outside, but I knew they were still there. I felt them. I'd never done anything like this before, but I have to be honest; there is a certain perverse thrill in danger! I just wish I knew how it would all turn out. That would make this a true adventure. But, as I said before, this was one ending I couldn't create.

I managed to get down the stairs without breaking my neck and stood quietly at the bottom. I still couldn't hear anything. I tried to adjust my eyes to the darkness and my ears to the sounds outside. All I could hear was something pounding a steady beat, which I realized after a second came from my chest. I tried to slow my breathing and just concentrated on that for several seconds. It didn't work.

There was a hazy shaft of light coming in from a high casement window across the cellar. I made my way toward it carefully. I hated cellars. I have this phobia about the creatures that usually inhabit them, such as mice, rats, spiders and maybe even your garden variety of snake, none of which I'm fond.

There were years of junk piled up all around me. I almost impaled myself on what appeared to be an old lawnmower and various other implements of destruction. But, I managed to get across the musty cellar quietly and without any further damage to my poor, hurting body. I finally got to the old window, which was the only source of light in this musty emporium. It was a little above eye level, and I found I could see out into the side driveway if I stood back a few feet. I shifted off to the side so I could see the road and saw part of the black and white that was parked at the end of the driveway. Two cops stood next to it gesturing towards the house. I strained my ears, but could not hear what they were saying. Then they abruptly turned and walked back to the front of the house and out of my line of sight. I scratched my head nervously. They weren't going to give up so easily. Where the hell were Mac and Tom? Actually, if they were smart, they wouldn't show up now. They wouldn't have to lie then. But I hoped they'd lie if they had to. I wondered about that for a second. The program dictates rigorous honesty for any type of success and growth, but there had to be exceptions. Hell, Mac and Tom had almost fifty years of sobriety between them; they'd figure something out.

I was up on my tip toes peering out of the dirty glass to see where they were headed, when something moved past the window directly in front of me and stopped my heart for what I hoped was the last time. It was the other two cops that had been at the back door of the house. I just saw their shoes and part of their legs as they walked slowly by heading to the front of the house. Did they know I was here? How could they? I slid down next to the wall and waited and kept listening.

I heard loud voices and then a car door slam, and another. Then I heard a noise sent directly from heaven, an engine starting. I slowly rose to my feet, stepped back and looked out the window, just in time to see the cruiser backing out of the driveway. I watched it slowly pull away and the other cruiser follow. They were gone. For now, anyway.

That was a little too close for comfort. I couldn't sit here and wait for them to come back, and I was certain they'd be back to question Mac and Tom. I then made one of the more questionable decisions of my life. I was tired of being hunted. It was time to assume the role with which Eddie was more familiar, the hunter! I felt a renewed purpose and a surge of energy. I wasn't done yet. The best way to describe how I felt up to that point was like that sick feeling you get in the pit of your stomach when life rears its ugly head. It feels like someone has kicked you in the stomach, and hard! But now, I was mostly pissed. I love my life, and whoever is behind this threatens my very existence.

Someone has gone to a lot of trouble to frame me for the murders of Carla and Shawn Kiley! From the looks of things, it was not going to get any better unless I found out who was responsible and why, and drag him by the hair to the police station myself. That is, after I kick his ass from here to Boston.

They taught me in AA that it is OK to feel and

express my feelings. Well, I thought angrily, look out who ever you are. When I find your sorry ass, I'm going to express myself, all right. I didn't pull myself up out of the gutter, kicking and scratching, to have someone try to throw me back down there. I've come too far, suffered too much, and learned a hell of a lot about how to live a good life, to quit now.

I crept up the stairs with a new lease on life and headed to the phone. There was still no sign of Mac and Tom, but I wasn't going to sit around waiting for them, although a faint, little voice told me that I should. I had to call Chris. I needed to see her somehow today. I needed to feel her arms around me, and I wanted to feel safe for a moment. It was a state of mind only she could bring me to. But I didn't want to call her from Tom's phone. I'd wait and find a booth.

My next thought was that I still hadn't called Ray. In my state of complete exhaustion, I forgot to call him last night. I knew he'd help me if he could, and I knew his daughter, Justine, worked at The Prudential in Boston. Maybe she could pull down a screen for me.

I got the number for Montego's from an operator and dialed. They have that tone of voice that makes you feel guilty for not using the phone book. I look at it this way, if everyone used the phone book, that woman on the other end of the line wouldn't have a job. She should have thanked me. I felt myself smile for the first time in what seemed like years. It was probably yesterday sometime. My old self was quickly returning, and it felt good. There are days that I enjoy being in a pissed off mood.

"Montego Ray's," a deep female voice answered,

laced with that familiar Jamaican accent, shaking
me back into the present. I slapped at an ant on the
counter that was trying to cart away a few crumbs of
my bagel. I managed to sweep him and the crumbs
off onto the floor. Jazz answered just as I was looking
for a way to clean up the mess I had just created.

"Jazz." I said quietly. "It's me, Nick. Don't say a
word. Just listen. Is Ray there?"

She cut me right off. "We not open yet, Honey.
Call back in a half-hour, the kitchen be open then."
She called everybody Honey, with a long O. Except
when she was at war. Then look out! She had words
I had never heard before and really wasn't sure what
they meant.

"Ray gonna be there?" I asked her.

"I already tole you, mon. You got trouble hearin'?
Call back in half-hour, and we take your order." Her
thick accent belied caution. I could hear the noises
of the bar slowly coming to life in the background.
Jazz wasn't stupid, so there must've been someone
there. Probably looking for me.

"Love ya, Jazz. I'll call back in exactly half an
hour."

I hung up quickly. She'd tell Ray to be in his
office when I called back. I could picture her bitching
to whoever was there about stupid people callin'
for food before they were open. And who the hell
was thinkin' bout lunch this early in the morning,
anyway? Jazz liked to bitch; it made her happy. She
was probably the only living person in the world that
Ray was afraid of, and he freely admitted it. He said
it made his life simpler when he finally accepted that
Jazz was the boss.

I glanced up at the clock in the kitchen and saw
that it was already nine-thirty. I felt good; it was

early, and I had already made some positive moves. I would feel even better when it was night. There was less chance for me to be seen and it would be easier to move around.

I needed to get out of that house. Nothing would get resolved by me sitting there. I'd try calling Mac and Tom a little later.

I thought I would sneak out to my place tonight and get the things I needed. I had the insurance file and the letter to the Wellfleet police that I wanted to check out somehow. Something happened that was serious enough for Carla to have called the police in for help, and I wanted to know what that something was. It was one of several things I asked Ray to check into for me. I hid the file in my secret spot, and I was relatively sure that no one would find it. When I had renovated the house, I hollowed out a spot in one of the exposed beams in my bedroom and made a rectangular hole on top about one foot long, four inches wide and four inches deep. I cut down the piece I took out and it made a perfect, fitted top. The only way to get to the chamber was to stand on a chair or ladder and feel along the top of the beam and to know it was there. It was where I hid things.

The police would probably be watching my place from the front, so I could crawl up from the beach side, slip inside, and get out before anyone noticed.

I waited the few minutes and finally got through to Ray. He showered me with words I don't think I've ever heard before and then agreed to meet me at later that night at the Governor Bradford in P-Town, where we were less likely to be noticed. I told him what I needed, and he told me he'd try. I felt better already; at least I was taking some action.

I started out the door and realized that I hadn't

called Chris yet. So, I went back to the phone. More than likely her phone was also tapped, so I decided to put a call in to her pager. She had one of those Alpha Mates, on which you could leave a message that would read out on the beeper. I was brief.

I'm OK. Call you later. Love N.

I thought briefly of our little sailboat, *Serenity*, moored down in Wellfleet, but realized that wasn't an option, either. Where was I going to sail to, Europe? Besides, I didn't want Chris involved in this at all, even though I longed to see her and hold her close. I always felt safe and secure when we were together. She was the love I have always craved, but which always eluded me. They say you attract what you are. So, I felt pretty good about all of that. I'd see her soon. But first, I had business to take care of. I also managed to sneak in a quick prayer.

I took a deep breath and headed out to the garage and borrowed Tom's old Country Squire, complete with genuine wood-grain side panels, chrome dash, and AM radio. She was old but I knew she ran; Tom made a religion of his car and kept her purring. As I pulled out, I knew I had to find a safe place to lie low until it was time to meet Ray in P-Town.

I also knew I needed to back away from this situation and gain some objectivity if I wanted to make any headway. I was too close, and I was having a hard time seeing the obvious. But, somewhere in the deep, craggy recesses of my mind, the rusty wheels started to turn ever so slowly. I resolved to try to relax and enjoy this brilliant day cradled in the protective arms of Mother Nature at the beach, and maybe some of the answers would come. I'd decide what to do there, where I was focused and at my best.

I guided the old station wagon up Rt. 6, turned into the National Seashore, and followed the sandy road through a maze of small dunes littered with scrub brush, pines and tall sea grass. I loved this part of the Cape. The salt water, the beach, and the wind are so much a part of my being that I feel connected and at peace there. Race Point was one of those special places for me. I loved to walk the long sloping beach at sunset, climb up into the endless stretches dunes, or just sit and listen to the surf rage on. I'd sit there in the sand, close my eyes to the wind, and breathe in the crisp salt air. Chris taught me how to do these things and now we savor them together when we can.

I couldn't push things too far from my mind. I was pissed. My life was just beginning to get comfortable. I was happy; I was sober, and I was doing what I loved to do. I had enough money to live on, and I couldn't ask for a more wonderful woman in my life than Chris. Then BANG! I landed smack dab in the middle of this certified nightmare!

I felt sad. I missed Chris terribly. She was my strength and my anchor when I got low. There were times when we would just sit, holding hands, or she would rest her head on my shoulder, both of us silent, for what seemed like hours. I never wanted to be anywhere else. Life was a lot more than OK in those moments. I needed to talk to her. I shook my head in that internal torment, wishing it would all go away. The tears welled up in my eyes and I knew that I had to think clearly, so no emotional distractions. I pushed Chris gently from my thoughts for the moment.

I parked at the far end of the sandy lot, got out, and trudged up over a small dune and down the heavy sand toward the water. The beach was crowded as it always was in August. It looked like a solid sea of brightly colored umbrellas with the moms reclined in beach chairs reading the latest John Grisham, dads baking in the sun with a cold beer not far from their grasp, and children playing tag with the ice-cold surf and digging castles in the sand. I saw couples walking down by the water holding hands and lovers lying close on blankets away from the crowd. I felt a part of it all and most times I felt lucky.

I picked a nice, secluded spot at the base of a dune about a half-mile down the beach and sat. The surf was coming in, and I felt the salty wind on my face as I leaned back on my elbows and squinted into the horizon. The sun was a bright orange fiery ball set against a sky that was still and clear and blue as could be. It will be a beautiful sunset tonight, I thought. I watched a few gulls circle overhead and then soar over the water looking for lunch. I picked one and watched him for a while. He circled over a spot about twenty yards out and glided lower and tighter with each pass. I watched him pick his spot and dive hard into the churning water, breaking the surface and then streak away with his prize struggling in his beak. It's funny, but I never saw that happen before. I wrote a poem years ago about this place and remembered how at peace I felt after I wrote the first stanza. I'd never forget those words as long as I lived.

> *This is the place that I come to be at one*
> *with that someone I'd lost along the way,*
> *a long, long time ago.*

I must've lay there in the cool sand for hours

watching the surf and the small boats inch across the horizon, and I might've even dozed off a bit. It was therapeutic to say the least, but I awoke restless. I sat up, stretched, and shook the sand and cobwebs from my brain.

I was thinking about how I've always been able to reach in and grab whatever I needed to get it done. No matter what it was. It's like some of the martial arts philosophies. Stop, close your eyes, Butterfly, and go deep to find your center. Once you get a clear understanding of who you really are in relation to the rest of your environment, you become able to deal with it totally focused. Deep shit, huh? Well, it didn't work this time. I was still clueless, but I made my decision. I knew I was going to play it out; at least for now.

It got a little chilly as the late afternoon sun began to set and my stomach informed me I was not being very considerate. I looked around and saw that many people had packed up for the day and were headed back to their hotels or condos to get ready for dinner. There were still a few stragglers who hadn't gotten red enough or had fallen asleep as I had. I needed to move, so I stood, brushed the sand from my ass, and trudged back up to the car. I had enough time to grab a burger and a cup of coffee before I had to meet Ray. My diet in the past few days had surely gone astray, but that was something I could justify easy enough, so I pushed that to the far recesses of my no-so-guilty conscience. I 'd better pick up a paper, too, even though I really didn't want to see what was in it.

The newspaper was never a high point in my life before all this happened, and I doubted it was going to start now. I had a narrow view of reporting journalists, although that's where I started. I was never a whore, who would compromise my values to twist a story just so, and that's why I had a hard time fitting in that world. It pushed me harder to become independent and to be the master of my own keystrokes. But don't misunderstand me. There were still rules in the publishing game. That is if one wanted to eat. Those rules I could live by. I tried not to cross any lines, and I was in a fairly safe and time-tested genre. Eddie Kane never got grizzly or graphic in the sex scenes. I didn't feel that I needed to do that to sell books. People seemed to like my characters and they bought my books. Hell, I liked Eddie Kane. He was more alive to me than anyone. I also knew that Eddie was me. He was born from within. He was the adventurer I would be if I could be. That's why I had renewed confidence and a misguided lack of fear. I knew Eddie would solve the case.

I reached in my bag and pulled out my notebook. All writers have a notebook—you have to because inspiration has no clock. Mine was a small leather bound notebook with a zipper and pockets inside. Chris bought it for me our first Christmas together. I had to have a certain kind, and I mentioned once that I never found the right notebook to carry around. They were usually so cumbersome and awkward. But this one I loved. Anyway, I put down the facts that I knew. The first was that Carla was attacked at the warehouse and has subsequently died. Fact two, Shawn Kiley, who was still my main suspect in Carla's attack-murder, was also dead, murdered in back of Ray's! The problem was that I liked Kiley for motive on Carla's attack. He could have knocked her up, and she decided to blackmail him. Kiley probably figured the only way he could save his hide from his wife, or anybody else for that matter, was to eliminate the source of the problem. I also believe that Mr. Shawn Kiley was well aware of the way their company insurance policy read, and that he, the grieving partner, would cry all the way to the Bank with a half a million bucks as a reward: No Carla, no baby, and a lot of cash. That would be called a win-win situation. But now I'd have a hard time proving that Shawn did anything. He'd been my main man in this whole thing. It was also possible that he was the one who attacked Carla and someone else caught up with him for a totally different reason. He had a penchant for getting involved in some slimy stuff, and I knew he liked to gamble. And who was that Trish at the bar? She was hot and not the type to fall for the likes of Shawn Kiley.

Whatever it was that I had the bad luck and poor timing to be caught in the middle of, I knew one thing; these people weren't playing around. Two people were already dead, and the baby. That makes three, and they, whoever they might be, are looking for me in addition to the police! Who the hell else would want to kill Carla? I hoped Ray could fill me in and was able to get the information that I'd asked him for.

I drove back to Wellfleet and grabbed a burger and coffee to go. When I passed the new Police/Fire & Emergency Center in Truro, I gave them the old one finger salute. I knew it was childish, but it's one of those little things in life that made me feel better. The irony of it was that they were probably all in there going crazy trying to find me. I thought briefly about parking in their lot and finishing my burger. That'd be one hell of a story to tell, but I decided against it for obvious reasons. It's called common sense.

I headed out to P-Town on 6A, which is a neat little road crammed on both sides with motels and guest cottages and always some pain on a bicycle in the middle of the road.   Where do they think they are with those cute little helmets and black spandex shorts, France? No, I am not jealous. Not even a little. I'd never have worn those things in my best days. I'm really not a spandex kind of guy.

I pulled Tom's Country Squire wagon into the parking lot of the Holiday Inn just before getting into Provincetown and drove down to the end of the motel's lot. I parked next to one of those fancy Japanese four-wheel drive vehicles that cost more than my house, got out, and stretched gratefully.

I looked around me and didn't see anything out of the ordinary. The Cape was relatively quiet this time of evening. Most people were back at their rented condos or hotel rooms finishing dinner and getting their kids ready for bed. A few people were across the street walking down on the beach. A big black retriever was chasing some gulls further on down by the rocks, and a couple of kids were chasing the dog that was chasing the gulls.

Dusk was settling in nicely and with it came a refreshing breeze. I reached back into the wagon, grabbed my jacket, and slipped it on. This was a nice time of day, I thought. I loved dusk, but I also cherished the early mornings up on my roof looking out over the bay, without the stress of this situation.

Chapter 17

I saw Provincetown across the bay in its splendor. It was a sight I never got tired of. The tide was in, and the small boats anchored in the harbor were bobbing and reflecting the lights coming from town. I felt a nostalgic twinge as I looked over at the spotlighted Pilgrim Monument standing watch high above the town, and the old Long Point Lighthouse that guided ships in the same way it had for hundreds of years. Provincetown is one place for which time has almost stood still. It has a charm and beauty that's hard to describe. It has a history of being one of the first settled colonies in America and one of the initial landing points for the Pilgrims. There were beautiful old sea captains' houses lining the cobblestone streets on the outskirts of town adorned with bright gardens and white window boxes. Reaching out to the sea were two long docks that held some very old fishing boats and dirty trawlers with their high booms and miles of netting resting next to big, gleaming pleasure crafts with trendy sayings painted across their sterns. The narrow streets were lined with small shops, busy pubs and restaurants, where thousands of people ebbed and flowed every day of the summer. Along with all of this was the predominantly gay community. They don't bother me; I don't bother them. I've learned to see past all that. I can't judge anybody, that's God's job, and he does it a hell of a lot better than I do.

I hope that was politically correct. I really am working on that. Chris says that I need to get in touch with my sensitive side and be more open to people who are different than me. I do try, because it makes Chris happy, and she's worth it. Hell, I'd start growing flowers if it would make her happy. Guess I was in love, which was not one of the things I've done well in my past. I'm working on that too. She told me that women just want to be listened to and then gave me that damn book, "Men are from Mars, Women are from Venus." I never told anyone except Chris that I actually read it, enjoyed it, and maybe even learned a thing or two about listening. What I got from the book was that women need to vent verbally more than men and they don't want us to fix their problems. They already know the answers, but they just need to be listened to and encouraged. The last thing they want is for us, meaning men, to try and solve their problems for them. Also, the paradox is that it usually is us, meaning men again, that is the root cause of their problems. You have no idea how much that little revelation elevated me in her eyes. It got me a lot of points, and it would be criminal not to mention, a noticeable increase of incredible physical reinforcement, if you catch my drift. Man is never too old to learn despite his motives.

I struck off towards town at a leisurely pace, not wanting to garner any unwanted attention. A new silver BMW convertible passed me slowly and the man behind the wheel winked at me and tooted his horn. I smiled through my teeth and gave him a small wave and continued on, not looking back at him. He got the message and buzzed off in his little silver phallic symbol. I laughed, thinking that I still have that old magic. I'd have to tell Chris about it, but instead of a gray-haired queen in a BMW, I'd make it a blonde vixen in a Porsche. She wouldn't believe me anyway. You see, Chris has this sixth sense when it comes to me stretching the truth a tad. I tell her its artistic license to exaggerate a bit, and she tells me once again that I'm full of the stuff that makes the grass grow green.

Commercial Street runs off route 6A and heads directly into the heart of Provincetown. It's a great place to grab a seat and watch life unfold before your very eyes. I would pick out people and just watch them. I've even followed someone I found intriguing for a bit just to watch their habits and what they do. Downtown was usually so crowded that you could follow someone and they'd never know it. I did it for research on my last Eddie Kane book. I wanted to learn how to follow someone without being noticed. Mac gave me some tips, and I practiced on live subjects; it was fun. I actually picked out someone and followed them all day: got their name, found out where they lived, found out where they worked and banked and who, complete with name and gender, their significant other was. It was great, and I didn't get caught.

There was an ancient oak tree that lived among the cobblestones in front of the old town library and that's where I liked to sit and people watch. It's a small wonder Norman Mailer called P-Town home. It's a virtual gold mine of subject matter. I love to daydream when I walk or drive. It relaxes me and works as kind of a meditation, but I knew I'd better slip into a more cautious mode. It was time to sharpen my senses and listen to my instincts. Provincetown has a lot of cops and most of them are on the streets, and more importantly, a lot of them know me. I wasn't all that confident in my altered appearance.

I looked at my watch and picked up my pace a bit. It was time to meet Ray. The Governor Bradford Inn, one of the oldest establishments in Provincetown, was located at the corner of Commercial Street and the world. It was another great place to sit back with something cool to drink and watch the chaos of life unfold. They have these great backgammon tables with tall stools beside huge windows that look out onto the beating heart of P-town.

It is a real heart, you know. You can hear it begin to thump in May, and it beats steadily and gets louder and louder as the days become warmer and warmer. It pumps the life-blood into its veins, in the form of thousands of tourists. Provincetown is probably the most alive place I've ever experienced.

In the summer, people seem to converge on the corner outside the Governor Bradford to watch a certain veteran cop turn directing traffic into an art form. This guy was a trip to watch, spinning and pointing, giving short blasts of his whistle while strutting like a rooster back and forth in the intersection; never a mix up. Never a car out of line and never a tourist caught on the crosswalk. It's as if he had a sixth sense and eyes in the back of his head. One of those TV tabloid shows did a segment on him once; it was his personal moment of glory. Just one small example of what gives the Cape its own unique identity.

I approached the Governor Bradford at a leisurely pace, looking as if I was in no hurry to be anywhere in particular. I was just blending in, hands in pockets, and taking in the sights. It was busy downtown and there were a lot of people in the streets.

I paused by a large window, which was on the Commercial Street side of the Governor Bradford and looked at my reflection. No, I didn't look like the Nick Thomas everyone was in such a frenzy to find. Chris would get a kick out of this get up, but she'd be upset because I cut my hair off and shaved my mustache. She always told me that she loved my thick gray-brown locks and my salt and pepper mustache. The hair would grow back, probably a lot grayer though, if I managed to survive this ordeal.

I put my hand to the glass, shading my eyes, and looked in to the dimly lit bar. I could see several couples eating dinner in the booths against the far wall and a smattering of people at the bar watching a baseball game. I didn't see Ray yet. I turned and scanned the street and didn't see anything that concerned me, so I ducked into the bar. I walked quickly down to the opposite end of the bar away from the TV and the sports fans and found an open spot facing the door. I almost shit myself when something hard poked me in the middle of my back and a deep voice behind me said,

"Don't move!"

The hairs on the back of my neck stood straight up and all of the blood in my body drained down somewhere near my feet, until it dawned on me that I knew that voice.

"Ray. I'm going to kill you! You just gave me a heart attack!"

"And that's not a nice choice of words for a man in your shoes, Mr. Nick," he said over the din in the bar. I turned around shaking my head. I wanted to hug him but Ray informed me once that he was not real big on hugs from other men.

Ray was about as incognito as he could ever be, wearing a brown leather cowboy hat on his gleaming head, a black tee shirt that had Nixon on a Harley giving the finger to the world, size twelve snakeskin cowboy boots, and faded jeans. He looked like someone you didn't even entertain the thought of messing with. Sort of like a black Indiana Jones on steroids. I wouldn't laugh at him even if he showed up in a diaper holding a rattle. He had that look.

Ray gave me a big smile with his gold tooth gleaming, slapped me on the back and said it was good to see me, but the look in his eyes told me what I didn't want to know. He was worried. Hey, so was I!

"That bad, huh?" I asked, knowing the answer already.

"The cops want your sneaky ass bad, mon." he kept staring at me, looking me up and down slowly, and then added with a smirk.

"Just tell me one thing Nicky, OK?"

"You name it Ray! I really need your help.

He is one of the few that can get away with calling me Nicky! Chris is the other, and she only does it when she's mad at me. She has a way of saying it through her teeth, and scrunches up her face like she smells something bad.

"I be real curious about your new haircut, mon. You switching gears on me?" he looked around the bar pointedly "Cause you in the right place fo it."

"Ray, quit screwing around! This is serious. Talk

to me. I don't think we should hang around here all night."

"Chill, mon. Order me a beer and then we talk. We get something to drink and go sit in the back. Relax, no one here knows who the fuck you are, or even cares. But, we sit where we can see the door just the same."

A loud cheer went up at the other end of the bar. Everyone else in the bar seemed to be absorbed in the game on the tube. The Yankees were up at Fenway kicking some serious ass, and I loved it. Even though I lived up on the Cape, I'd been a Yankee fan since I was a kid. My dad used to take me to the old Yankee Stadium and fill me full of hot dogs and popcorn. He would drink a lot of beer and I'd dream. I felt the presence of Babe Ruth and Lou Gherig and guys like Billy Martin, and Maris, and don't forget "The Mick".

It was me who came up in the ninth with two out and the bases full. Yes sir, it was me that would dig in my spikes and stare down the pitcher and it was me who crushed that hanging curveball into the upper deck. I could hear the roar of the crowd as I rounded the bases, tipping my cap to the crowd with my fist held high, and then finally being mobbed at home plate by my frenzied teammates.

I waved at the bartender, who was seated on a stool behind the bar and busy force feeding himself from a large tin of potato chips. After trying to motion to him politely with no result, I rapped on the bar with an ashtray to get his attention. He scowled in our direction, got up off his stool, and walked grudgingly down to where we were standing. He was a short, pudgy man with a big, long head, a gray goatee, and rimmed glasses. He had on matching coral blue polyester pants and vest along with a purple silk shirt open to the bellybutton. I really hated to bother him. He was wiping the grease from the potato chips on his pants as he came up to us. This somehow made dinner a bit less desirable. During the long trek from his seat he had managed to produce a toothpick from somewhere and stuck it in his mouth.

"Get you guys something?" The toothpick in his yap bobbed up and down as he talked. I had a real burning desire to help him find a more suitable place for that toothpick.

I smiled politely and asked him to get Ray a Corona with lime and a Coke with lime for me. He made a little huffing noise and shuffled off to get our order. I was still hungry, but I figured I'd grab a slice of pizza from one of the little places on the way out of town. I knew it would turn into a big production if I wanted food here. The burger I had on the way didn't even make a dent.

The barman came back with our order, and we retreated to a booth at the far wall. The inside of the bar was dimly lit and rustic with barn board paneling and all kinds of shit hanging on the walls and ceiling. There was even a small, old wooden row boat suspended from the center of the barroom. It was dark in there, and that suited my purpose fine. It didn't seem like anybody cared who we were, as long as we didn't interrupt their game.

"Well Ray, did you manage to find out anything about the insurance policy for Shawn and Carla's little business?" Ray's only daughter, Justine, worked for Prudential and had access to certain information that I didn't. I was curious if it would back up what Maxine told me. I made a mental note to send her some flowers—Justine, not Maxine, of course. Then, I thought about sending Maxine Gill, the insurance lady, a nice, little present the next time I cleaned Bob's litterbox. I make a lot of mental notes and seem to forget most of them. I should get a pad. Eddie Kane has a pad. I have to get a pad. I made a note of that.

Ray brought me back. "Yeah mon, it seems the big question is who's gonna benefit from the payoff. Word has it that it's still pointing in your direction." he paused, taking a long pull from his Corona. I watched him in envy as I saw the ice-cold, amber liquid disappear down Ray's bobbing throat. I even saw the green wedge of lime floating in the foam as he set the beer down on the table. It was as if it happened in slow motion. That beer did start to look awfully good. "Let me lay it out for you." he continued.

I groaned, fearing the worst.

"Whoever set your ass up did a good job of it, mon." He reached in his pocket and pulled out some folded papers and slid them across the table to me. I unfolded them and began to read as Ray continued. "That's the policy that was written when they set up the business. Justine faxed me this copy. If you tell anybody where you got it, you gonna need the insurance." He looked me dead in the eye to make sure he made his point even though he knew I'd never dream of crossing him or putting Justine in any jeopardy. Justine is his baby. I shook my head "yes." I understood completely. He nodded with satisfaction and went on.

"Some nice lettuce. A million clams goes to the surviving partner and if they both happen to die, they each set up a contingent beneficiary to receive the payoff. Guess who Carla's was, my man?" I didn't like the way he was looking at me.

I suddenly felt anxious. "I know, Ray, it was me. But I didn't know that before. No way, man," I said with exasperation. "She hated my guts. Why would Carla name me as beneficiary to anything? The only thing she ever left me was pissed off."

"She didn't always hate you, mon, and she probably forgot to change it after you two love birds separated for good." he laughed softly. "Justine says that it would seem real curious if the policy holder's next of kin were not named as the contingent beneficiaries. The insurance company might want to know why."

Ray took off his leather hat, leaned back, and ran his huge hand over his gleaming head. I swore he shined it, but he got real upset when people asked. So, the masses speculated quietly.

We stayed quiet for a moment and I listened to the sounds of the bar. The television with the game building to a climax, glasses clinking, lighters clacking and clusters of talk and laughter. I could even focus and hear the opening of a bottle of beer.

I closed my eyes and leaned my head back into the comfortable leather of the booth. If I were the cops, I sure as hell would think it was me! Nobody in the world had more motives than I did, and most people knew how much I disliked Carla. I used to joke about it constantly. Some joke now!

"Who else, Ray?" I asked miserably. "Who else on this stinking earth would benefit? What about Kiley's old lady, hot-to-trot Karen? She was his contingent beneficiary, right? Or it could have been one of their kids. I don't know the daughter, but Ian is a strange one. You know the one that's a cop in

Truro? I know him from AA. But he still gave me a parking ticket once. He came up to me the other night and gave me a hug. Can you believe that?"

My head was spinning. There had to be an obvious answer; there usually was. There was no doubt in my mind that the money figured in here as the main motivator.

"Right again, Nick. She's the one set up to get the cash and instead of the million, she could possibly collect a couple of million if you wind up dead or in the slammer for murder. Very neat package, my man. Think she's up to it?" Ray leaned forward, resting his massive chin on his hands pensively, with his elbows on the table.

"I saw her yesterday. She tried to climb all over me. She's dangerous."

He shook his head and said, "You be dippin' into that yourself, mon? That's some crazy shit. You go to jail for sure then, mon."

"Ray! How can you say that?" I said defensively. "You know how I feel about Chris, and you've got to know that I'm not out looking for trouble. That lady is trouble with a capital "T". Besides, Chris would kill me. I'd be safer in jail! I just said that Karen Kiley is hot-to-trot, and that's all. And I think that she's definitely worth checking out. Shawn was my prime suspect, but now that he's checked out, she seems like the one with the most to gain. And believe me, man, she hasn't shed many tears over old Shawnster waiting to be planted six feet under. See if you can find out who she's playing around with, will ya? She would've needed help."

I then told Ray about the incidents at the cottage including the shots fired at me yesterday morning. He told me that he'd get to the bottom of it. We thought we could rule out Karen Kiley for the actual shooting, so there had to be someone else involved.

The bartender shuffled back over to our table and asked if we were all set. Same toothpick, hand turned deftly on extended hip. I thought it was real nice of him to ask. We told him we were fine. He gave Ray a warm smile and then shuffled off to the next booth on a mission. I started to comment but Ray held up a warning finger. "Don't go there, mon. I'd have to hurt your ass."

"Almost couldn't help it," I laughed. "You two would make a nice couple."

He swore at me in tongues I didn't recognize.

There was another roar from the bar and it appeared like the game was over, as some of the patrons got up from their stools, slapping each other on the back, laughing, and saying their good-byes. I didn't catch the score, but by the looks of the guys at the bar, the Red Sox must've pulled one out. I hated it when that happened, because I always ran my mouth about how the Yankees would give Boston a spanking. You could imagine the abuse I received when the tables turned.

The TV caught our attention as the leader for the 10 o'clock News came on. The pretty blonde anchor on channel 7 was saying something about the body of a female Caucasian with red hair, somewhere in her thirties, was found washed up on the beach in Wellfleet. Foul play suspected. Her identity is not known at this time. Anybody with information . . .

What is going on? Another body? God, I hope I didn't know this one. The only redhead that I remember was the one with Kiley at Ray's the other day. I hope it wasn't her. I had to search my memory for her name. I think it was Trish something. Or maybe she didn't even mention her last name. That would be too much of a coincidence if it turned out to be that same woman. Three homicides in two days! This was definitely a record for Cape Cod. The anchor went on to say that the authorities were still searching for a local writer who lived in Truro. They flashed a more recent picture of me on the screen. It was the one from my last driver's license, which still showed me with a full head of hair and my bushy brown mustache. I liked that picture. I felt somewhat safe for the moment. Her next statement was the icing on the proverbial cake. That sick feeling started to gnaw at my gut.

"If anyone has information on the whereabouts of this man, please contact the State Police C.P.A.C. Unit in South Yarmouth or this station. There is a twenty-five thousand dollar reward being offered for information leading to his arrest and conviction." The anchor-woman didn't look so pretty anymore.

"Oh no, Ray. You know what that means." I said, head in hands.

"It means I'm taking you in, mon." he laughed. "I could use the cash. Need some stuff done on the Corvette. Been waiting for a little extra cash to pop up."

"You're a ball of laughs Ray. I'll give you the twenty-five grand if I get out of this alive. I already owe you a jeep. You know what this means, don't you? This means that every hot shot on the Cape is going to come looking for me and I pity anybody who looks even remotely like me. The cops ought to know better than this, it's going to create chaos, and somebody innocent is going to get hurt. I don't want that, Ray. I wonder what bleeding heart idiot put up the reward."

"Look mon, keep your head on," he said in quiet voice. "I'm going to talk to your buddy Peck and shake him down for some info. I'll tell him that you're innocent and that they're barking in the wrong bush. He may not like it, but he'll listen to me. He came sniffing around the bar this afternoon with his Brooks Brothers suit and an attitude, asking me and Jazz a lotta questions. I told him I'd see what I could do. He said that if I heard from you to have you call him. I don't know, mon, but part of me thinks he's a square guy for a cop, huh Nicky?"

"Yeah, he is. Remind me to send him some chocolates. But right now he wants my ass real bad. He's upset at me for sure. I called and left a message for him this morning. I think it was today. Christ, I don't even know what day it is. I got more questions than time, my man. But yeah, I'll try and get back to him. I've been putting it off."

"What you going to do now?" Ray asked. "You got a place to lay low, mon?"

"First of all, I'm going to go out to the house and get some necessities. I might even try to get my bike out of the garage. I know they probably have the cottage staked out, but I'm not worried about that. They won't know I was ever there. Let's set up a time for me to call you later and we'll work from there. I need you to check out our dear Mrs. Kiley and her men friends. I'll see what I can scare up on the insurance angle. I know time is running out and if I don't move fast now, I could be somebody's valentine in some maximum security lockup for a long time."

"You'd make a good wife, mon. You cook?"

There are times when Ray got on my nerves. This was becoming one of them, but I knew all he was trying to do was to cheer me up in his own way and besides I needed his help.

"Ray, please focus on the situation at hand. Don't count me out just yet, OK, mon?"

"Yeah, OK mon, call me at midnight at the house. I'll make sure I'm there, and I should have stirred up something by then. I'll talk to Peck, too, and feel him out. Don't get Justine into any trouble 'bout the insurance stuff you hear?" He wagged a big finger at me and held it there.

"OK already," I said and grabbed his finger. "Ray you have my word, and that's always been good with you, right?"

He pulled his finger out and reached his paw out over the table and tapped my cheek a few times with his open hand, smiling. That was about as affectionate as Ray got.

"Stay safe, my brother. I'll talk to you roun' midnight. And don't try to be a hero, mon."

He jammed his leather hat on top of his head, pried himself out of the booth, and left the bar without another word. I sat there for a moment, finished my soda, and then walked out into the cool August night.

Chapter 18

I made my way cautiously up the beach toward my cottage on my stomach. The sand was cool and damp, the wind was blowing the heavy salt air over me, and the surf was loud. I felt like I was in a bad 1940's war movie, and I was Audy Murphy or John Wayne leading a silent assault. I was on some obscure beachhead in the South Pacific. Actually, my thoughts went even deeper as I realized that I was acting certifiably insane. Here I was pretending to be a character out of one of my books, hiding from the cops, and trying to play investigator. And the dude I was looking for was probably responsible for killing several people; shooting at me, and making it appear damn convincing that I was the bad guy. He was real, and he was dangerous.

This was one script that I wanted to rewrite for sure. It'd be fun if I knew what the outcome would be. In my books I write the outcome. If I don't like the ending I change it, or if I deal Eddie into a mess he can't get out of I simply switch the cards. I could do that there. But, this was different. This was a real, bona fide situation, with real police, real dead people, and real bullets coming out of real guns. I could get shot. More than likely, I would get arrested for a murder or murders that I didn't commit. The problem I had with turning myself in and letting justice take its course was that I didn't have a whole lot of faith in having them see things my way. The frame seemed like a very good one, so I knew that I was dealing with a cunning opponent. I knew that whoever it was out there was toying with me, and I knew that he, she or they were out there watching me. I shivered at the thought. He could be crawling behind me in the sand ten yards away and I wouldn't be able to see or hear him. He could be waiting on one of the small sandy bluffs in back of my cottage with his rifle and a night scope, biding his time, waiting patiently for me to show. He'd know that I eventually would. The hairs on the back of my neck stood up, and I looked around carefully. All I saw was a lot of black, a dark starless sky, and the wind and the surf inching in loudly.

Why not try some of the deductive reasoning that I used in my books? What would Eddie do now? I'd spent a lot of time in the past trying to get inside the criminal mind so I could better write about them. It opened a virtual Pandora's Box. I found the frightening ones exceptionally intelligent and obsessively focused on some dark, evil side of life. I didn't say they had any common sense or social skills, and I certainly don't admire anyone who could or would take a life.

I was near the cottage. I strained my ears for any noise, any sound that wasn't supposed to be there, but all I heard were the waves lapping closer and closer in a building cadence. My heart was exploding with adrenaline and my mouth was dry as I crept closer to my home. I'd never had to sneak up on my own house before. Well, maybe in my drinking days, but not lately.

I had to try to get into my cottage. If I could just get the keys to my Harley and roll it out of the carport quietly, then I could push it down the road a bit and be home free. The problem was that the keys to my bike were hanging in my kitchen by the back door. I needed fresh wheels. Ray took the keys to Tom's wagon and said he would have someone take care of it.

The main thing I was after was that damn insurance file. I didn't know why I hadn't taken it when I left the house. I think I figured that this would be all over by now with a happy ending. But it's not and I think that file held the key. I could show it to Peck and he would listen, maybe. I also wanted some fresh clothes, and I toyed with the idea of getting my .45 out of my desk, but quickly thought better of it, because more than likely I'd be the one who got shot. I was better off unarmed even though there was still someone out there with a persistent desire to kill me.

I looked over and saw that Rudy's kitchen lights were still on, but the rest of his house was dark. He was probably up having his nightcap that I knew consisted of a dollop of tea in a big cup of good brandy. He told me his doctor recommended that he follow that practice to which he complied with religious fervor. I'd bet he went through a few doctors before he found one who told him what he wanted to hear. Oh well, God bless him. He wasn't hurting anybody. Besides, I've used more than one of his strange habits in my Eddie Kane books. Salute to you, Rudy!

I strained my eyes in the darkness and made out the shape of my cottage against the night sky. There was a lot of cloud cover and no moon was visible, so it was really dark. Even though it wasn't all that cold, I felt a chill. It was high tide and the waves crashed to the shore about twenty five yards away, making it impossible to hear much. I thought, with some satisfaction, that no one would be able to hear me either. I also felt something else. I felt a sort of energy from the danger. I should have been scared out of my pants. But, Eddie was alive! I was focused on the task at hand, and I felt charged and invincible. That should've worried me right then and there.

I proceeded cautiously towards my back deck staying low in the sand. My favorite character was Magnum. I'd love to be Thomas Magnum. I could see him crawling up a dark beach in pursuit of justice just as I was. I felt a little better about what I was doing even though the thought of Captain Artus Peck and his exuberant horde was never far.

I slapped myself back to the moment and rested my head on my hands, tasting the sand and smelling its dampness. If my friend was out there watching, I wasn't going to give him an easy target, so I tried to become one with the beach. I stayed low and ate sand as I realized that what I was doing was not all that bright. But onward I crept. My house was completely dark and there was no sign of life anywhere. I wondered where my feline adversary, Bob, was. He was probably really mad at me for not being there and very, very inconvenienced. Maybe Chris came and got him or at least fed him for me. She had her own key, of course, and she would've been concerned about poor kitty. That smelly cat had it made. He'd be so sweet and lovable to Chris.

She'd pick him up and cuddle and kiss him and he'd eat it up and the whole time he'd be looking over at me with a big smirk on his puss. And yes, cats do smirk, at least this one does. He and I do not like each other, and we both know the rules.

My cottage loomed ahead about twenty feet away. I rose up and threw a small rock at the side. I heard it hit the wood siding and clatter to the deck and I waited. Nothing. All I could hear was my heart pounding in my ears and the steady tempo of the waves crashing onto the shore behind me. I crouched and sprinted the remaining few yards to the cottage, flattened against the side, breathing hard and then peered around the corner. I saw that my driveway was empty. I looked around further and saw my MG in the carport. At least they didn't impound my car. Yet! So, I was reasonably sure that my old friend, my 1968 Harley-Davidson FLH, would be waiting and able. I just needed the keys. I should have taken them this morning. Eddie would have taken them. And Eddie wouldn't have left the insurance file either. I flogged myself for lack of foresight and resolved to learn from Eddie. Hey, I was new at this.

The house looked dark and deserted. I figured that it was now or never. Maybe the cops assumed I wasn't stupid enough to go back to my own house and called off any stakeout. I remained crouched by the corner of the cottage looking up the driveway toward the road and saw and heard nothing. I stood and was about to go back around the rear of the cottage and go in through the slider when a shiver went up my spine. Something cold and hard pressed against the back of my head just behind my right ear. I didn't even have to look to know what it was. I raised my hands slowly and whoever was holding the gun exerted upward pressure forcing me to stand. I stood.

The voice behind me said, "Keep your hands where I can see them and don't even think about being brave, because I'll blow your ass all over the side of your pretty little house." He pressed the gun harder into the back of my neck by my ear. "I knew you'd show up."

I nodded. Whatever you say, brother, you got the gun! I also knew that I'd heard that voice before, but I couldn't quite make the connection yet. The gun, which felt big and cold, was pressed firmly behind my ear.

I wasn't in any position to bargain, so I said, "You got it, Partner. Just relax and take it easy. I'm not armed or going to do anything stupid. Just tell me what you want me to do." I didn't want him to get nervous and pull that trigger.

He shoved me hard and then shouted at me with more urgency, "Put your hands against the house and spread your legs. Come on, hurry up, Thomas, you know the drill!" I did as I was told. He patted me down roughly, checking for weapons and found none. Christ, I was a writer. Eddie was the P.I. who carried that nasty little 9mm Beretta Cougar, a compact but powerful semiautomatic with a ten shot capacity. And I wish I had it now. Then again, what would I have done with it? Could I, Nick Thomas, writer, friend, lover of life, actually pull the trigger? I don't know that I could.

The man pushed me from behind and I stumbled forward. "Turn around slowly and put your back against the house. Keep your hands up. That's it. And now slide down to the ground," he ordered. I did exactly as he said and then I did a double take when I saw who it was. I remembered Vinnie Sax from the Truro Police Department. He was a rookie about the same time I was winding down my notable and somewhat renowned drinking career. He was a loner with an attitude, and from what I remember of Sax, he was always a bit larger than life; Italian as they come, with jet-black, wavy hair, tall and lithe with a clean-shaven face and big square chin with a huge dimple on it. Vinnie Sax was his own biggest fan. His uniform was always meticulously clean and pressed. He never had a hair out of place and he had this sneering, insincere smile. And he also had this habit of getting too close when he talked to you. I hated that. There is a space that we all feel is somewhat sacred that usually extends out about two feet around us. I don't like too many people closer to me than that as a rule, with the exception of Chris. That was different. But Sax was a space invader.

I always thought he watched too much TV. He wore his official aviator sunglasses all the time-literally. I remember doing a short character bio on him after we met. You never know when you're going to need a character like Vinnie Sax to thicken a plot. Eddie Kane would eat Vinnie Sax alive. Oh, and I remembered that he hated to be called Vinnie. He insisted on being called Vince. In his eyes there was a lot of difference between Vinnie and Vince. I thought so, too!

I did as he ordered and waited for him to speak. I had to become Eddie now or else I'd be scared shitless. Eddie wasn't afraid; he'd do whatever he needed to do—whatever came next.

My eyes adjusted to the darkness, and I saw him clearly. I groaned inwardly. He was grinning at me like a cat that had a nice, fat mouse cornered. He was dressed in dark clothing, and looked like something right out of a James Bond movie. He had on black jeans, a black long sleeve sweatshirt and, believe it or not, a black woolen watch cap pulled down over his ears. The only thing missing was the charcoal on his face. Reality prevailed when I focused on the ugly Smith & Wesson .357 that was still pointed at my head. How come the barrel of a gun always looks bigger when it's pointed at you? His adrenaline must be pumping, I thought, so I knew I'd have to be really careful with this guy. I did not want to get shot by this NYPD wannabe.

He moved several feet out of the shadows, and I saw that the gun was still trained on me. It was almost pitch black on the side of the house; his face was just visible, but not real clear. The noise from the rising tide was building along with a brisk wind blowing off the bay.

"Sax, right?" I yelled over to him.

"Just keep your hands where I can see them, Thomas. And shut the hell up! OK? This is the way it's gonna be. I'm gonna talk. You're gonna listen, got it? And if I want an answer, I'll ask you for one, otherwise don't even breathe, man." he said in a low, urgent voice, looking around nervously.

Wait a minute! Something didn't feel right here. Why did he have to be quiet? And what was he so nervous about? He's a cop, at least the last I knew he was. He should be calling this in on the radio, which I did not see on him, or screaming for his backup. He was doing neither. These facts suddenly struck me as very odd. He had to have a backup somewhere close by. His outfit was a bit on the bizarre side, but somehow believable. Who knows what the Truro Police have resorted to? But something told me he had something else on his mind. And I was not sure I wanted to know what it was.

I kept my hands raised over my head and sat with my back against the side of the house. All of a sudden I seemed to have a lot of time. I nodded my head back and forth several times, not saying a word. I wanted to see what he had in mind and how he played this out. Right now, he had the gun so he was in charge.

"Now listen to me carefully, Thomas." he came closer and squatted down in front of me. The Magnum was still leveled at my head. "First of all, you and me are gonna take a little ride and then we're gonna have us a little talk."

I leaned forward and opened my mouth to speak, but he jabbed the gun closer to my mug. I closed my mouth.

"Think about this, Thomas. I could blow your head off right now and nobody would shed a tear. In fact, they'd probably give me some kind of medal for doing it. So your best option right now is to listen to me and do what I say."

I nodded yes. This fool was up to something all right, and for the time being, I decided to keep my mouth shut and do exactly as he said. Of course, the decision was easy due to the fact that he had the gun and it was pointed at my head.

In one of my earlier books, Kane's Capture, Eddie was held for days by a serial sociopath who killed for fun and kept Eddie alive for sport. Eddie played along and studied the psycho for a weakness, a flaw, a thread to unravel, and he found one, and then used that to turn the tables. That's what Eddie did to survive. And that's what I'd try to do with Vinnie. I had to find that thread.

Vinnie kept looking past me towards the driveway and then over his shoulder behind him. He was acting more like a fugitive than a cop. OK, Vinnie, exactly what is going through that miniature brain of yours?

He came closer and crouched down in front of me and said, "Now that I have your attention, this is exactly how we are gonna do this, OK?"

I nodded and smiled through my teeth. My attention? I'll show you attention!

"I'm gonna help you, Thomas. I'm not gonna turn you in, because I don't think you're guilty, and I really want to find out who is. The why, that you are asking yourself, is because if I catch the killer I will look real good in ink. We all have motives, Thomas. Mine is a little glory and maybe a promotion. Who knows? Maybe I get in the movies. Huh? You never know. One of those cop things on TV maybe. They all think I'm stupid, but I'll show them. Yes I will!"

I couldn't see his face real clearly, but I'd bet his eyes were shinning and quickly approaching psychotic. It was then that I began to worry—a whole lot!

He prodded. "Well, what do you say to that, Thomas?"

"I'd say that you have my attention, Sax. You have the gun. OK, we take this ride, and you tell me what's on your mind. I won't try anything funny. You have my word."

"I know you won't run, because the first time that I think you are up to something, I'll blow you six ways to hell, capish?" He gave me a big, toothy grin. If he only knew how foolish he really looked.

"Cool! Then I suggest that we get out of here as soon as possible. Is there a unit out on the street?" I asked him. He nodded yes with a smug smile. "Don't worry about him. He's not with us right now."

"Vince, tell me you didn't dust the cop out in front of my house. Please tell me that!" But he just stared at me with that stupid smile on his face.

Great! I thought. This delusional maniac who thinks he's James Bond killed a cop in front of my house. Guess who they are going to like a whole lot on that one? Cop killing was one of those unwritten, shoot on sight, offenses. I might as well let this jerk kill me now.

"Relax, Hemmingway.   He's not dead, just sleeping for a while. On your feet now, time to go." He still had the gun on me, and I prayed that he was telling me the truth about the cop.

"You can put that thing away before somebody gets hurt, Sax. You got my word that I won't try anything. And can I please get into the house a second? I need a few things?"

He thumbed the hammer back on the Magnum and leveled it at my puss again. OK, sorry I asked, forget going in the house. If I needed a gun I'd figure out a way to take his. Eddie Kane would be proud. I think.

"Let's walk, Thomas. My car is parked down by your neighbor's driveway, and you're gonna drive. I still don't trust you a whole hell of a lot."

Guess what, Vinnie? You're not high on my trust list, either! But, I wanted to see where this was going. I had a feeling I was getting close to some answers. I didn't believe for a minute that Vinnie was capable of tracking down anything for the reasons he gave me.

Pete Nolin opened his eyes cautiously and strained his ears. He hadn't heard anyone move or walk by for quite a while now, and he could hear the cop outside his door snoring in his chair. He knew the cop was there because when the nurse came in to check his IV, he cracked open his eyes as she was leaving the room and saw the cop leaning against the wall in a metal folding chair with a magazine propped up on his lap. Pete waited for what seemed like eternity, listening to the cop rustling pages in the magazine, trying to stay awake, and then finally losing the battle about twenty minutes ago. The hallway was quiet.

Pete figured it was somewhere between eleven thirty and twelve because he'd heard the chatter and commotion of the nurses at shift change. He was pretty sure that was usually at eleven o'clock and that was a just a little while ago. He knew it was now or never to make his move and get out of here or else he would never see the light of day again.

The police must've tried to contact his mother by now and possibly found her in the cellar. No. They would have been back here in a flash if that'd been the case. So far they think he killed the Irishman and that was bad enough. As soon as they realized that he was conscious, they would be back to interrogate him. And then it would be all over. Pete couldn't talk to people like the police. They made him nervous.

It was dark in the hospital room, and he waited until his eyes adjusted. He slowly tried to sit up and was promptly greeted with a pain like he'd never known. It seemed like every bone and muscle in his body was on fire, and his head felt like someone was peeling his skull back with pliers. His entire chest, from high on his breastbone to below his waist, was covered in gauze bandages secured by a copious amount of white tape. He reached over and peeled off the white tape that was holding the IV in his arm and pulled out the needle slowly. He quickly placed the tape back over the puncture on his arm, where a bright red spot of blood appeared instantly. It hurt like hell to do that. He felt dizzy and groggy and his legs felt sore and raw where he must have lost some skin. There was a thick bandage on his left knee, but it didn't feel like there was anything on his right leg at all. He could wiggle his toes on both legs, though, and he knew this was a good sign. Pete hoped like hell that he'd be able to walk. They must've been giving him huge doses of pain-killers, because he didn't feel the pain that he thought he should've and that was OK with him, too. He would love to grab some drugs on the way out for later. He knew he was going to need something, but only if the opportunity presented itself and with a minimum of risk. First priority was escape. Jail was not an option. Pete knew that he could not go to jail. He looked down at the electrodes taped to several areas of his skin and prayed that they were not hooked up to any type of alarm. There were several on his chest above the stiff bandages and one on the right side of his head near his temple. He watched the monitor screen on the stand next to his bed which showed zigs and zags every time he moved, but made no noise. He reached over and switched the unit off, laid back down and covered himself up, waiting. He strained his ears, trying to filter out the pounding in his chest, for any type of reaction to his shutting off the machine. He waited for about five minutes and there was none, so he peeled the electrode wires off and laid them carefully over the top of the machine. He smiled to himself as a plan began to formulate. He might need those wires again.

Pete sat back up, ignoring the pain that raged through his body. He felt a stabbing pain in his ribs and there was a high school marching band playing in his head, tubas, cymbals, and all. He slowly rested one foot on the cold tile floor and found that he could put a little pressure on it and was able to bear the pain. The next one was surprisingly painless and he knew then that he'd be able to walk. Not run, but walk. He sat there on the edge of the bed and looked around the room for something to put on over his hospital gown, which he could tell didn't cover much, because he was cold. His clothes were nowhere in sight, and he didn't see anything that even resembled a robe. He figured that they didn't think he was in need of anything to wear for a while. He couldn't leave the hospital like this. He needed clothes and there was only one logical source.

He stood slowly and winced as the pain shot up his left leg and vibrated up to his head like a tuning fork. He grabbed onto the bed railing and inched his way towards the door, forcing himself to stand upright and gritting his teeth with each small movement. The heavy bandages around his ribs pulled painfully on his skin as he straightened up. He felt dizzy and was fading in and out of blackness. Only sheer will kept him conscious. He grabbed an empty, hard plastic cup from the bedside stand in one hand and pulled the stainless steel crank handle of the bed out of its socket with the other. The L-shaped handle was about twelve inches long and weighed three or four pounds, he guessed. Perfect.

He painfully made his way towards the door, hoping that the night nurse would not pick this time to make her rounds. He stood silently by the door and listened. The only sound he could hear was the cop outside still snoring in his chair. Pete tried the knob and turned it to the left with care. When the knob was turned all the way and stopped, he pulled the heavy wooden door open a crack. He could see the policeman clearly now, leaning back in the metal folding chair, with his eyes closed. Pete pulled the door open a little more, poked his head out, and looked down the bright hall in both directions. There was no one in sight.

He closed the heavy door without a sound and stepped back and to the side, behind where the door would swing open. He raised the crank handle above his head and threw the empty plastic cup on the tiled floor. The cup hit the floor with a loud clatter, bouncing once then tumbling and rolling noisily to the inside of the door. Pete held his breath and raised the handle a little higher above his head. His shoulder was throbbing and it felt like he might have ripped out some stitches. It felt warm and sticky under his gown, but he didn't have time to worry about that now. It was too late. He had already made his move.

He heard the policeman grunt and then the scrape of metal on the floor as he got up from the chair. Pete's chest was pounding and he felt dizzy. Just hold on . . . a minute more.

"What the hell was that?" Pete heard the policeman ask himself.

A narrow shaft of light knifed into the room as the policeman pushed open the door a little and looked into the dark room. Pete couldn't see the cop's head just yet. Come on, get in here! Another shaft of bright light darted into the room and found its way to the empty bed. The cop pushed the door open wider, and Pete saw an arm with a long black flashlight extending into the room. The cop was no fool and was being cautious. Pete didn't count on this. He'd hoped that the cop would just come charging in after he heard the plastic cup drop and then Pete would bop the sucker on the head with the crank handle. His heart was about to explode and his eyes burned as beads of sweat trickled down his forehead. The only thing between Pete and the cop was the thick door-an inch and a half of wood and metal. Pete held the handle poised and steady over his head. He heard the cop breathing heavily only inches away. His hands felt sweaty and cold as he held his breath.

The door opened more and the cop began to enter the room slowly. The beam of his flashlight was playing around the corners of the room, back and forth. Pete saw the cop's shoulder and then his head become visible, slowly from the other side of the door. Without a second of hesitation, he brought the crank handle down on the cop's head as hard as he could and was rewarded with a sickening crack. The door crashed against Pete as the cop went down in a heap. Quickly and quietly, Pete slipped out from behind of the door and pulled the unconscious policeman into the room over the slick polished floor. He then stepped over him and looked out into the hall. Still nothing. He felt his throbbing temple and wiped the sticky blood on the side of his johnny. Maybe things would work out after all.

He closed the door and dragged the unconscious policeman behind it. The cop was not small and

Pete was hurting, but he was pumping fire—pure adrenaline. He couldn't explain where his strength was coming from. But make no mistake about it; it was there!

The policeman was a little taller and somewhat heavier than he was, but not by a lot, so Pete quickly undressed him and struggled painfully into the uniform. Pete didn't know much about guns and was nervous as he buckled the heavy, black leather gunbelt around his waist.

He just wanted to get away. He didn't want to hurt anyone else. He only wanted them to leave him alone, even though somewhere deep in his disturbed mind, he knew they could never leave him alone now. He'd killed once and now they'd never let him be! Pete knew one thing in his heart; he'd never go to jail! He'd never let them lock him up like some kind of animal. Momma used to lock him in his closet when she and Daddy got drunk and wanted to fool around. He closed his eyes and remembered the musty, dark closet, remembering the drunken laughter and the sounds of sex. They would sometimes pass out afterward and leave him till morning, and then beat him for pissing his pants. No, that would never happen again. Pete made a silent pledge to himself as he finished putting on the unconscious cop's uniform. He'd die before he would go to jail.

He felt the hard, carved wood and steel handle of the weapon strapped to his side. It was heavy and cold. He shivered as he ran his fingers along the polished steel butt and felt where the clip slid into the handle and locked. He pulled his hand away. He never had held a gun before. He never had any reason to. Guns meant death, and Pete was afraid that it was going to be him who would die.

Pete jumped when he heard a phone ringing somewhere down the hall. He froze, unconsciously holding his breath and listening. The silence was thick with the exception of the muted ringing. His eyes wandered down to the unconscious cop and saw that he had a nasty gash on the side of his head where he'd hit him with the crank handle. Oddly enough, there wasn't a lot of blood around his head. He saw blood and hair on the crank handle, but there wasn't much. Maybe he'll be OK, thought Pete. He thought he saw the cop's chest rising and falling slightly, so he must be breathing. Pete really hoped he didn't add killing a cop to his list. He knew he didn't have the strength to put the cop into the hospital bed and hook the monitor wires up to him as he was planning, so he left the cop on the cold tile floor.

"Hello?" a voice called from right outside his door. Pete's heart stopped. Someone was in the hall directly outside his door. It was female. Must be the night nurse looking for the cop. Where did she come from?

"Officer? Are you in there? There's someone on the phone for you. Hello?"

Pete froze as he saw the knob begin to turn. He quickly reached down and picked up the already bloodied crank handle. Shit, he really didn't want to hurt the nurse too! Oh well, you gotta do what you gotta do, he thought.

The phone rang again down the hall and Pete saw the doorknob spring back as she let it go. He felt faint as he exhaled. He figured it was now or never and to hell with the damn nurse. He took a deep breath and opened the door and stepped quickly out into the hall. The bright light hurt his eyes, and he had a hard time focusing as he looked toward the nurse's station. He saw the nurse's back as she spoke on the phone. The other direction yielded a reward as he spied a red illuminated EXIT sign at the end of the hall, about twenty feet away. He did not hesitate and headed directly for it.

"Officer? Hello?" the nurse called to Pete from down the length of the hall. "You have to call your station right away."

Pete, with his back still to her, raised his arm in a waving gesture, mumbled, "OK," and kept on walking toward the exit door.

He prayed the door led to a stairway, and it did. He didn't hear if the nurse replied or not as he opened the door and headed, as fast as his hurting body would allow, down the stairs. The number on the wall informed Pete he was on the third floor, so he figured he had four small flights of stairs to negotiate, two per floor. He didn't have time to look at himself in the mirror before he left the room and imagined that he was probably a sight. His hair felt sticky and he knew there were visible cuts and bruises on his face and arms. He'd never pass close scrutiny as a cop, but all he needed to do was make it out of the hospital, and he'd be home free.

Pete stopped and listened carefully. He didn't hear anything in the stairwell in either direction, so he proceeded cautiously, but painfully down the cement steps toward the first floor. He leaned heavily on the steel railing and had to stop every few steps. Pete didn't think he'd be seen. Most people were lazy and used the elevator. Besides, it was almost midnight, so there shouldn't be a lot of coming and going.

Pete assumed there would be another cop in the

lobby, or at least a security guard and he knew it would be just a matter of minutes before someone discovered he was missing and raised the alarm. The nurse would find the unconscious cop when she made her rounds and that had to be soon. Then all hell would break loose. He felt the gun with his hand. He'd try to find a less traveled exit instead of using the main lobby and risking an inevitable confrontation.

Chapter 19

There were several large questions looming in my mind about my new buddy, Vince, which had me concerned as we drove west on 6A away from my cottage. Let me clarify that last statement; I drove, and Vinnie was behind me in the back seat with his gun pressed against the back of my neck. He had his left hand on my shoulder and the gun in his right. Needless to say, I was a bit wary about hitting any bumps. And if I weren't so convinced that all this was leading me in the right direction, Vince would have been impaled on that nasty .357 of his a long time ago.

Eddie Kane was wary but not afraid and this is how I had to be if I wanted to live. It was all so bizarre. I was becoming Eddie Kane again and with that realization I found I could justify this insane behavior, and almost like it. Mind you, this was not Nick Thomas, writer of fiction, saver of errant souls. This was Eddie Kane, an alter ego I'd created to be all I wanted to be, when I needed to be. I felt a strength that I'd never felt before.

I looked back at him in the rearview mirror. "Do

you think the gun is necessary, Vince? I mean, that damn thing could go off by mistake, you know!" I asked him as calmly as I could manage.

"Just keep your eyes on the road, Thomas." he said, nudging my neck with the gun. "Come to think of it, it might not hurt for you to be a little worried about this gun. It'll keep you honest." He leered at me in the mirror with this idiotic grin on his waxen face. I didn't like him anymore.

"Sax, you are really starting to piss me off." I'd reached my boiling point. My patience, that I was so proud of a minute ago, had vanished. "Didn't I hear you say that you believed I was innocent and that you were going to help me, or was I hearing things?" I asked him over my shoulder, through clenched teeth. I gave the Camaro more gas.

"Slow down! That doesn't mean I trust you, Thomas. I could be wrong about you. I'm not taking any chances."

I heard a lot of fear in his voice and I sensed there was a lot more to this than meets the eye. What was he so afraid of? If the cops stopped us he could say that he had me in custody, which was true. No, there is something else going on here and I'd bet the farm that he was high on something. If I were to guess, it would be cocaine. He had that glassy-eyed, agitated, dry mouthed, jaw clenching look. Unfortunately, I knew that look all too well. I knew there was no sense in agitating him further right now. Patience, Nick, I told myself. Eddie would wait and watch—play the game. And that's exactly how I would play it.

I came to the intersection of Route 6 and then asked my new friend what he wanted me to do. He gestured with the gun for me to turn right on Rt.6. How could I resist? I down shifted the Camaro at the intersection, looked both ways, and nailed it, spitting sand, and rock in all directions. "Hey!" he cried, shoving the Magnum hard against the back of my head. I could feel his hot breath on my neck as he leaned forward and hissed in my ear, "Be careful of my car or I'll decorate the windshield with your brains. I'll kill you right now, Thomas, I swear I will! And nobody will care either way! I'll be a hero. Now slow down!"

I somehow doubted that he'd mess up his pretty car with my blood and brain tissue. Besides, I thought that he thought he really needed me for something or I'd be dead. For what reason he needed me was the mystery—the million-dollar question. I also felt that he was not working alone on this. Vinnie was just not that smart. I didn't buy his story about trying to find the real killer for a second, and wondered if he actually thought I was that stupid!

"OK, Vinnie, relax. I just got carried away with this fine Detroit machine. I'll be cool! By the way, where are we headed?" I asked him.

He ignored my question and kept watching the road. I was getting the creeps from this guy. It was like he was possessed or something. His eyes were wide open with lots of white showing and there were beads of sweat on his forehead and cheeks. I'd love to run this car into a tree. He'd freak and it'd serve him right, but he also might shoot me in the process. I didn't, for a moment, forget the fact that he still held the .357 a mere inch from my skull . . . for the moment.

I saw the lights of Truro approaching quickly up ahead, so I kicked the Camaro down into third and slowed a bit as we approached a changing light. It was just turning yellow so I nailed the big V-8 and roared on through the intersection. I was beginning to have fun.

"Thomas, if you get stopped the joke will be on you, so slow down!" he screamed in my ear.

Remember when you were young and there were those cartoon characters that had a devil on one shoulder and an angel on the other? Well, my devil wanted me to choke him in the worst way, but the angel told me to go along with him just a little longer. I listened to the angel, which was new behavior for me. The devil had been my buddy for many years, or so I thought. Vinnie had someplace to go and something on his mind, and I wanted to know what that agenda was. This was more than I had to go on up until this point, so why not? Eddie would be patient and so would I.

"Take the next right up here and use the blinker, will you?" Another friendly nudge from the magnum emphasized his point. He was going to be very sorry that he ever saw that gun, because every time he goes to the bathroom for the rest of his life, he will be reminded of that Smith & Wesson .357 magnum. Enough is enough!

I did as he asked and pulled onto a small, darkened road that wound around some small dunes and would eventually end up somewhere near Wellfleet Harbor. I slowed the powerful Camaro and hit the brights. I saw the lights of a few small houses and cottages on both sides of the road as I wound the car slowly through the darkness.

"Up here on the right, about 50 yards. Pull in the driveway and go on up behind the house. There, the yellow one. And go slow, asshole, the driveway is bad." That turned out to be the understatement of the century. He leaned over the seat and pointed with the gun where he wanted me to turn. I wondered if he could learn to converse without it.

The front end of the car bounced fiercely as I plunged into a crater sized pothole at the mouth of the driveway. The cold barrel of the .357 dug into my neck as we bounced with the car. He screamed something unkind to me, which I blissfully ignored. He wasn't going to shoot me, at least not yet, I hoped.

The car's headlights washed over a shabby, yellow clapboard ranch that was set back off the road in a dark tangle of overgrown shrubs and trees. There were no lights on in the house, but there was a small motion sensor by the side door which tripped on and spilled light onto the driveway when we passed. It felt like I was driving in a mine field as the car bounced up and down slowly when I rumbled past the dark house. The overgrown weeds around us came up to the car door, sweeping noisily against the sides of his precious car as we drove by. I could see a rusted Ford pick-up resting on blocks up ahead of me at the end of the driveway, next to a small ramshackle garage that was barely standing. I parked the Camaro next to the truck and looked back at Vince. He didn't say a word, as he seemed preoccupied with checking the yard.

"Nice place." I commented.

He looked back at me and said, "You know Thomas, someday someone's gonna close that wise trap of yours for good!"

Vinnie had no sense of humor, and you know what? Mine seemed to have escaped as well! I shut off the motor, pulled up the emergency brake with my right hand and quickly reached back over my right shoulder with my left hand, grabbed his wrist and twisted as hard as I could. I heard some nice little crunching noises. A few of the small bones in his hand would need some type of therapeutic care in the very near future. I surprised myself. I had never actually hurt anybody like this before. I turned in my seat and reached up with my right hand and plucked the gun from his crippled hand. Oh, I almost forgot, he was screaming now. I let go of his hand and grabbed him by his hair and promptly shoved the big, ugly barrel of the Magnum in his mouth. Vinnie stopped screaming and his eyes got real big. I had a good slice of his attention now. And in that quick stroke of bravery, Nick Thomas disappeared completely and Eddie was alive! I liked the feel of the heavy gun in my hand. I was in control.

I got real close to his face and hissed through clenched teeth, "Now you listen to me and you listen hard you greasy punk!" I poked the gun into the roof of his mouth. "Do you understand me?"

Vinnie nodded as vigorously as he could with the gun still in his mouth and I kept it right where it was. It seemed to be a good attention getter. This was stuff I wrote about. I loved it! "Now, Vinnie, let's try to get this on the first try. I haven't had a real good couple of days, and consequently I'm not in the best of moods. You can understand that, can't you?"

I liked watching him shake his head like that, with the gun sticking out of his puss. I was beginning to like it a lot! It was another character defect that I might have to work on someday. I knew I shouldn't react out of anger. I should show a more understanding side, even to my adversaries. Not tonight though, I was starting to have fun!

"Now here's the deal, Vinnie. You and I are going to get out of this car, real slow, and then we are going into that poor excuse for a house. Do you live here Vinnie?" I think I heard the word "Yes" filter around the barrel of the Magnum.

"Is anyone else in the house, Vinnie?" I had a firm grip on Vinnie's hair with my left hand and I perfected this nice little technique of twisting his head a bit when I asked him a question. I think Vinnie liked it too because his eyes were wide open and he answered me each time with renewed enthusiasm. This time I believe he said "No!" to my last question. It was hard to tell. I think he needs to work on his diction a bit. A lot of life is how one presents oneself.

"I wish I had more time to lecture you on keeping a nice home. It's more important than you know, because it's a direct reflection of the image you have of yourself. Did you know that, Vinnie?" I thought we were well on the way to becoming the best of friends. You can always tell when you've made that special connection with people.

There was another enthusiastic nod. By God, I really think Vinnie was getting the hang of this. Eddie had a sarcastic side, and he had turned the tables now. I, Nick Thomas, was just along for the ride.

"Now, here's where it gets a little complicated, Vinnie. First, we are going to get out of the car and if you do anything to piss me off, any more than I already am, I will blow your head off." I was pretty sure I had his unwavering attention. I wondered what it would take to actually pull that trigger, to consciously end someone's life in some insane moment of truth. I prayed it wouldn't come to that. I also hoped Vinnie wouldn't sense just how scared I was.

"You know, come to think of it," I said, "I might as well shoot you right now, because everybody thinks that I killed Carla. There are those who think I also killed Kiley. Where in the reality of it all, Vinnie, I didn't hurt a fly. Yet!" And I looked him right in the eye. I probably looked a bit psychotic myself at that point. I continued, "What's one more body, right? As a matter of fact, Vinnie, if you say one word right now, I am going to shoot you. In fact, I'm beginning to think I really do want to shoot you anyway, Vinnie. I'm growing fonder of the idea by the minute. Now get out of this goddamn car, unlock the door, and find me some food and some hot coffee fast. My mood just might improve and then you and I are going to have a nice talk. I'm anxious to hear what you have to say. Trust me, Vinnie, you want me in a better mood as soon as possible!"

Eddie was beginning to scare me. I wondered if there was more to this Eddie Kane thing than being an alter ego. I prayed that I wasn't developing another personality. I was researching MPD for my new book and it was awful scary stuff. I didn't have time to analyze that now, so forward we went.

We, that is, Eddie and I, followed Vinnie closely into the ramshackle house, with the gun jammed firmly in his back. I was already speculating what this Cretan had festering in his refrigerator. That slice of pizza and bag of chips I'd inhaled on the way out of town was but a faint memory and I was still famished. All this mystery and intrigue lent to a hearty appetite, which even under normal circumstances, was ravenous. If you couldn't already tell, food is an important facet of my life.

I followed Vinnie into the ramshackle house unaware of the sleek black car that was parked on the other side of the run down garage.

There was that wonderful smell of greasy bacon frying in Vinnie's grungy kitchen. It was actually an improvement over the smell of decaying garbage and mildew, I thought, and man, was I hungry. The smell of bacon frying was an aphrodisiac to me, as was most food. Chris says I get more turned on by the sight of a fat Maine lobster stuffed with crabmeat than her in a negligee'. That was definitely not true, but she always fed me first just in case! Smart woman!

"Don't forget the toast, Vinnie." I said, waving the Magnum at him, getting impatient. My stomach was rumbling with anticipation. "Got any jelly?"

"You know Thomas, this ain't no damn diner."

Ignoring his venomous look, I popped open the cylinder on the Magnum and checked it. Full. Good! I turned the nasty looking revolver over in my hand and inspected it more closely. It was a Smith & Wesson Model 19 Combat Magnum with a two and one half inch barrel; small, lightweight and very deadly. This was not your run of the mill cop piece, but great at close range. I learned a lot about small weapons when I was searching for the perfect gun for Eddie Kane, and this fine weapon was one in contention. But the smaller Beretta 9mm Cougar won out. I'd actually gone to the police range with Mac and was allowed to fire both, and I went as far as taking the mandatory safety course and got a permit to carry. I could, but never did. I'd never felt the need to carry a gun on Cape Cod before this whole nightmare. I watched Vinnie the whole time to see if he was brave enough to try a move while I was checking the gun. He might have been considering it, but wisely thought better of it.

"Now Vinnie..." I began.

"Look Thomas," he interrupted me angrily. "I don't like to be called Vinnie. The name's Vince and I'd appreciate it greatly if you could remember that. OK? We are not enemies here, you know. I saved your ass, Thomas. Remember that! Vince, OK?"

I nodded and decided that I'd be nice to him until he finished making my meal. I have a problem with rude people, especially when I'm going out of my way to be nice. I thought I was being nice here. After all, he was the one who started with the gun back at my place. But, I gave him some slack and said with a small laugh, "Sure, sure Vince, I'm sorry."

He came over and dropped the plastic plate down on the table in front of me with a clatter and went back to get the coffee. We were bonding. He came back to the table with two mugs of coffee, a chipped blue mug with a white Fleet Bank logo on mine and his sported a faded Red Sox "B". It figures, losers love losers. He sat down in the chair next to me and looked at me expectantly. I guess I rated his good china. I know the knife and fork he gave me came from a restaurant. I had the same set at home.

"Not hungry Vince?" I asked him between mouthfuls of bacon, eggs, and toast. "This isn't bad. Maybe you ought to consider a career change. That is if you live long enough."

He didn't answer me. I felt bad that he couldn't appreciate my humor. He eyed me and took a sip of his coffee. I could tell he was trying to read me. Good luck! The .357 was right next to my plate and he would have to reach across me to get to it. I think we both had a silent understanding that he shouldn't try that. I could see that his hand was swollen and purple from our discussion in the car. He would have better luck trying to take food away from a couple of starving Dobermans. I continued to eat. Well, shovel is probably a more appropriate term. Chris says that what I do with food doesn't even faintly resemble eating. It has a more primal nature. She says it with love, though.

I motioned Vince with my fork to talk. I had my mouth full and even I know it's rude to talk with food in your mouth. I noticed him looking out the window behind me trying not to be obvious. No wonder he was a lousy cop, I thought.

I swallowed quickly, wiped my mouth with the dishtowel he gave me, and turned around to the darkened window, scanning the yard and driveway the best I could. I shaded my eyes with my hand and got close to the glass. I kept one eye on Vinnie as I did this, of course. I didn't see anything, but decided it would be a good idea to take a walk around outside just to make sure. When I was done eating, of course.

"Expecting someone Vince? If you are, I suggest you tell me now or else I'm gonna be real upset. We're trying to establish some trust here. Right?" I took a bite of a buttered triangle of toast. I couldn't see anything outside except the part of the driveway that was illuminated by the weak porch light. I turned back to Vince and picked up the gun.

"Vince, let me explain something to you. I'm a man who is wanted for a murder, actually several murders, that I didn't commit and as a direct result of some insane misunderstanding, I have every jerk and their brother out there looking for me. So, at this particular point in time, I have very little to lose. If I think for a second that you are scamming me, I'm going to shoot you directly between the eyes. Frankly

I don't care. I'm way past that. So, now is the time to come clean with me and tell me exactly what your agenda is and what we are doing here, besides eating bacon and eggs. Which are great by the way. I hope I didn't forget to thank you." I smiled at him.

"Are you always a smart ass, Thomas?" He asked, looking at me over the rim of his beloved Red Sox mug. I thought I scared him, but he barely blinked. He put his mug down on the table with a thud, folded his thin, white hands in front of him, and went on. "Because it seems that you need me a hell of a lot more than I need you. Let's put things in perspective here. OK? I'm not the one the cops, which by the way, I'm one, are looking for. You are!" He jabbed a finger at me and then leaned back in the kitchen chair, looking really smug. I kept eating, but held my hand on the gun and my eyes on him every second.

Vinnie rolled his eyes toward a greasy spot on the ceiling, as if pondering some great wisdom, and continued. "Now here I go out and find you, tell you that I believe that you are innocent and offer you my help. I mean, I really put myself out on a limb here to help you and this is the thanks I get. I could get in a load of trouble over this, you know. Talk about trust." He had this way about him that everything he said came out like a whine. And I was genuinely touched by his sacrifice.

I think he wanted a hug. I finished my eggs, mopping up the last of the yoke with the toast. That was my favorite part. The yoke. I didn't answer him or even acknowledge that I heard him. I was at one with my food, or so I acted. I held up my empty coffee mug and raised my eyebrows. He snatched it from me and got up to refill both of ours.

"You are indeed a jerk, Thomas. There is little doubt about that." He sounded far away and I was very tired all of a sudden. It had been a long day both emotionally and physically. I had to get things in perspective with Vinnie so I could get some sleep and this seemed as good a place as any to do just that.

"OK Vinnie. Sorry. OK Vince, as soon as we finish our coffee, I'd like you and I to take a quick look around outside. It'd make me feel a whole lot better and then we're going to hash this mess out. I assume that I can crash here tonight?"

"Sure, Thomas. Whatever you say."

He was being nice to me, and I should've been worried. But all I wanted to do was crawl up in a ball somewhere and go to sleep. I was fighting to stay awake with everything I had. I stretched my arms over my head and yawned, but my eyes refused to stay open.

The words were hard to form. "Look Vince, do I really need this gun?" I said slowly, looking over at him standing by the coffeepot. He was beginning to look fuzzy. I thought I saw a strange smile play on his lips. I didn't understand and the Magnum felt like it weighed a thousand pounds.

"What's the matter Thomas, you tired?" It sounded like he was taunting me now. But I couldn't respond right away. It seemed like minutes passed.

We both jumped when the kitchen door flew open and slammed against the wall behind it. My heart stopped and jaw dropped open when Karen Kiley came charging through the door with a pistol in her hand and a wild look on her face.

"Shit honey, you scared the hell out of me," Vinnie whined.

She looked at Vince in disgust and then over at me. I couldn't focus on her very well. I squinted one eye and she was still blurry and my head was heavy. Their voices were far away. Karen was close to me; I could smell her strong perfume. It was musky but powdery in the same breath. I fumbled for the gun on the table, but couldn't find it. My head felt heavy when I tried to look around for it.

Vince came over to the table and he stood over me as I slumped forward a bit then caught myself. "That stuff works good, huh baby?" he said.

Karen's voice answered from a long way off, "Maxine got it from some pharmacist friend who has the hots for her. She told him that she needed it to play a joke on somebody. Some joke, huh? And the dumb shit gave it to her. He looks like he's almost out."

She walked over and grabbed me by the hair, pulling my head up. It was like I was watching the whole thing on TV with the mute button on and it was in slow motion—very slow motion. Karen let go of my hair and it was like I didn't have any muscle control. My face crashed down onto the table sending the plate and the remains of my breakfast flying. I stayed with my face down on the table not moving. But the funny thing was that I could still hear them. I pried one eye open and watched Karen turn back to Vince and then level the small automatic at his chest.

Vinnie looked surprised and stammered, "Karen, what . . ?"

"What is going on, Vince? What happened?" she snapped at him stopping him cold. "He had a gun on you when you came in. A goddamn writer! And you're a cop? What a joke!" her voice was low and menacing. She took two steps toward him with the ugly little semi-automatic held firmly out in front of her. Vinnie backed up and put his hands up in front of him. He looked scared. He should've been.

"Karen, please put the gun down. Everything is under control. We got Thomas just like we planned . . . er you planned. I grabbed him outside his cottage and he was there just like you said he would be. Come on honey, put the gun away." He pleaded, reaching for her.

"Did anyone see you Vince? Anyone at all?" she asked him with a disgusted look on her face. He shook his head no. I was fading by the second.

She slowly dropped the gun to her side and then slipped it into the pocket of her blazer. Then she stepped into Vince's arms and nuzzled her head under his sinewy neck. She reached down and rubbed her hand over his crotch. "OK baby, I just had to be sure. We can't make any mistakes right now. We're too close to the jackpot. OK, baby?"

Vine responded and began kissing her neck, but she pulled away, always the tease. "I missed you, honey," he pleaded with her in a pathetic voice. "I don't like to be away from you. You know that."

She dismissed him with a wave of her hand and looked over at me. "Vince, we better take care of Thomas first. Do you have the cuffs and rope you said you would have?"

"Yeah, yeah." He said thickly. "Hold on here a minute. I'll be right back. They're in the trunk of my car. Don't lose that thought. OK, baby?"

He grabbed his keys and disappeared quickly outside, leaving Karen standing in the kitchen watching me.

She strutted over and grabbed me by my hair

again. "Remember that night at Ray's?" she hissed in my ear. She sounded as if she were miles away. I couldn't answer her but I remembered vaguely. I felt her breath on my face again, "Screw you! Nick Thomas, mister famous writer. You turned me down like I was some piece of bar trash. You and that little fish doctor, what's-her-name. So high and mighty!" she hissed in my ear. "But, I got you now, Mr. Big Shot. Maybe I'll talk Vince into tying you up naked and I'll screw you silly while Vince watches. What you think about that, Shakespeare? Maybe I'll cut your dick off with a pair of scissors and put it in Vinnie's refrigerator." She laughed in my face and stumbled a little. She wobbled against me, leering, and high on something.

At the moment, I didn't feel like laughing. I could see that she was dangerous, and I didn't want to tangle with her when she was messed up. I couldn't anyhow. I couldn't feel my arms or legs anymore and her voice came from far away.

The door slammed closed behind us and Vinnie came back with two sets of cuffs and a coil of heavy rope slung over his shoulder. "We gonna stash him in the cellar tonight? I got it bolted up pretty good. He won't go anywhere and nobody's gonna hear him down there. He'd have to be Harry Houdini to get away. It'll be safe."

"Sure Vince, we'll put him downstairs, but first I think we should have a little fun." she purred, rubbing back up against him, running her tongue slowly along his throat and kissing his neck wetly. He dropped the cuffs and rope right there where he was standing.

Vince pulled back and looked at her with a puzzled smile. " Sure Honey, what do you have in mind?" She put her mouth to his ear and whispered something to him I couldn't hear. I closed my eyes for the last time and dove into the black water.

⬻⫷⫷⫷⫸

Pete found his way out of the hospital through a door marked Maintenance Personnel Only that had a crash bar, which he pushed open from the inside. Luckily, no one happened by because he knew he'd never pass muster in the cop's uniform, and he was in no mood for any more confrontation tonight. The maintenance door led out to an area with a high chain link fence that seemed to be humming with electricity. It was a transformer and he noticed a large HIGH VOLTAGE sign on the fence a few yards down. He bristled involuntarily and could almost feel the prickling current in the air. He looked out onto to what looked like a small gravel access road that led around the back of the hospital and was dimly lit by two flood lights mounted high up on the building. To Pete's relief, the area appeared to be deserted. He let the door close quietly behind him and stepped into the shadows next to the building. He leaned against the cool brick wall and listened as he rested. The pain was everywhere in his body. The IV meds had just about completely worn off by all his activity.

He knew that he didn't have much time before the cops descended upon this place with a vengeance. Pete didn't know if the cop upstairs was alive or not, but it was not something that would keep him awake nights. They were going to get him soon enough and he knew it. What he knew and they didn't, was that he wasn't going to any jail. Period! They must know about Momma by now. And more than likely they think he killed that fat Irishman, too. Hell, they probably are going to try to pin that Thomas woman thing on me, too. He patted the leather holster on the heavy police gun belt nervously and knew that he'd have to use the gun eventually, even though he was not very familiar with it. There was always a first time for everything. It couldn't be that tough. Just point the gun and pull the trigger and BAM!—you're dead.

It is unusually quiet back here, Pete thought. All he could really hear was the humming of the high voltage lines overhead and the stiff rustle of the night breeze through the trees. It was cold and he was beginning to slow down due to the severe pain racking his body. It seemed that the adrenaline rush from knocking out the cop and escaping from the room kept him going for awhile, but now that he was somewhat still, the pain was flooding back over his body in a steady wave. He knew he was going to have to fight to stay conscious.

Pete knew that he must be in Hyannis. It was the only large hospital on the Cape. He laughed to himself because he realized that it didn't make a difference where he was now. He had no home to go to, no one to answer to, and no job. No one! Even his girls in the magazines were far away back in his desk. Fuck them too! It's a new game now—simple survival. All because he had the bad timing to deliver that woman's food that night and he saw her lying there in a pool of blood, dark, crimson blood. He never did anything. It was all her fault. He wouldn't have killed Momma; he wouldn't have been in the parking lot at Ray's the night the Irishman got killed and he wouldn't have smashed into that Lincoln and be here. One horrible minute and his life had changed forever and he knew that he could never turn back. It was life or death now. There was no in-between any longer. Pete thought of a drink. A drink would be good, some 100-proof vodka would do the trick, but there was a fat chance of that now.

He thought about what he was going to do and decided that he was going to go out in a blaze of glory and last as long as he could. Why not? He figured he would take a few of them with him. He'd be like Rambo. What did it matter now?

He wished he could have stolen some drugs before leaving the hospital, but the opportunity did not present itself and he wanted to get out of there as quickly as possible. But really, what could they have done, arrest him? He laughed weakly to himself and finished with a racking cough. The pain was becoming unbearable, but he knew that he couldn't risk going back inside. He was not ready for a fight just yet. The pain was draining every bit of strength he had. He had to save his energy.

He jumped as he heard tires crunching slowly on the gravel of the access road heading in his direction. He looked around and limped painfully across the road where he ducked behind some hedges. He strained his eyes in the direction of the sound but didn't see any headlights, but he could still hear the car slowly coming towards him. Could the sons-of-bitches be coming for him now? He looked behind him and all he could see was a steep hill leading to what looked like a residential area. He'd head towards those houses if he could negotiate that hill. But it looked awfully steep and he wasn't exactly feeling nimble. Pete knew his leg was bleeding now. It felt wet and sticky under the heavy uniform pants and he felt something running down his leg. The wounds on his chest were still burning and he felt dizzy and nauseous. But, he wanted to try to make it up that hill before more cops came around the other side.

Too late! He saw the dark shape of a police cruiser come around the building and into the light. He could make out two cops. The one on the passenger side was shining a hand held spotlight into the hedges that bordered the road where he was hiding. They were going slow and checking every inch. This was it, Pete thought. He felt his heart about to explode. Although it was a cool night, he was bathed in sweat. The police car was about twenty yards away, and he wasn't sure if he would be hidden from the spotlight or not. He knew he had to move out of there and fast! The hill behind him looked steep but he really had no other choice besides going across the road in front of the cops. Either way, there was a big chance that they'd see him before he got very far.

Then he heard noises from behind him on the hill. He spun around and fell to his knees from the sudden movement. He wiped the sweat and blood from his eyes with the uniform sleeve and squinted into the darkness where the sounds were coming from. His heart sank when saw two figures moving quickly in his general direction with what looked like two nasty German Shepherds straining on their leashes. The dogs began to whine and bark excitedly. They must have his scent because they were headed directly towards him. The cruiser on the road stopped about ten feet in front of where he was hiding. They must be in contact by radio, Pete thought. They had him surrounded. Here we go! It's show-time!

Pete unsnapped the leather holster and pulled out the gun. It was a scary looking thing and felt heavy in his hand. He knew it was one of those semi-automatics with a clip, but that was about the extent of his knowledge. The situation was out of his hands now. It was either fight or surrender and he already promised himself that they would not take him alive. There came a certain and total freedom in that realization. He could do anything he ever wanted to do and didn't care about the outcome. He was ready to die. So fight it was!

He stood up on shaky legs and looked over the hedge and came almost face to face with a huge, young cop about ten feet away, walking around the front of his cruiser. They stared at each other in total shock. Pete was the first to react as he raised the heavy gun and squeezed the trigger. He wasn't prepared for the recoil as the powerful handgun exploded in his hand. He saw the big cop fly backwards and land heavily on the hood of the cruiser behind him. He must have hit the bastard. Everything seemed to be moving in slow motion now. Good! Pete felt a rush and turned to see where the cops with the dogs were. Then there was yelling and more shots. He heard another explosion and it felt as if someone hit him in the shoulder with a sledge hammer, as he was thrown backwards into the hedge. His mind was screaming, I have to get up. His shoulder was on fire. He reached over and placed his hand over the wound and it was immediately covered with warm and sticky blood. Pete knew he was hit bad, but the total insanity of the moment drove him on. He wasn't done, yet! He grabbed a handful of hedge and tried to pull himself. His hands were cut and bleeding from the sharp branches, not that he felt them or much else at this point.

A bullhorn sounded from somewhere. "Stay where you are and put your hands in the air."

Pete tried to yell, but it came out garbled. He tasted blood in his throat and it made it hard to yell. He raised his right arm and tried to extend the gun in the direction of the two cops with dogs who were now only about ten feet from him. He couldn't see them, but he knew they were there. He felt a darkness start to wash over him as he squeezed the trigger and fired a shot that went harmlessly into the air over their heads.

Pete was already unconscious and didn't feel the next two slugs rip into him, or anything else . . . ever again.

Chapter 20

I came to again for the second time in the past few hours. After considerable concentration and process of elimination, it appeared that I down was in Vinnie's cellar. It was cold, damp, and completely dark, with the exception of a small glow from a crack in the furnace door. That's how I figured out I was in the cellar. The old furnace would rumble to life every few minutes spitting hot air up into the old house, sparing none for poor little ole' me. It was chilly at night and the small warmth from the furnace felt good.

What happened the first time I was awakened I won't tell you. Use your imagination. Suffice it to say that if I ever and God be my witness, get free from this rope, there will be two extremely sorry people upstairs. You can take that to the bank!

Vinnie was not really as smart as he would like to think. Number one, he tied my hands in the front, which will make it much easier to work the knot, and number two, he didn't tie me to anything. He must've been in a hurry to do an encore with sweet Karen. What a sick bitch that one was. I can't believe what she did to me and that idiot, Vinnie, just sat there watching, playing with his pecker. I guess what really pissed me off is that I couldn't control my response and she got exactly what she wanted. She is a very sensuous and sexy woman, but in the same breath, an extremely sick and dangerous one, too! She was a veritable Black Widow in high heels. I wondered if they were the ones who killed and ate their lovers when they were finished with the mating act.

I realized that my pants were soaked through and my ass was numb. Vinnie so thoughtfully threw me in a corner that had a good sized puddle of water and I could hear water dripping over my head, splashing just a few feet from me. My head was resting against the cold cement block wall that felt dirty and also very damp. Vinnie, Vinnie, shame on you. I thought we had this talk already. Better Homes and Gardens won't be pinning any blue ribbons on you any time soon.

My head was throbbing and my mouth felt like somebody dry cleaned my tongue. And believe it or not, even my hair hurt. At least they had the decency to put my clothes back on. I'll have to thank them properly when I get the chance.

The more I focused on Vinnie, the madder I got. He was a dead man. He just didn't know it yet. And then there was Karen Kiley. Now just where and how does she fit into all this? It didn't make sense. Or did it? Wait a minute! A small light bulb clicked on somewhere in the far recesses of my mind. The cobwebs started to clear away from whatever they drugged me with, leaving me with the equivalent of a massive bourbon hangover. Remember I was an expert at hangovers. My guess was that it was some sort of Phenobarbital cocktail or possibly chloral hydrate, which Vinnie slipped into my food or coffee. It's too bad. I thought Vinnie and I had begun to bond. Oh well, I guess you can't save everyone. AA says to pray for those who have harmed us. Believe me, Vinnie, you're in my prayers! I pray to get just close enough to put my hands around your greasy neck!

Of course it made sense now that I'd had the time to digest it all. Karen had set me up. You almost had to admire the shear cunning of it all. What she did was to figure out what her goal was and then work backward on how to get there. First, she must've been the one behind the attack on Carla and made it look like me. She probably had Vinnie do the actual deed because it was sloppy. Vinnie could mess up a wet dream. It was no secret that Carla and I did not get along and there was definitely no love lost between Carla and Karen. After all, Carla was playing hide the salami with Shawn, and Karen knew it. Then Karen had her sorry-excuse-for-a-husband snuffed outside a bar, which was his second home and not out of character. He was last seen in the company of that red head, Trish, and they had left the bar together that night. Ray said she could've been a hooker. He never saw her before and neither had I. All of this left me wanted for the murder of Carla, the baby, and more than likely, Shawn.

I could just imagine Karen choking back a sob and dabbing away the tears to sign the check, and then go bask in the sun. And she never got her hands dirty. She had that idiot, Vinnie, convinced that she'd take him with her. That, I somehow doubted. It was shrewd killing Carla first. It threw everyone off the track and had the dogs out chasing me and, in the same stroke of genius; it shed a lot of doubt about Shawn's moral fiber and character. Then, she had him taken out: quickly, ruthlessly, and quite anonymously. All she had to do was make sure that I was either dead or in jail for good and then just sit back and wait for the check to come. I had to hand it to her. It wasn't bad. She probably had Vinnie do all the dirty work and all she had to do was keep the idiot happy for a while. Guess what Vinnie? This would prove to be the most expensive piece of tail you ever had and more than likely the last. If Karen didn't get to him first, and he ended up in jail, I'd get Ray make sure that a certain few people in prison would give Vinnie a good old jailhouse welcome. Vinnie would be wearing a garter belt and nylons for some dude named Bubba in no time. I liked it. Pay-back is a mother. Oh, and Vinnie? I really don't think you'll be spending any of that insurance money and neither will your sweetheart, Karen, if I can help it.

But I couldn't help wondering why I was still alive. If Vinnie were smart, which he isn't, he should've put a bullet in my ear back at the cottage. What did they have to gain by keeping me alive? Maybe Karen didn't trust him to do the job properly. Maybe they just needed to figure out a way to make me disappear completely. That way nobody would ever know for sure if I killed Carla. That would make sense.

At least I knew the who and the why. The who being Karen Kiley and Vince, and the why was money. When isn't it? If I turned up dead or convicted of a major crime, Shawn's beneficiary would get the whole banana. And take a wild guess who that was?

Vinnie was the weak link. I could work on him, as long as she wasn't around. Karen was a psychopath. She proved that by having two people killed in cold blood for money, and one of them was her husband of twenty years, not to mention tying me up and raping me. But Vinnie could be talked to. I'd have to make him see how expendable he really was and how cunning and dangerous Karen Kiley could and would be. It was my only chance. I didn't have any great delusions of being rescued. She'd kill me the first chance she got if she thought that I could ruin her plans in any way. But, they should've killed me already. Don't get me wrong. I'm glad they didn't. I just wasn't sure why they didn't. That part didn't fit.

The house was quiet, with the exception of the incessant water dripping in my corner of the cellar and the old, tired furnace moaning and groaning every once in a while. There was no light anywhere. Vince must have sealed up the casement windows. The lovebirds were probably asleep after their night of drugs and debauchery. I figured that they both snorted their collective brains out and were wired for sound. I saw it in Vinnie's eyes. Looking back at my visit to Karen's house, she was wired then, too! I judged it to be about five or six o'clock in the morning. I waited a while listening. And there was still no sound from above.

I was a hurting unit, and I didn't want to assume that I had a lot of time left, so I had to try to get free now. I closed my eyes and tried to focus my mind on the task. OK. Eddie, where are you? First of all, I'd work on the heavy knot that bound my wrists. I could move my hands a little and my fingers still worked. I needed the right tool; a nail or something thin and sharp that I could slip into the knotted rope and try to loosen it. A small crack of fiery light came from around the furnace door and threw a small pool of light in front of it. That was about ten feet away towards the middle of the cellar.

I rolled myself over into the puddle on the wet floor and got on my hands and knees. My hands were tied in front of me and my legs were bounds tightly around the ankles, so this maneuver was both painful and difficult.

I rested again for a moment, waiting, listening and still no sound came from the house above. OK. I rolled over on my back slowly and grabbed at my shoes. This wasn't going to be as easy as I thought. I gripped the heel of one shoe and pulled it off, thinking I could slip the rope over my ankles and off my feet. It was a silly thought and all I got was a wicked leg cramp for my efforts. The rope was tight, and Vinnie had not only bound my ankles together, but had also looped the rope through the other way between my legs and cinched it tight several times. I decided to forget the rope on my legs for the moment and head over towards the furnace where I might be able to find something to loosen the knot that bound my hands. It'd be easier to work at the rope on my legs with my hands free. I inched forward, putting my hands out in front of me and pulling my body ahead. It was a slow and painful process. My knees were already raw from the damp, rough floor.

I had a few feet left to go as I rested for a minute on my side. The cramps in my legs felt like somebody was sticking a knife into my calves and twisting. But, I knew I had to keep going. They might be getting up relatively soon. I wondered if Vinnie had to report in to work this morning. Part of me hoped he didn't, because I didn't relish the thought of being alone with psycho woman. That was enough to motivate me. I got back up on my knees and started inching again towards the light.

To my relief, the area near the old furnace was warmer, and I figured I'd stay there for a while and warm up. I turned around and leaned my back against the side of the furnace. The thick iron was hot, but bearable, and felt great on my cold and cramped body. It was still kicking on every ten minutes or so. I strained my ears and looked up at the ceiling. The house was still silent.

I searched around to see if there was anything that might help me. It looked like the floor had been hastily swept recently and there really wasn't much in the way of anything lying around. It appeared that I was in a partitioned part of a larger cellar. I made out a heavy wooden door a few feet beyond the furnace, and the only other thing I could make out in the room was an old washer and dryer against the wall in the corner. There was nothing on the walls, no boxes, and no garbage. What the hell kind of a cellar was this? No junk! It appeared that Vinnie had been expecting me. Our meeting at my cottage was not by chance. Karen probably assumed I'd head there eventually. That woman scared me. It's amazing where you will find a totally psychotic and criminal mind. It could be your wife, your mother, your neighbor, or the boy next door. And someone that insane had a certain element of genius and was a very dangerous prey or in this case, a predator. They knew no fear, and Karen Kiley was such an animal, and I had no doubt in my mind that she'd shoot me dead without giving it a second thought.

I noticed that the support columns for the floor were made of thick, rough hewn, 6x6 lumber which had long since seen better days. The constant water and dampness in Vinnie's cellar had rotted the bottoms of these columns and it looked like Vinnie or somebody nailed some pine boards to the bottom to give them some sort of support.

I crawled over to the column that was about three feet away and saw that there was a piece of 1x6 pine nailed to each side of the rotten post. I tugged at one of the boards. Because the post was so damp and rotten, it pulled free from the bottom easily. Whoever had nailed the boards into the post used an assortment of nails. I had little doubt that I'd find one to suit my purposes.

I heard a noise from above and stopped what I was doing. It was a toilet flushing and then footsteps. I gave the board another tug, but it still wouldn't pull completely free from the top. The wood was not as rotten higher up. I'd have to come back. I turned and crawled as fast as I could back to my corner and repositioned myself back in the cold puddle. I laid my head back against the damp cement wall and closed my eyes. My heart was pounding and my mouth was dry. I just prayed that whoever came down did not see the wet trail I made to the furnace and beyond.

I got back none too soon as I saw a light go on in the other part of the cellar. It filtered under the wooden door and through the cracks of the wooden partition wall. I heard some heavy footsteps coming down the stairs and knew I was about to have a visitor. I hope he planned on feeding me. No matter what the situation, food was still very important to me. If I were going to die, I'd prefer to do so on a full stomach. I knew that if Vinnie was my prisoner, he could expect a nice full-course breakfast.

You really believe that? I got a bridge to sell.

There were more noises from above and I assumed that they both were awake now. I heard keys jingling and a lock opening. He must've had a padlock on the part of the cellar where I was. The door opened and in stepped Prince Vince with what looked like a mug of coffee and a bag from a doughnut dump. I always said that Vinnie was a nice guy. Didn't I? I was kind of hoping for some eggs, bacon, homefries and toast, but this would do.

"Rise and shine Thomas. This is your big day." He walked over to where I was and gave me a savage kick in my side. I groaned, still making believe I was out. I opened my eyes slowly, wincing in pain from the kick, shaking my head.

I looked up at him and smiled with all my might. "Well, good morning, Vinnie, nice to see you! I see you're a morning person, too. I always say, wake up with a smile and the whole world smiles with you." I braced myself for another kick, but it didn't come.

"You know, asshole, for someone about to die, you are an awful wise-ass. No wonder your old lady left you."

"That is a matter of interpretation, Vinnie Boy. Is that for me?" I gestured towards the mug with my head. "Thanks man. I don't care if it's drugged. I just need some coffee. Am I to assume this my last meal? And you went to all this trouble."

"You never know, Thomas," he smiled, setting the coffee and the bag with the doughnuts on the wet floor next to me. I made a note to include etiquette in a future conversation with him.

I thought it was a good time to plant a seed. "Vince, all kidding aside, do you really think she is going to let you live? Think about it man. Once I am out of the picture, she won't need you for anything. All you are is a loose end, my friend."

"Shut the fuck up Thomas," he spat, kicking me

again and spilling most of my coffee. Served me right. "You don't know what you're talking about. Karen and I are in love."

I laughed. I mean I really laughed even though it hurt. "Come on Vince. That psycho bitch . . ."

We both jumped when a voice behind Vinnie screamed, "This psycho bitch is gonna put a bullet in your mouth, Nick Thomas, if you don't shut it!" Karen appeared in the doorway, wearing only a tee shirt and looking very, very mean. The tee shirt she had on was too small and came only a little below her waist and there was her finely sculpted patch of pubis for me and the whole world to see. I'd seen more of that than I cared to disclose. She had no shame at all. She walked towards me barefoot, oblivious to the water on the floor and stood tauntingly over me. I could see her hard nipples through the cotton shirt, and her eyes had a faraway look to them. She was excited, but there was something else. Cocaine. It had to be, I thought. Not many people are this psychotic without some type of help, especially this time of morning.

"Want some breakfast Nicky?" she taunted, straddling me and pulling my head roughly between her legs. I tried to turn my head away, but she had a firm grip on my hair. She was beginning to really piss me off. I smelled the musky scent of sex on her. She moved back laughing with a wild look on her face. She was totally out of control and had lost all touch with reality.

Vinnie freaked out and grabbed her roughly. "Jesus Christ, Karen. What is wrong with you? Don't you ever get enough? It's bad enough with that sick bitch Maxine," he cried. "We're not doing this again. I mean it."

"Shut up, Vince."   She hissed at him and then looked back at me, wetting her lips. "Bring him upstairs now, Vince. I want him again." she commanded, yanking her arm free. "And don't you ever touch me like that again. Do you hear me?" Her voice was low and guttural. It sounded like the deep howl of a scared cat. He looked at her numbly. Maybe he was seeing the real her for the first time.

Something told me poor Vinnie's minutes were numbered, too. Notice that I didn't say days or even hours? And I don't think it even remotely occurred to her that she could ever get caught. Most psychotics didn't. She was over the line and didn't know where fantasy ended and reality began. And what was this mention of a Maxine? That got my interest in a hurry. The Maxine I met? The anal insurance lady I met in P-town? Where did she fit in here?

Vinnie snapped me back to reality. "No way Karen. I gotta draw the line somewhere. Don't you understand that I love you? I don't want you having sex with someone else. I can't stand it. This is not how you said it would be."

I rubbed my eyes with my bound hands. Vinnie... Vinnie...Vinnie! Hello! Is there anybody home in there? What a dramatic scene this was turning out to be. This was getting good. I've paid money at the movies for stuff like this, and needless to say, I'd rather be watching this from the safe seat of a movie theater. However, I did know better than to antagonize someone like her, especially if she was high. That's the elusive trait called common sense. Karen had seemingly gone over the edge and killing me would probably not be a problem for her. So, I played along with her. I might even try to play up to her and get her off guard. It was worth a try. The old

Thomas charm has worked more than once.

"Excuse me Karen, honey, but am I out of line by asking why I am here and what you plan to do with me?" I asked, drilling her with my eyes, smiling and running my tongue slowly over my lips. She thought she knew what I was thinking.

"In time sweetheart. In time." she purred coming closer to me again. "You want me again, don't you Nicky Baby?" I shifted my glance to Vinnie then back to her. She got my meaning. I'd rather sleep with a snake, but she didn't know that.

Clearing my throat, I said, "I just want to get out of here alive. What would I have to do to make that happen? You name it baby."

"You just sit tight, Thomas. You never know what could happen." Vinnie answered. "Come on Karen. I got a cure for that itch you seem to have developed." He reached for her and she moved to him. I could see the raw heat from her as she wrapped herself around his leg and began kissing his neck. His hands traveled to her bare bottom and gripped her firmly. I'd had enough. They were going to get it on right here in front of me on an empty stomach.

"Guys! Please have a little mercy on me and take that upstairs." I said winking at Karen. Vinnie was in another world and didn't notice. The more I watched him the more I was convinced he had a snoot full of powder, too! What a pair they were.

"Oh we'll be back, Nicky," she said slyly, running her tongue over her lips back at me. "That you can count on."

They left me sitting in my puddle.

Chapter 21

It had been a quite a while since Vinnie and Karen had disappeared upstairs to continue whatever debauchery they were in to. I really didn't care what they were doing as long as they left me alone for a bit longer. I'd managed to squirm and crawl back over to the rotten post where the pine boards were hastily nailed and succeeded in prying one of them loose. It had several nails sticking out of it, which would do very nicely for my purpose if I wasn't interrupted. I dragged the board back to my little home in the puddle and listened. My whole body hurt. My hands and knees were raw and bleeding from trying to crawl across the rough cement floor holding onto the board. I didn't know what had been worse the past several days; the physical torture that my body had been through or the emotional and mental stress. I think both took their toll. When this was over, and I prayed to God that it would be soon, I vowed that I would grab Chris and take off for two weeks somewhere in the Caribbean where I would do nothing but lie in the sun, eat like a pig and make love. Actually, I'd probably sleep for a week, and I wish I hadn't thought of food. I was starved. Vinnie's idea of breakfast, stale doughnuts, barely made a dent, and by now you know all about my appetite.

I heard some muted sounds from above, but I couldn't really make them out. Knowing the subjects, I think I could safely assume they weren't up there holding Bible study.

I worked the knot on the heavy rope that bound my raw wrists with one of the rusty nails that was sticking out of the board, and I wasn't having much luck, but I did manage to take a nice gouge out of my wrist. The rope cut in and burned the open gash. Damn, just what I needed. I was already weak from the trauma and lack of nourishment. I knew that if I were going to make any kind of move, it'd better be soon. They'd soon tire of their games upstairs and then they would come for me. This was real and I was scared. They had every reason in the world to dispose of me as soon as possible; actually one million good reasons. I found myself caught up in the building insanity of the situation. This was like a scene I would write, but it was easy to have Eddie undo the knot in the rope because all I had to do was write that way. I couldn't do that here. I had to stay calm and focus on what I needed to do to stay alive. Those two upstairs thought they could kill a bunch of people and waltz away to some island with a wheelbarrow full of tax-free cash. I think they watched too much television. The problem was that I wasn't dealing with rational people. Those two were high as kites on coke, and I think Karen really believed that she could get away with it. Vinnie was history either way. The scary thing was that if I disappeared, the suspicion would always be on me. And I couldn't dispute a damn thing if I were dead.

I realized that I was the only thing standing between Karen Kiley and her dream. Guess what, Nicky? I was a dead man! So I did the only logical thing I could think of at the time. I summoned Eddie for a quick consult and he gave me some quick, rational advice. I had to escape, and I had to accomplish it soon. I figured I had a half-hour at the most, and more than likely it would be less. The dragon lady would come for her prey, and that was me!

I did something that I should've done earlier. I prayed and just sat back for a couple of minutes and regrouped. Strength does come from within. I opened my eyes, took a deep breath and began again on the knot. I was rewarded immediately as I managed to get the nail under part of the knot and loosen it a bit. I rested, focused, and worked it a little more. I pulled and pried with my cramped fingers. The knot finally came loose, and I quickly unraveled the rope from around my wrists. I took a second to rub some circulation back into my wrists and then went immediately to work on the ropes that bound my legs. They were impossibly tight, and I had trouble loosening the knots with my bruised and bleeding fingers.

Suddenly a loud boom echoed throughout the house and I didn't need a degree in rocket science to know what it was. Someone fired a gun upstairs and it was a big one. I heard a thud and then Karen screamed. "My God! Oh, my God. Vinnie? Vinnie?"

I knew one thing for certain. My time was up! I wasn't certain if Vinnie shot Karen or visa versa. But whoever was still standing up there was going to be coming for me and fast. Silently, I prayed that it would be Vinnie. Believe that? I'd rather face him than Karen with a gun any day. I heard the front door slam and running footsteps. I worked the knot that bound my legs with renewed enthusiasm. It still wouldn't budge. Vinnie had really pulled that knot tight.

A shot echoed throughout the house and then another. Then an eerie silence settled in. I heard Karen screaming and screaming.

Whatever was going on up there I knew it wasn't good. I picked up the board again with my cut and bleeding fingers and began picking at the rope with one of the rusty nails.

"Come on!" I prayed aloud. "Please!"

I heard footsteps again above me. I still couldn't tell if it was Vinnie or Karen, but they were heading in the direction of the cellar door. I worked furiously at the rope and it began to separate at the knot. My heart was pounding as I was trying to listen and work at the same time. My eyes burned as sweat trickled down into them. I wiped my head and face with my damp sleeve and ran my hand through my hair. I was glad for the moment that I'd cut it all off. The cellar door opened with a loud creaking noise and my heart stopped when I heard the voice.

"Nicky? Nicky? They killed Vinnie." Karen sobbed and screamed down from the top of the stairs. "Vince is dead, Nicky. I have to lock the door. They're coming for us, Nicky. They're coming for us. But we have some unfinished business, you and I."

I worked the knot furiously with renewed motivation. Who killed Vinnie? I didn't hear anyone else, but I heard her footsteps run toward the rear of the house. What was she up to now?

I just about had the knot undone. My arms were cramping from my frantic efforts. Ahh! I had it.

The knot came loose and I began unwinding the rope from around my legs, which felt very numb after having been bound for so long. The rope was off and I stretched my sore legs straight out. They screamed in thanks. I kept my eyes on the door and my heart in my mouth.

Then all hell seemed to break loose. More shots rang out rapidly in succession from inside the house. What the hell is going on? I scrambled to my feet and I heard glass shattering and more gunshots. These came from outside the house. Cops? I sure the hell hoped so. I lost count of the shots fired from inside the house. I tried to keep a mental note of how many were fired just in case I'd need to know. I saw Clint Eastwood do that in a movie once and it impressed the hell out of me.

I heard Karen running towards the cellar door and then bound noisily down the stairs. I limped to the door and leaned against it. I heard her fumbling with Vinnie's keys to unlock the little room I was in. I stood back and called out to her.

"Karen. What is going on out there? Talk to me, please!"

"Can't find the right key." I heard her say, and then I heard the keys drop to the floor. "Damn it!" She screamed in frustration. Then the wooden door exploded as she fired at the lock, shattering it and the whole latch.

"Five, or was it six?" I tried counting her shots. There might be one left. I wasn't sure now.

The door flew open and I stepped back into the shadows behind it as Karen charged in with the .357 extended in front of her. I saw her look frantically to the corner that I was supposed to be in and then it dawned on her where I might be. "Nicky?" she whirled around and saw me immediately.

She didn't hesitate for a second. She closed her eyes and pulled the trigger of the Magnum, and I kissed my ass good-bye.

Karen stood only about six feet from me with the ugly barrel of the Smith & Wesson leveled right at my chest. A few things happened at that precise moment in time. First, she closed her eyes as she squeezed the trigger, and second, there was a very loud and very distinct click as the hammer of the gun dropped on an empty chamber of the gun. And last but not least, there was a loud crash as somebody, hopefully, the police, smashed the front door in.

"Six," I whispered, breathing hard. "It was six!"

Karen stood there looking at me and then slowly at the gun that was still pointed at me, not comprehending what had just happened. She was a mess; her hair was a wild mass of tangles and she had blood and dirt smeared all over her naked body. I couldn't tell if the blood was hers or Vinnie's. Fitting finale for her I'd say. I stepped over to her and plucked the empty gun from her hand as she just stood there with her mouth open and body trembling. She was confused and scared. "Nicky?" she whimpered, but her eyes were far away. I really felt sorry for her at that moment. I didn't even want to inflict bodily harm on her for what she had done to me, not to mention the other people she had killed. She was a sick lady and she needed help. All I wanted to do was to get out of this smelly cellar, take a long hot shower and eat everything I could lay my hands on. I heard shouting from above and a lot of running footsteps.

"Hey! Police! Down here." I managed to yell. "Hey you guys. It's OK!"

A voice from a bullhorn filled the cellar. "Whoever is down there, you will lay on the floor on your stomach with your arms extended in front of you. If we see any movement at all from anything we'll shoot first and ask questions later! Do you understand me?"

"Yes!" I answered and then I tried to pull Karen down next to me, but she had sunk to her knees and was half sitting, half-lying on the cold and wet cement floor, naked and bloody. She looked delirious to me and all the fight was gone from her body. It was over. I looked at her sadly. Strangely enough, I didn't feel anger or rage towards her anymore.

A moment later, two cops in black commando gear charged down the stairs and faded to either side of the door. Then one suddenly crouched in the doorway and the other in back of him to his right with guns drawn. I didn't move and Karen just sat there whimpering. I watched the guns and they didn't waver. The one crouched had a spot marked on my forehead and the one behind him had his gun trained on Karen.

The cop in the doorway barked in a military manner, "Any more?" I shook my head and raised up a little to show him I wasn't armed.

"Move again and you're dead," he barked matter-of-factly. He looked to Karen and yelled over his shoulder. "Secure here. Somebody bring me a blanket. Now!" This guy had no sense of humor; probably was fresh out of the Marine Corps, one of Peck's elite, no doubt.

A very large shadow started to descend the stairs and with it came a perfectly tailored blue, double-breasted Armani suit and inside that suit was, none other than, Captain Artus Peck with a green army blanket folded neatly over one arm. He calmly walked over to where Karen was collapsed and draped it over her. He shook his massive head and looked up at me with a raised eyebrow and gave me a dark look.

"Had a feeling I'd find your sorry ass today! This will be a good day now. And do you want to know why?" I shook my head. I had the feeling that he didn't want me to answer just yet, so I listened. He was upset, so I was probably better off letting him vent.

"Yes sir Thomas, today you going to jail. Gonna be my guest hopefully for a long, long time."

There was a lot of commotion going on upstairs. It sounded like there was a platoon of cops crashing through the small house and I heard doors opening and then slamming shut. Peck looked at Karen still laying on the floor in a fetal position and sobbing. "She the one behind all this?" he asked me.

"Yeah, her and good old Vinnie. By the way, have you seen Vinnie? Vinnie Sax, Captain. He's a Truro cop."

"Was a Truro Cop. He's upstairs. He appears to have a few holes in him, though. Big holes," he said.

I nodded. "I told him she was going to kill him too, but the dumb shit didn't believe me. He said she loved him. How'd you find us?"

"Neighbor was getting his paper and heard gun shots. Said there was a sniper outside and was shooting at the house."

"Sniper? I thought Karen dusted Vinnie."

"I don't know who dusted who, hero, but I do know that Vincent Sax, a brother police officer, is upstairs by the front door with a very large hole in his forehead, and it looks like a rifle wound, not a close up pistol shot," he said. "I don't know how guilty he is, but I'd like to be sure before I pass judgment. Kind of like I did with you." He bent over and picked up one of Karen's hands. The blanket fell away to the wet floor. Her hands were covered with sticky blood and I noticed there was blood spattered on her face and hair and there was even some gray viscous matter streaked on her breasts.

I thought she must've been right behind Vinnie when he took the bullet. And it must've been my resourceful friend out there somewhere who'd been shooting at me. I told Peck my deductions but he ignored me. I thought he'd be impressed and want to give me some sort of citation.

He dropped Karen's hand and pulled the blanket up around her shoulders, covering her naked breasts. He seemed to do everything in a deliberate manner; slow but sure. Peck looked at the lead cop and nodded toward Karen. "Get her out of here. Get her down to the hospital but I want her under wraps. Do you understand?"

"Yes sir," the young cop answered and picked Karen up with the blanket wrapped around her like she was a small child. She was whimpering and completely limp, as all I could see of her was tangled hair and bare legs as he carried her up the stairs.

Peck said to me, "You know what I'm going do, my friend? I'm going do you a favor. Actually I'm going do society a favor and put your ass in jail. And if I have my way you'll stay there for a long time. Your next book is going to be a prison romance novel."

I kept waiting for a twinkle in his eyes or the beginning of a smile. But there was none. He looked at me like I was a cockroach on his counter and he had a big, rolled up newspaper.

I spread my arms wide and groveled a bit. "Come on Captain, I didn't do anything. Except maybe disappear for a little while and do a little checking on my own. After all, I did have a vested interest in the outcome of this fiasco. I just wanted to make sure you consummate professionals didn't miss something."

Then Peck smiled and his eyes did twinkle as he took out his cuffs.

Chapter 22

For the second time in a week I found myself in the back of a police car. This one was a little nicer, but it was a police car just the same. Peck stashed me, handcuffed again, I might add, in his gleaming Crown Vic with the motor running and the AC purring comfortably. I almost was glad that it was over and that I didn't have to hide any more. Peck knew damn well that I didn't kill anybody, and he also knew that he wasn't really going to toss me in jail. I hoped! But I knew he was extremely annoyed at me for giving his men the slip for so long and obstructing justice and just plain messing things up. Peck was a hard man to read; he was as big and tough as they come, but he was also fair and compassionate at the same time. He had six kids, a loving wife and a whole bunch of dogs and cats and whatever else big families have. And he helped me a lot when I was first trying to get sober. He made me keep my community service commitments that I earned by driving drunk, and he saw to it that I went to the AA meetings. This time I think he just wanted to teach me a lesson. OK already, I get the point so you can let me out now. This all fell on deaf ears in the air-conditioned car.

I watched them haul what I assumed was the remains of Vinnie out on a stainless steel gurney in a black zippered bag and put him into the coroner's van. I also caught a glimpse of Karen huddled in the back of another detective's Crown Victoria before she was whisked away to wherever Peck was going to hold her. It was either the hospital or jail. I didn't think that there'd be any other options open to her at this point.

Peck came out of the shabby house and started down the steps, but then he stopped, bounced up the two stairs, and ducked his head back in while holding the screen door open. He looked like he was talking to someone inside, and then he turned abruptly and headed toward the car. Good. I hoped that I could talk him into something for my stomach. A cup of coffee, maybe a stale doughnut, even a piece of bread would work. I wasn't fussy; I was starved, and I had to literally stop myself from conjuring up an imaginary breakfast in my mind's eye. That would've been masochistic, but so Nick.

Peck didn't look at me or say a word when he got into the car, so I tried to strike up a conversation. "Captain, I . . ."

"Shut up, Thomas," he snapped over his shoulder as he put the car into gear. "I need a few minutes to think about all this. Right now I'm so mad at you I could . . . oh, never mind. I'll talk to you when I'm ready."

He was pissed, and I had the sense not to push, so I leaned back against the heavy leather seat and closed my eyes. Even the vivid visions of food faded as far away as did I.

⌁⧸⧸⧸⧸⌁

"Wake up, Thomas.   Wake up!" Peck barked over his shoulder. My eyes snapped open. I must've drifted off. I'd slept all the way from Wellfleet and saw that we were getting off Rt. 6 in South Yarmouth. My mouth was dry, and I had a dull headache behind my eyes and my hands were chaffed and raw from being cuffed. The rope Vinnie had tied me with last night took off a lot of my skin and now the cold, heavy nickel-steel handcuffs seared into the open wounds.

"Wake up, Thomas," Peck yelled back to me. "Now!"

"I'm awake," I managed to mumble. "Relax already. Hey Cap, I'm hungry. Think you could find it in that big, generous heart of yours to stop and grab some breakfast before we go in? I can't remember when I ate last. I'll do anything, I'll tell you every gruesome, hairy detail, but please let me get some coffee and food."

"I don't have a heart, Thomas. Never did." But then he asked me, "You got any money on you?   If you want to eat you better have the cash. I'm not the Red fucking Cross." A glimmer of hope sprung from within the deprived depths of my soul. He was softening up. I could feel the love. Well, maybe that was pushing it a bit, but I knew breakfast was close. And about then I would've sold my mother for a cheeseburger.

"I don't know what I got, Cap. At this point I have no idea. I'm not real sure what day it is and you want me to know what I got in my pockets?" I got brave. "Look, I know you're pissed, and I don't blame you. But, take a second to think about the

THE NINE IRONY   273

couple of banner days that I've had. I've been shot at, chased, beaten up, drugged, and accused of murder, and other things that I don't feel I want to share with you. It's been the week from hell. Believe that, my friend!" I was worked up. "And you know what? I'm beyond caring if you or anybody else is pissed off at me. Do what you have to do. OK?"

"Feel better?" he asked me.

"Yeah, I do. Damn Captain, you know what I went through when I sobered up. I had to scratch and claw my way back from hell, and I did it. I changed. I got my life back and I live gratefully, and I help when I can. This shit almost took me back where I didn't want to go." I felt drained. "I just want to put this behind me."

He nodded. "Let's eat first. Then we go in and talk," he declared. "OK?"

"That works for me."

Peck glanced back at me over his shoulder and said, "We'll fill your belly and clear the cobwebs, because we got a long day in front of us. And I want you with a clear head and a lot of answers. And if I even think for a second that you're bullshitting me, you'll be singing soprano down in the state prison glee club. I'll come see you in the Christmas Pageant."

"You're a riot, Peck. No bull, I promise," I assured him. He grunted and he went back to ignoring me as he drove on.

But he did stop at a Burger King, took my cuffs off and let me have a go at it. I spent eight dollars and sixty-three cents on myself, which I justified with each bite, and Peck had a small coffee that he stubbornly paid for himself. When we pulled into C.P.A.C. headquarters at about ten-thirty, I was nursing an overstuffed belly to the point of nausea and was clinging with dear life to a 24 oz. cup of jet-black rocket fuel. Just let someone try and take this coffee away from me, I thought with resolve. I practiced a crazed Jack Nicholson look in the window a few times in case anyone tried. The look with the eyebrows cocked funny and a lot of teeth showing. I have strange role models.

It had turned to a rainy August morning with thunder clouds rolling overhead and the air now cool. We arrived at C.P.A.C. headquarters and pulled in. It was a depressing looking two-story brick structure with white trimmed windows on old Route 28 in South Yarmouth. There was a gray flagpole out front sporting the stars and stripes flapping in the morning breeze. Someone had made a few weak attempts at flowerbeds and landscaping around the building, but everything was brown. The grass was brown and the bushes were brown and the flowers were dead. There was a black fire escape climbing the right side of the building and a large dirt parking lot to the left. This was the home of the State Police Anti-Crime Unit that Captain Artus Q. Peck headed and this was where I was destined to spend a lot of time in the next few days. I could barely conceal my enthusiasm.

Peck parked the Crown Victoria, shut off the motor, and then turned in his seat toward me. He filled the front of the car like a bear in a phone booth and all of a sudden I felt very small. He pointed a finger the size of a deli sausage at me and said, "I'm very aggravated at you right now, Mr. Nick Thomas. Who did you think you were? You watching too much TV, or maybe you were believing some of that crap you write about?"

Hey, that was below the belt, but I still didn't dare tell him that I was Eddie Kane. He'd lose it. So I looked up at him and didn't speak. I just nodded as humbly as I could. After all, he did let me eat, so that bought him some humility on my part.

He continued, "I believed in you five years ago and you didn't let me down, and I believed in you again a few days ago when I agreed not to arrest you. But you waited and really stuck it to me this time. You lied to me and you made me look like a fool to the people that pay me. I don't like to look like a fool, Thomas, especially to those pompous asses. I take that real personal." He had a way of simplifying things. His big smoky eyes bored a hole in me. I hate it when he does that. Even though I was innocent of the more serious offenses, I couldn't hold his stare.

I started to say something but he held up his huge paw and commanded silence. He produced a key, leaned over and unlocked the cuffs again. "We're going to go inside, and we're going talk a long time," he said.

I nodded rubbing my raw wrists. "I'm ready. Let's go."

When Peck let me out of his car I turned and saw Chris's Jeep parked in the small visitor's area and right then I knew life would be good again. She was always there when I needed her the most. It was that feeling I've lived my whole life for.

Peck guided me through the wooden double doors on the side marked Authorized Personnel Only, and Chris flew into my arms. I smelled the fresh scent of apples in her hair as she kissed me tenderly with her eyes closed. I held her tight and the tears came, both hers and mine.

"Oh Nick, I've been so worried. I love you. You OK?" she asked me, stroking my hair and looking into my eyes. "Just hold me a minute."

"I'm glad you're here," I whispered into her ear and kissed her lobes gently.

She pulled her head away from my chest and looked at me with her big green eyes and said, "Where else would I be?"

Peck cleared his throat in back of us. I'd forgotten he was there for a moment.

"OK Captain, I get the hint. Let's go get this done."

He looked at Chris and said to her, "I'll be as fast as possible, and then maybe, just maybe you can take Mickey Spillane here home." He took me by the arm and we walked through the door to the inner offices.

"Don't think you're off the hook for a second, Thomas. I just didn't want that nice lady out there to worry. How'd you manage to get such a nice woman anyhow, Thomas? Huh? She's young, pretty and I'd say she's reasonably intelligent, except for the serious lapse of judgment in your case."

I smiled. "It's my charming personality and let's not downplay my dazzling intellect."

"Shiiiiit!" he commented laughing, finally.

The Cape Cod Times

Bodies Pile Up
Man Linked to Murder in Provincetown

AP- Hyannis, Cape Cod- Last night a suspect in several murder investigations was gunned down by the Hyannis Police when he attempted a daring escape from Cape Cod Hospital where he was admitted following a serious car accident.

Police sources say that the suspect's name was Peter J. Nolin, 33, of Wellfleet. He was apprehended leaving the murder scene of Shawn Kiley, also of Wellfleet. He was also wanted for questioning in relation to the assault and eventual death of Carla Thomas of Truro. Police say Nolin was fleeing the rear parking lot of **Montego Ray's Nite Club and Restaurant** in his 1982 Ford van when he collided head-on with a parked car. LifeStar then flew Nolin to Cape Cod Hospital where he was in intensive care in critical condition. Nolin apparently regained consciousness, brutally attacked a police officer that was assigned to guard him, and walked out of the hospital with the officer's uniform on.

Nolin was quickly spotted by a Hyannis police patrol and he began firing on the officers.

The police returned fire and Nolin was killed

by two bullets to the chest, in addition to his already critical wounds.

A search of Nolin's mother's home last night found one female, a Caucasian woman identified as Louise Alice Nolin, 73, with whom Peter had lived, wrapped in a construction tarp in the hatchway of her home. The medical examiner confirmed that she died from a knife wound to the chest. Nolin is also a suspect in that homicide.

Chapter 23

As I waited outside Peck's office, I wasn't sure how I felt that morning. There was a certain sense of relief that it was all out in the open, but I couldn't shake the feeling that something wasn't quite right. Something was still missing, and I couldn't put my finger on it. I'd always thought that it was Vinnie behind the incidents at my cottage. Now, I wasn't so sure. They found no one lurking in the bushes or even any evidence of anyone outside Vinnie's house. I overheard it was a large caliber bullet fired from a rifle at long distance that killed him. So, there was still someone else involved besides Vinnie and Karen. And all evidence or lack of it pointed to a professional. It hit me then that I, personally, was not out of danger. I was puzzled. This guy could've gotten to me more than once, and now I felt like I was a loose end for him. But what was his motivation? And who was he?

It was Monday and this whole thing started last Thursday night, a mere five days ago. It felt like a lifetime. I wasn't even completely sure that I was going to walk out of there a free man. I really didn't do anything against the law with the exception of evading the police and lifting that insurance file. I'd told Peck where it was and he immediately sent some detectives back to my cottage to retrieve it. He got pissed off at me all over again about that.

I closed my eyes and rubbed my temples. I was too tired to think. I didn't think whoever was after me was going to try something in here. But Chris . . . I had a moment of panic and jumped up from the bench. Peck's secretary, Alice, looked over and shot me a wary look, shaking her head silently with her hand steady on the telephone. Peck told her to make sure I stayed put.

"Alice, I need to see Chris. She's out in the main lobby. She could be in danger." I was out of breath all of a sudden. "Please?" I pleaded. "It's important." She gazed over at me coolly with a face that's heard it all, but then she softened and smiled. "I'll call down and have her brought up," she said punching a couple of buttons on the phone. "I don't think the Captain would mind."

I smiled at her and said, "Thanks. It's been a rough few days."

Alice, was an attractive and stylish woman in her fifties who had been around the department for a long time. She was efficient, tight lipped, and most thought she actually ran the department. She helped me coordinate a few D.A.R.E. events for the kids and we got to be sort of friends in the past few years. But, even Peck walked softly around Alice. He was no fool. She commanded his respect, which was not an easy feat.

I was deposited, surprisingly enough, under my own recognizance on a carved up wooden bench outside Peck's office. Inside was the omnipotent

Captain, with some anal-looking woman in high heels and a man's suit from the District Attorney's office and a rumpled, gray-haired man with a red nose who looked like a lawyer, with the femme fatale, Karen Kiley. I'd been sitting there in the hall when she was brought up, cuffed, shackled and wearing a lovely one-piece, prison-gray jumpsuit. Her hair was matted and uncombed, her eyes puffy and swollen without any trace of makeup; she looked like the beaten animal she was. When they led her past me I caught her eye and saw nothing but pure hatred. She started to come at me, but the deputies pulled her back and pushed her toward Peck's door. She glared at me as she passed and I swore I heard a low growl from deep down in her tainted, greedy soul.

I'd spoiled her best laid plans. It was I, or actually Eddie and I, that got between her and that fancy umbrella drink on that white, sandy beach somewhere where the water was warm and the cocktails cool. But, I thought happily, the only white sand she was going to see would be at the bottom of an ashtray.

I held her gaze with my own anger. I'd every right to be pissed. My whole life had been turned upside down because of her, the greedy little bitch. I was really happy that she was the one in shackles instead of me. "Nice outfit, Karen, it does something for you," I said.

"Hope you rot in hell, Nick Thomas, you...you... bastard...you!"

"You're going need somebody to keep you company," I answered.

She spit at me from about five feet away but missed and then the deputy pushed her roughly through Peck's door and into the already crowded office. The door slammed, rattling the thick glass pane with Peck's name painted on it in black letters with gold trim. Below his name was one word: COMMANDER. I was surprised he didn't spell it with a "K". I sat and counted my blessings that I was out here and they were all in there! I closed my eyes once again and leaned my head back against the cool cement wall and waited for them to bring Chris up.

Ten minutes later one of the deputies that had dragged Karen up earlier arrived with Chris. But, this time his demeanor was considerably different. He almost walked into the wall when he opened the door and stepped back so she could enter first—what a gentleman. He was all smiles and babbling like an idiot as he led her over to me. He looked down at me in instant disapproval and then flashed Chris this smile that was all teeth and told her that his name was Roy and if she needed anything, anything at all.

What a turd. "Yeah, OK Roy, that's wonderful. Thanks a lot. You've been a great help. You can go now," I said wearily, as I stood up and hugged Chris.

Roy looked at Chris, shot me a look of obvious disgust, turned, and stalked off down the hall shaking his head.

I laughed and said to Chris, "I think he was quite taken with you."

"He was sweet," she said innocently. "And he was very helpful. I would never have figured out how to open these heavy, old doors all by myself." She batted her pretty brown eyelashes at me and puckered her lips. We both burst out laughing.

"Let's sit," I said, taking her by the arm. "We need to talk."

For the next twenty minutes I recounted the

events of the past several days the best I could, given the circumstances. And I told her that we both could be in danger until whoever was out there was caught.

She grabbed my arm and blurted out, "Oh, God, Nick, that reminds me."

"Reminds you of what, baby?"

"Ray gave me something for you." She jumped up, reached into the rear pocket of her jeans and pulled out a folded up piece of paper and handed it to me. "He said for you to be cool with this info and to watch your step. Whatever that meant."

"What's it say?" I asked.

"I didn't read it. Ray said not to, and that I'd be better off not knowing."

I put my arm around her and said, "He was right. I don't want you involved."

"But I am involved, Nick. You just said I could be in danger, too!" She whispered a bit too loud.

I nuzzled my face in her rich hair and kissed her. She was right. But, I held in my arms the one thing that made sense in my life and I didn't want to lose her, now or ever. I sat back and started to unfold the piece of paper when I was startled by someone who'd walked up to us unnoticed. "Hey, Nick! Hey, Chris."

We both looked up into the smiling freckle-faced Ian Kiley. He was all I needed. I forced a smile, folding the piece of paper back up and tucking it into my shirt pocket. With some effort I stuck out my hand. "Hey Ian. How you doing?"

He took my hand and smiled more. "I'm cool, Nick." Then he looked around nervously and nodded towards Peck's door. "My mom in there?"

"Yeah, she is, Ian. But she's in rough shape," I

said. "I don't really know much or the why."

The smile faded and he looked anxious. "Was she with Sax?" he asked.

"So you knew."

"I knew. I knew about Vince, and I knew they were into some serious coke. And I also knew that my old man was fooling around with Carla. I knew too much, Nick. I should've said something, but I didn't know what. Something tells me you knew, too."

I shrugged and didn't say either way. He sat down next to me and leaned back against the wall. "I've had a hell of a home life, Nick. It's no small wonder I'm a drunk. First it was the old man. Now there was a first class, award-winning asshole if I ever saw one, and he was supposed to be my role model growing up. And let's not forget dear mom with the whips and chains in her closet. And then, of course, she and that crotch-sniffing Vince Sax snorting themselves six ways to hell."

I just couldn't find any compassion for him and for some unknown reason, I never could warm up to him. He was too neat, too perfect and now he was whining. His red hair was short, his face clean-shaven and his clothes were always pressed and creased. That kind of stuff irritated me. I didn't even know you could iron blue jeans.

He turned and asked me again, "You haven't heard anything, Nick, have you? I mean, do you know what's going on?"

I shook my head. "All I know is that she and Vinnie kidnapped me and were happily planning to feed me to the sharks out on Race Point. So don't get all choked up if I don't share your pain about your childhood. I've had a few bad days lately myself."

He nodded too quickly and put his hand on my shoulder. "I know. I know. Hey, what can I say, Nick? I think she was trying to collect the insurance cash from Dad's and Carla's little enterprise. She knew she was the beneficiary. And she would've collected a wad if you disappeared," he said chuckling. But he looked nervous as his eyes kept darting toward Peck's door.

"How'd you come to know all that, Ian?" I asked. How would he know about the insurance? I had the damn file hidden back at the cottage.

"Oh, Mom must've told me that once, I guess. I really don't remember where I heard it. It's a standard thing, isn't it?" He was squirming. The little turd was lying to me and I knew it. I looked at him closely and felt Chris nudge my ribs at the same time. It was then when something jogged my memory. "Hey, who's your girlfriend now, Ian? You seeing anybody special?" I asked casually.

That hit a nerve. He spun around to face me quickly. "What you want to know that for?" he asked now on the defense. His red face dotted with patches of rich freckles was inches from mine. But he wasn't smiling anymore. His eyes were hard and small and his expression tense.

"That's none of your business." His voice rose as he spoke. Alice looked over at us and caught my eye. I raised my eyebrow and shrugged my shoulders. "Easy Ian, chill out, I was just making conversation. That's all, buddy. Relax."

His bloodshot eyes studied mine and then he said in a harsh, low voice, "Thomas don't you even dream of dragging me or anybody else into this mess. You got me?" I smelled the faint odor of liquor on his breath mixed with a mint of some sort or mouthwash. But there was no mistake about it. That was a subject I knew all too well. He'd definitely been drinking and it was still morning. Not to mention the fact that Ian was supposedly a recovering alcoholic, not an active one. I also noticed that his eyes were red and slightly dilated. I wondered if he wasn't sampling the coke himself. But, I wasn't about to push him then.

"Sorry, Ian. I didn't mean to upset you," I mumbled. Eddie was urgently whispering in my ear, but I knew that this was not the time to confront young master Kiley. He was too agitated and a little too volatile for my mood.

He jumped up and began pacing back and forth in front of Peck's door. It seemed like he was manic. "I want to know what's going on in there. I need to see if Mom's all right." Now he was the concerned son again.

"Go on in, Ian," I chided, not really being serious. Nobody in his right mind would dream of barging into Captain Artus Peck's office on any occasion. But he jumped up, marched up to Peck's door, turned the handle and walked in slamming the door behind him. Chris gripped my hand as we watched in amusement. Alice made some kind of gasping noise I didn't recognize. We heard Peck scream some obscenities. Ian babbled something unintelligible and then we heard Peck tell him to shut the fuck up and sit down. Now, this was getting good!

They were all in there a good hour before Chris nudged me. I'd fallen asleep and she just sat there, holding my hand and letting me snooze. I opened my eyes to see Peck's door open and his big woolly head sticking out into the hallway. "Alice, call the deputies. I need them to escort Mrs. Kiley back to her accommodations." He looked over at us on the bench and pointed at me. "I'm going to want to talk to you now. Chris can come in if she likes, unless you have a problem with that." I shook my head and squeezed Chris's hand as we stood. "No problem. Thanks Captain."

He grunted and said, "Let me get these people out of here first." Then he went back inside his office, closing the door.

I squeezed her hand and said, "Maybe we can get out of here soon."

Before she could answer, Peck's door flew open once again and the woman from the DA's office marched out with the rumpled little lawyer with the red nose on her heels, trying to talk to her. It appeared that she wanted no part of any type of deal. Good! Karen deserved whatever she got and no less. Then Karen appeared in her prison garb with her hands and legs shackled. Her gaze was down at the floor as she shuffled past and Ian was right behind her, whispering in her ear as they walked.

He had a strange look about him, I thought, and it wasn't one of concern or compassion. He almost looked threatening, his face was dark and his eyes were sharp. His motions were quick and agitated. Somehow he didn't look like the innocent boy he wanted everyone to believe he was.

Then he must've said something to trigger his mother because Karen stopped and snapped her head up and hissed at him, "You little cocksucker. Who do you think you are? You gonna threaten me here in front of God and everybody? And you think you'll get away with it?" She reached up with her cuffed hands and clutched his shirt roughly. "I've changed my mind. I'm gonna tell them it was you. You don't scare me you little piss-ant. And I'm sorry

I ever gave birth to you," she hissed in his face. It looked like she actually scared him for a minute. Chris and I watched this with our mouths open. But, Ian recovered quickly, realizing that we were watching him.

He pulled away, smoothing his shirt and then said to the deputy, "Please take care of her. She's been through a lot and doesn't know what she's saying."

Karen lunged at her son again, "I'll kill you if you let me hang out to dry by myself!" She managed to get her hands on his neck, but the deputy pulled her off and threw her against the cement wall, face first and held her by her shackles. She screamed in pain as the deputy jerked her arms back and upward. But then she turned her head, looked right at me and said with surprising calm, "It was him, Nicky, he was behind it all. Him and his girlfriend, Maxine. Tell Peck. Please tell Peck!"

The deputy dragged her away and Ian looked at us. "I don't know what got into her, Nick. I just want to help her, and now she trying to blame me for something I didn't do."

"And I'm the Easter Bunny," I said to him, getting off the bench. I'd had enough. Besides, part of me believed Karen. He probably was involved somehow and that was good enough for me.

"Sit down!" a voice commanded behind me. It was Peck. He'd been on the phone, heard all the commotion out in the hall, and came flying out. I sat.

"Kiley, you got two seconds to get the hell out of my house before I throw your red-headed ass in jail. You got that? Cop or no cop." Ian didn't miss a beat and was gone without even answering.

Peck looked at me and barked, "Get in here now, Thomas. You too, Chris." He sounded weary. Then in a surprising act of kindness, he asked Alice to get us all some coffee and I didn't argue.

For the next hour and a half, I recounted the last five days' events. Peck would listen, ask a couple of pointed questions and then prod me to continue. I already told him all I knew about Carla the first time he interrogated me, but he wanted to hear it all again, slowly, over and over again.

I kept asking him about Karen and Ian, but he kept ignoring my questions and asking his own. We were all tired and our nerves wore thin as the afternoon dragged on. Around four o'clock he finally told us to go home. I could see that it wouldn't do to argue with him and maybe he heard me anyway about Ian. He told me that he'd be in touch tomorrow and for me not to leave the house. He looked at me over his huge mahogany desk, with his hands folded and eyes white.

"Nick, you go home. Let Chris make you a nice dinner and you go to bed. I don't want to hear that you went anywhere. I'm still very upset at you, and I'm not sure that you're off the hook, yet. I have to give that some thought, but if I hear that you went near anything that has to do with my investigation, I will make sure you spend some time in jail. Are we clear, Mr. Thomas?" The scary thing was that he said all that in a calm voice. I almost wished he would yell. The Peck I knew I could con, yelled.

I nodded with as much sincerity as I could muster and Chris gave him her solemn promise that she'd watch me like a hawk. He smiled at her, scowled at me, and then told us to disappear. Thank you, God!

Chapter 24

I can't describe what it felt like to be home, up on my roof, looking out over my bay, with my moon almost full, and my lady love curled up next to me. There was a soft evening breeze coming off the water, and the air was just cool enough to be cozy. It felt like I had been away for a long time.

When we came home earlier, Chris led me upstairs by the hand and proceeded to show me how much I was missed. We made delicious love for what seemed like hours and then fell asleep exhausted in each other's arms. I awoke much later to find the bed empty, and heard Chris come out of the shower. I dragged a pillow to the end of the bed and lay there watching her brush her full, chestnut hair in front of my long mirror, naked and beautiful. I believe you can tell a lot about a woman by the way she brushes her hair. She was slow and sensual, using long and lingering strokes. And she could look at herself without embarrassment or self-consciousness, but in no way narcissistic. She knew exactly who she was, no more, no less and was content with that. I was a lucky man.

"You watching me, you?" her eyes danced at me from the mirror, still stroking her hair with a pearl handled brush.

"I think I'm in love," I answered. "You know, I wish I could freeze this moment, this feeling. This is what life is all about, baby—true love." She turned and walked slowly toward me, smiling and twirling the brush on its leather strap. Uh oh. "Its called lust, Romeo. Have any of that left?"

"That, too!" I confessed, laughing. "And I think I can muster up some lust if forced." She stood in front of me and put her bare foot up on my shoulder and ran her delicious toes up and down my arm. "I never had to force anyone, Gramps," she teased, and to which I responded in silence by slowly kissing her shapely ankle and working my way up her long, tanned leg.

We woke hours later hungry enough to eat a horse, so we decided to get up and find that horse. While Chris dressed, I went downstairs and looked for a long time at my CD collection and finally chose an old Elton John favorite of mine, *Madman Across the Water*, to enhance the mood. Chris came down and our eyes smiled a lot as we danced close in the fading evening light. Thank you again, God.

Later, we found some hidden treasures in my refrigerator and whipped up a feast of roasted chicken seasoned with garlic and basil, brown rice and shallots. And I'd be remiss not to mention some butter-sautéed mushrooms and country biscuits browned ever-so-slightly in the oven. Chris even found a box of brownie mix with walnuts that I had stashed for severe emergencies and shocked the hell out of me by baking them for our dessert. She said we deserved to be evil. That worked for me. I've always been able to justify almost anything with a little encouragement. Now seriously, who in their right mind would risk losing a woman who was not only young and beautiful but could cook, too!

I'd stoked a nice fire in the living room and we ate sitting on the floor, leaning back against the couch. The music and the food prompted a brief appearance by Bob, my ever-so-loyal feline, to show us how annoyed he was at being left alone for so long. He then decided it was too strenuous, so he waddled over and curled up next to the fireplace to rest. He lay there with his head on his paws and glared over at us while we ate. I really thought he should take a vacation-maybe find a girlfriend. It would mellow him out. He needed a life.

It was then I had the idea. "I think we ought to go somewhere special to celebrate. How about some warm water and white sand?" I asked, putting my arm around her. "I want to go to some little island down in the Caribbean, lie in the sun, make love to the woman of my dreams and eat like a pig for a couple of weeks. What you say, good-looking?"

"Didn't we just do all that?" Chris laughed, leaning back against me. "It does sound wonderful. When do we leave? I got the vacation time if you got the cash, Bubba."

I squeezed her. "Let's see what happens this week and then we'll go for it. I love you. You know that, don't you?"

"I know," she sighed, purring against me. "And I love you, my crazy, mixed-up writer guy. But, please promise me that you won't go playing detective on your own again. Please?" She turned and faced me with her arms around my neck. Her soft eyes searched mine for truth. "I never want to lose you. You hear me?"

I smiled and kissed her again. "It wasn't on purpose, you know. It all kind of just happened and then all of a sudden, I was Eddie. I can't really explain."

She pulled back and looked at me with one eyebrow raised and asked, "Eddie? What about Eddie? You didn't tell me about any of this, Nick Thomas. What on God's earth does Eddie Kane have to do with any of this? Or do I dare even ask? Did you tell Peck about these delusions? You didn't tell Peck. This you have to tell me."

"Don't ask, and hell no, I didn't tell Peck. He'd put me in a padded cell and eat the key," I laughed and kissed her again. "Someday I'll tell you the whole story, or maybe it'll be my next Eddie Kane novel, where he helps this writer out of a jam. What do you think? Wait for the book?"

"I think you're nuts. That's what I think." We both laughed and retreated to our haven on the roof to watch the sunset and drink our coffee. We were rewarded with a sunset done in pastel chalks with smudges of pale blues, darker hues of purples and then all rubbed softly in oranges and reds as the fading yellow sun dipped below the calm horizon. It was a masterpiece of non-symmetry and awesome beauty.

CKKK8

I don't know what time it was when all hell broke loose. I was sleeping on my side and Chris was snuggled into my back with her arms wrapped around me. The gunshot exploded through my dream and brought me wide-awake and onto the floor. I reached up and pulled Chris off the bed and down on the floor next to me. Her eyes were wide and confused. "Nick? What's going on?"

"I don't know," I whispered and put my finger to my lips. Then we heard yelling from down on the beach and then another loud shot. It was then that I smelled something funny. Something was burning. "You smell that?" I asked her, and then it registered. "Oh shit, it's the house, honey. Come on! We got to get out of here, now!"

I raced over and grabbed the jeans and sweatshirt that I'd had on earlier and jammed on my boat shoes. I looked over and saw that Chris was almost ready. She was just lacing up her sneakers and ready to roll. I grabbed her hand and started for the stairs when another shot rang out. This one shattered the huge glass window that faced the beach. We both fell to the floor when the window exploded and were covered with fine shards of glass. I reached over and found Chris's hand and we bounded downstairs into the thickening smoke, coughing. I couldn't see where the fire was and my eyes were burning. But I knew we could not stay in the house.

I thought I heard sirens off in the distance. I prayed they were coming here. We got to the bottom of the stairs and saw that the fire was outside on the rear deck and beginning to spread. I grabbed the extension phone on my old desk under the stairs and tried to dial, but the line was dead. Of course it was.

"Dead?" Chris asked with her eyes wide, and I nodded.

"We got problems. The deck is burning, so whoever is out there knows we've got to go out the front door. He's already put a bullet in the window upstairs. We'd be sitting ducks up there. It looks like he's come for me," I said with surprising calm. "I know who it is now. It's Ian Kiley."

Chris nodded and pulled on my arm. "Come on, Nick, let's get out of here." She looked out the back and coughed from the heavy smoke. She ran over to the couch and grabbed an old throw blanket that we kept there for cold nights in front of the fire. "I think we should go out the back, Nick. Let's wrap up in this blanket and head for the sand. We can make it. We have to do this now. The smoke is bad."

There was another explosion and more glass shattering. We dropped to the floor in the kitchen. We still heard the sirens in the distance. I prayed again that they were coming here. I crammed the blanket she'd grabbed down in the sink and turned on the water, trying to soak it as quickly as possible while Chris found a couple of heavy cotton dish towels for our faces.

"Let's do it!" I yelled and we wrapped the wet blanket around us and over our heads. We turned and ran for the large sliding glass doors that led out the back toward the beach. There were a couple of small obstacles between safety and us. The most obvious was the twenty-five feet of intensely burning deck on the other side of the door. The other major anxiety was that there quite possibly could be someone with a night vision scope on a large rifle patiently sitting on a dune waiting for us to do something this stupid.

We held hands and crashed together through the screen door and out onto the burning deck. I heard another shot in the roar of confusion and could've sworn it buzzed by my head. We lunged forward, coughing through the smoke and flames to the other side of the deck, where we flew off the end into the hot sand in a heap. Another shot exploded and thudded into the sand by my head. Then there was a blast from behind us and I thought it was all over for us. There were two of them!

I rolled away from Chris to get a look and couldn't quite believe what I saw. Crouched about ten feet away, behind a small dune, wide eyed and insane-looking, was my neighbor, Rudy Kemp, in his bathrobe, with his shock-white hair standing on end, holding a big, ugly, smoking shotgun!

"I saw him, Thomas. I saw that red-headed little shit sneaking around in the sand and I saw him pour gas on your deck and put a match to it," he screamed over the pounding surf. "And he saw me, too, and shot at me. That's when I ran back to the house and got my gun." He held up his double-barreled relic proudly.

"Stay down, Rudy," I screamed over to him. Another shot rang out and smacked into the deck post a few feet in front of us. Rudy stood and fired his shotgun in the direction of the unknown sniper. It looked like the recoil from the old shotgun knocked him backward into the sand, but when I looked closer, I saw a growing red spot on the front of his white t-shirt under his open bathrobe. Chris screamed and crawled toward him.

"Chris, get back here!" I yelled to her.

"He needs help, Nick. He's been shot," she cried.

"I have to help."

If I would have stopped and given the matter more thought, I probably wouldn't have done what I did next. The shooting had stopped for the moment and I poked my head up and tried to focus my eyes into the darkness behind the burning deck. Then I saw him. At first, he was just a black figure limping toward the dunes about twenty yards away. When he looked back I saw his face aglow as the flames from the deck reflected off his skin.

I felt rage well up inside. Ian Kiley! I knew it. I screamed as loudly as I could over the pounding surf, "Kiley, you're done!"   The sirens from the distance were getting closer by the second. "They're coming for you, dirtball!"

His face widened into a huge grin as he stopped and snapped off a shot from his handgun in my direction. Wood splintered in front of me as I was using the deck for cover. I ducked into the sand and waited for a moment. There were no more shots, so I raised my head just in time to see him disappear around the front of the house.

I looked quickly back to where Chris was tending to Rudy and called over to her, "How's he doing? You OK?" She looked up and shook her head, "He's bad, Nick. I don't know," she yelled.

"I'll be back, Chris. Just hang on. Help is on the way."

"Where are you going? Don't leave me, Nick!"

"I'll be right back." I yelled and scooted around the corner of the burning deck before she could protest further. I felt the heat from the flames and saw the fire licking away at the side of my house, and it looked like the roof was smoldering. I knew she'd be gone if help didn't arrive soon.

I put that from my mind and focused on Ian Kiley. I was Eddie again. I felt the rush of adrenaline and clarity of thought as I charged around the house. I was no longer Nick Thomas, fiction writer. I was Eddie Kane, saver of souls and champion of good and I felt invincible as he surged through my veins.

The sirens were about a mile away, turning off the main road and would be here soon. I reached the corner of the house and looked around it cautiously. I didn't see any sign of Ian. I turned and looked back toward the beach, but couldn't see Chris or Rudy, either. I said a silent prayer and took off around the front of the house.

As I rounded the corner, I saw him at the mouth of my dirt driveway picking up a small dirt bike that he must've hidden in the tall sea-grass. The sirens were close, and it sounded like there were a lot of them. I just prayed that there was a big, shiny, red fire engine leading the way or else my precious little cottage would soon be history.

I saw Kiley jump up on the kick starter and the little bike roared to life. Eddie Kane was coursing through my veins as I raced around the side of the cottage and straight toward the unsuspecting Kiley. He revved the dirt bike and kicked it into gear, spraying loose gravel and sand from the back tire. All I heard was roaring in my ears and pounding in my chest. At that point, I'd lost all reason. I knew he was still armed, but I didn't care. The little bastard wasn't getting away again if I could help it. He had done way too much to mess up my life.

He was about 20 yards away and I was racing full tilt toward him. He looked over his shoulder at me, and I saw him grin when he realized who was running toward him. He stopped the bike suddenly, reached down and pulled his gun from the waistband of his pants, raised it in my direction, and pulled the trigger. I leaped over a small rise in the sand and landed in a depression about two feet deep with a thud that knocked the wind out of me for a second. The bullet smacked into the sand inches above my head.

"Come on, Thomas," he screamed over the noise. "What you waiting for? I'm right here!" He snapped off another shot and then I heard him rev the bike and turn it in my direction. The crazy bastard was coming after me with his bike. I looked around me in the sand for anything I could use as a weapon. I felt helpless as I heard the bike only a few yards away. The sirens were on top of us now, but it didn't seem to faze him a bit.

I heard him scream above the noise, "Come on, asshole. Come on out. 'Cuz your ass is mine!"

I was afraid to raise my head. The wolf was at the door and he was knocking! I lay quiet in the sand for a moment and heard the throaty idle of the bike on the other side of the dune. I knew he couldn't see me from where he was and I knew there was no firm ground for him to set the bike on its kickstand and leave it running. So, I knew he was still seated on the bike probably trying to figure out exactly where I was. The advantage was mine this time. I knew exactly where he was, but he could only guess my location. Time was running out as I heard the squealing of tires and the blaring of sirens on the access road about a quarter mile away. He had to make his move now or never, I thought.

Then I heard him race the motor and come straight over the top of the dune. I rolled to one side, just in time, as his front tire landed where my head had been. I kicked out and knocked him off balance just as the rear tire came down and bit into the damp sand, sending Kiley flying off his bike and face-first into the sand. I scrambled up over the still running motorcycle and on top of him. The rear tire was still spinning, spitting sand everywhere. Kiley reached back and grabbed me by my hair and tried to roll me off of him, but I held on for dear life and screamed at him, "You son-of-a-bitch! You're not going anywhere."

"Fuck you, Thomas!" He rolled quickly to one side and caught me squarely in the groin with his knee. I doubled up in pain, my eyes blurred and watering, watching helplessly as he reached for his gun. He scowled and patted his side in frustration. "My gun. Where's my gun?" He screamed into the night and looked at me with wild eyes.

Two cruisers, and thank God, a fire engine, wheeled into my drive with others right behind. The night sky was lit up with fire, smoke and flashing lights. I looked back at Kiley just in time to see him dive into the sand to my left for the gun. I saw the ugly black butt of the gun sticking out of the sand and I rolled and tried to reach it before he did. My fingers closed around the grip, but Kiley was deceptively strong as he ripped my arm back and snatched up the weapon.

I don't know where my strength came from. I have to believe it was from God. I managed to grab his wrist and we fought. Kiley was on top and I was half-buried in the wet sand-exhausted and disoriented. The gun exploded next to my head and I thought it was all over. My consciousness faded for a moment, but I realized that I wasn't hit. Kiley's face was kissing close and I could see the burning hate in his eyes and feel his hot sour breath.

"Say good-bye, Nick," he smiled.

I still held his wrist tightly and tried to turn it away from me. I knew right then that I was going to die. There was too much going on to sort it out-the cops, the scream of the sirens, the fire, Chris, Rudy, and Ian Kiley about to end my life. My arms had no strength left, but I couldn't give up. We both shook as he tried to turn the gun on me and I pushed with every bit of strength I had. Our eyes locked and his sweat dripped in my face and with the last ounce of will in my body, I pushed but couldn't get him off of me. Another explosion filled the heavy night air and Kiley jerked as if he were hit by lightning. His eyes grew wide as he looked down at me incredulously, not comprehending what had just happened. I didn't know what had just happened. He tried to laugh and a sour stench escaped his lips. His smile faded and then his body went slack on top of mine. I felt his warm and sticky blood spreading over my chest and then all the noise seemed to be gone.

And that was the last thing I remember.

Chapter 25

It was a beautiful, cool afternoon. The sky was picture-perfect, the deep blue water sedate, and there was a nice breeze blowing off the bay. We were seated in one of the oversized booths in the back of Ray's with all the huge seaward windows cranked wide open. For me, being near the water brought alive my senses and also my connection to God, with an incredible feeling of gratitude. I'd just been to hell and back. I've been there before; maybe not to this extreme, but it was hell just the same. And I know that we've all lived through our own hells. Mine happened to be a 12-round, championship bout with alcohol that brought me to my knees-literally. But I learned how to stand up and live a good life. For today, I've won that battle with booze. I didn't pick up the bottle during this last ordeal. That's all that counted. And I knew that I was a lucky man.

My love, my friend and confidant, Chris, sat next to me in the huge, straw covered booth with her hand in mine. My good friend, Mac, was seated across the table, and Ray was perched on a stool against the wall beside the table, sipping his ever-present bottle of Corona with lime. There was some soft, island music playing in the background and the smell of wonderful food floated deliciously through the air. I felt warm and happy and very connected.

Jazz came over in a flurry and plunked down a huge platter of fried calamari in the middle of the table, clearing away empty glasses and dishes as she went. Jazz was a buffet of color, wearing a hot pink muumuu with huge orange and yellow flowers, natives paddling thin, brown boats into a red sunset, along with electric blue plastic sandals, and topped off with a yellow carnation tucked behind one ear. Only Jazz could wear an outfit like that and get away with it and look good doing it. Actually, I used her as a character in my Eddie Kane books. Eddie's neighbor in the city is a large, savvy Jamaican woman named Flo who is a clairvoyant. She uses chicken bones to see the future. That woman is Jazz.

"Now here we be, all one big happy family. Another Kodak moment, I think." Jazz chortled, winking at me and running her plump, bejeweled fingers though my hair. "A happy ending, no? Jazz wants to kiss everybody!"

"Happy ending, 'yes', my Jamaican vixen. And to put it in plain English, we lucky as hell," I answered, laughing and kissed her on the cheek. I held onto Chris's hand and continued to shovel the last of the succulent lobster bisque into my mouth with the other, nodding to the music as I ate. Ray had put on one of my favorite jazz CDs. It was Gato Barbieri who made love with a sax like no one else.

"Nick baby, you haven't stopped eating since you got here. Take a break, mon, there always be tomorrow," laughed Jazz. It was good to hear her laughter. It was good to be there. Actually, it was good to be anywhere in one piece.

"It's been a rough few days, Jazz darlin'. I can't remember worse." I mumbled, munching on a hot buttered breadstick. I was convinced that food was the healer of broken spirits and wounded souls and I was prepared to defend that staunch belief to the bitter end.

I wiped my mouth, held up the remains of the once proud and liberally buttered breadstick, and cleared my throat for attention. "But as I think on it, one time does come to mind." I paused for effect, my voice softened, and I glanced at each one of them. "Did I ever tell you about the time I was fishing for great blue Marlin off the southern coast of Panama with my publisher when we hit the granddaddy of all storms? A blow right from Zeus's lungs, I'll tell you." Ray's stool came down with a thud, his ebony face creased with interest, and Chris's deep green eyes were riveted on my face as she gripped my arm. I knew I had them: all eyes were glued on me. They were too easy. I closed my eyes as though I was remembering and continued my tale.

"It was a late September afternoon when the squall hit. The sky got dark fast, like someone pulled a huge blanket over the sea and turned off the lights. And the wind came at us like I'd never seen, battering us for what seemed like hours. The wind even ripped the short-wave antenna right off the flying bridge, so our radio was knocked out and we began to take on water. Two of the crew members were swept overboard and our little boat bobbed like a cork. And in the raging sea around us, I could see the deadly fins of the Mako sharks circling-smelling the blood of the seamen who had been washed overboard, falling prey to the sea. I'd about given up all hope." I spoke the last in a whisper. "I was ready to make my peace with my God and to die like a man."

The silence was heavy. "You never told me that. What, whatever did you do, honey?" Chris finally managed to ask, still holding my arm. "I never knew. I mean how did you ever get out alive?" Oddly enough, I detected a trace of disbelief from my loved one.

Ray looked at me and laughed, "Yeah Hemingway, what you do next? Take on those big, bad sharks? Or grow wings and fly home, mon?"

I looked up from my plate, staring at them, and then I couldn't keep a straight face any longer. "I woke up!" I blurted out. "Got ya!"

And we all roared with laughter.

Ray tossed his lime at me and Chris kissed my cheek. I smelled the soft scent of cinnamon and apples in her hair. Her tanned face was flawless and smooth as her eyes smiled into mine. God, I loved this woman. Life began to feel right again.

Chris squeezed me as I resumed my frontal assault on the calamari and she said, "This guy here's going to need lots of rest and relaxation. Last night he told me I was hired on as his personal nurse, so my first diagnosis was stress. My prescription for a speedy recovery is to take me to an exotic Caribbean island where we are going to lie in the sun, make mad, passionate love in the sand, and eat like kings."

She knew she had me when she mentioned the food part, but I kept my cool and asked with a puzzled look, "When is all this supposed to happen? Maybe I have amnesia from lack of food because I don't remember saying that? Was that before or after you seduced me?"

She flashed me her dazzling smile and laughed, patting my leg. "It don't matter, Big Guy, it's too late. I already called and booked the trip this morning. We have ten glorious days in the Bahamas where there is blue water, white sand, and very small bathing suits. We leave Friday morning and don't forget your Visa card, honey."

I heard the part about small bathing suits. "Just how small are the bathing suits?" I asked, straightening up in my chair. "And we're leaving when?"

"We leave Friday morning," she answered. Then she held her thumb and forefinger up about an inch apart. "And the bathing suits are this small, my dear, and in that vein, I've got something to show you," she said to me with a strange smile on her face.

I watched her reach down and pull a small, white paper bag out of her purse. It was about the size prescriptions come in, with a bright orange sun and an electric blue San Tropez Shops logo on the front. She held the bag up with ceremony for us all to see and then opened it slowly. The anticipation was killing me, but I played along. Her long, slender fingers parted the opening of the bag and peeked inside carefully as if there were a small animal inside or something. Then she crumbled it closed with a loud crinkle, quickly looking over at me with a smile.

"I don't know if you're ready for this, Nick Thomas."

"Come on, honey; enough is enough," I protested impatiently, trying to see into the little bag. "What's in there? Is it for me? A present?"

Again she smiled at me, "You could say that, big boy." And with that she began to pull something slowly from the fancy little white bag with the orange sun and blue lettering. I saw a flash of gold and then my mouth fell open and my eyes widened as she held up the smallest piece of material I'd ever seen. There were two shimmering, gold patches about the size of half-dollars with a thin lame' cord holding them together and then a piece of the same running down to a triangular patch that was equally as small on the bottom. I knew I was viewing the smallest string bikini known to man. I also knew that I was a very lucky man indeed.

"You...You're going wear that?" I stammered. It came out sort of squeaky sounding. I looked over to Ray for help. He smiled and shrugged his shoulders. "Jazz got one just like it." And we all laughed at that one.

"You always say I'm too inhibited," Chris said innocently, batting her eyelashes at me. I held up one of Ray's prized palm tree cocktail napkins and said, "Honey, there's more material in this silly napkin."

Ray shot me a wary look. "Don't be messin with the ambiance, mon. I'll tell Jazz. She still think palm trees grow on Cape Cod and I'm not gonna tell her different."

Chris laughed and said to me, "Be a good boy and I'll let you help me put it on."

I sighed and thought for a long moment and then I finally answered, "OK, if I have to." We all laughed and it felt good to be alive.

"I'm game for anything as long as they have food where we're going." I said, sitting back, patting my full belly. "I'm full now, but one has to plan for the future. My stomach was severely traumatized, so now I feel that I'd be very irresponsible to myself if I allowed that to happen again."

Chris laughed. "Don't worry, honey, I'll make sure that you are well taken care of." And then she added with a sly look, "In all respects."

"I didn't think I'd ever hear you say that you were full, Nick." laughed Mac. "You know, you sure put us through the mill the past few days, old buddy. Peck still would like a piece of your hide to tack on his wall, but I managed to calm him down. Just stay out of his way for awhile, OK, partner?" I nodded. The last thing I wanted to do was to butt heads with Peck. We didn't exactly see things the same way. He could be so intense. I had a more relaxed philosophy about life these days. And besides, I trusted Mac's judgment.

"Don't worry about me, Mac. It seems I'll be lying on the beach in three days with my lady-love here. Far, far away from the beloved El Captain." I pronounced it El Cap-e-taan, the way the Mexican banditos with the big, droopy mustaches did in the old cowboy movies.

Chris drained her lemonade and put her tumbler down with the ice cubes clinking. She asked. "OK, now, does anyone here know exactly what really did happen and why? I'm still a bit confused."

I wiped my mouth, waving yet another fresh breadstick in the air for silence. I hated to see them go to waste. "First of all, I am formally announcing that this is the plot for my next book. Now, the best I can figure is this: Maxine Gill, the insurance lady, was behind the whole deal from the beginning. She was the one who wrote the policy for CDI and saw her opportunity to cash in. She then manipulated Ian, the simpleton that he was, with the wicked ways of flesh and cocaine to plant the seeds of greed and crime into his already greedy head. Not only were Maxine and Ian lovers, but Maxine and Karen were also lovers. This Maxine was a piece of work. I guess we have to figure out who she didn't sleep with. She probably didn't trust Ian to get it done on his own, so she seduced the affection-starved Karen herself. Anyhow, between the two of them, they convinced Karen to eliminate Carla and Shawn and to frame me for both. That way they would get all the insurance money. Karen bought it and then promptly recruited her less-than-bright lover, Vinnie, to do the unpleasant deeds and to leave me holding the bag. That would leave a nice neat little package for Karen to collect and of course share with Maxine. But it didn't end there. Maxine would make sure that Karen was found guilty of plotting to murder Carla and her husband. Then all the money would go to her survivors, namely Ian and ultimately, Maxine. Karen self-destructed instead. Getting the money away from Ian would be child's play for Maxine. She really thought she had all the bases covered."

"Clever stuff. So where is Maxine now?" Chris asked. "She didn't get away, did she? You didn't tell me, Nick."

I swallowed some seltzer. "No, my dear, she didn't get away. Almost, maybe, but she didn't quite make it. See, folks, crime does not pay. And hot-to-trot Maxine Gill was no exception. Peck's men picked up her sneaky ass at Logan Airport last night and booked her on multiple counts of conspiracy to commit murder, insurance fraud and a shopping list of other charges. She's going grow old in jail, washing some bull dyke's underwear."

"You have a way with words, Nick Thomas,"

Chris laughed, punching my arm playfully.

"Lady thought she was slick, mon" chimed in Ray. "And she almost pulled it off. Gotta admire the complexity of the situation." Ray held a certain regard for criminal genius.

"True," I said. "If Karen and Vinnie had murdered me and dumped me off shore like they were planning, Maxine and Ian might be lying in the sun as we speak with those umbrella drinks and a fat bank account. And I'd be floating in the sea with some smelly fish stripping the flesh off my carcass. Scary, isn't it?"

"They wouldn't eat your ass, mon, fish be fussy," said Ray with a deadpan expression.

"Amen, to that," said Chris, patting my thigh. "I'm glad you're here."

"Me, too!" laughed Ray. "He supports my kitchen." We all laughed.

"OK, now that we have Maxine, Karen and Ian figured out, where does that psycho, Pete Nolin, fit into all this?" asked Chris, "Or does he?"

"He doesn't. Never did." answered Mac. "He was just another weirdo in the wrong place at the wrong time. I don't think he killed Kiley, either. I agree with Nick and think Ian Kiley did that. We figure Nolin was delivering some takeout food from next door as it went down or just right after. But, I'm glad that he is not with us anymore. I have a feeling that we would've been hearing from that sicko sooner than later, anyway. And after all, he did fillet his mother. Hell, he could've buried her in that cellar and we would never have found out if all this didn't happen."

I nodded in agreement. "It makes me feel awful lucky. It seems like all the psychopaths got together and collaborated on this one. Maxine did it all for money. Her motives were pure. But, look at mild mannered, suburban housewife, Karen Kiley, who was a closet nymphomaniac, cokehead and murderess. And let's not forget her freckle-faced, darling son, Ian, who managed to wreak havoc in my life with a smile and vengeance, and Vinnie Sax, the poor, ignorant bastard who killed for love, or lust, or whatever Karen had him thinking. Karen was like a black widow spider. She snapped big time and took out everyone in her way. They were both so fried on coke that I don't think either one of them had any sense of reality anymore."

Mac had told me earlier that the cops found several ounces of high-grade cocaine in Vinnie's house and had managed to trace it back to some missing evidence in a major drug case a few months back. The coroner did a tox screen on Vinnie and found that he had massive levels of cocaine in his blood and tissue samples. The same with Karen when they did blood and urine tests on her at the hospital. They were snorting their brains out. Literally.

"Good old Vinnie was a walking crime spree with a badge, all done in the interest of love. Scary thought, huh?" Mac added.

"What's going to happen to Karen now?" Chris asked. "Are they going to try her or commit her? She seems pretty screwed up to me."

"We don't know yet. The D.A. is staying low-profile so far," answered Mac. "First, they're going to determine if she's competent to stand trial. They've got a team of shrinks checking her out now. Of course, you know that her lawyer's going to bring in another half dozen shrinks to say that she isn't competent to try, or else they could try for an insanity defense. They are the rage now and very difficult to prove either way. Personally, I'd love to see her fry. She's responsible for at least four deaths that I know of. Lord knows if there are more. That's one sick lady, my friends."

Mac took a long pull from his iced tea with lemon and asked me, "Now tell me, Nick, what happens to all that insurance money?" I leaned back in the leather booth and put my arm around Chris, smiling broadly. "You know what they say, Mac. What goes around comes around. After all, I am the injured party here and I feel that I deserve whatever compensation the powers that be deem fair."

"Don't even tell me that you are going to get all that green, man," cried Ray, laughing. "It's not fair! But there is good to come from this, 'cuz now you can pay your tab. Remember you owes me a new Jeep, too!"

"All I'll say is that it looks like I'll be able to afford that vacation, Boys. Hey, come on, really. I earned it. I was chased, shot at, tied up, and whatever else I was subjected to. I forget the details now, not to mention the serious lack of decent food. But right now I'd like to propose a toast."

I raised my glass in front of me in tribute. "To all my good friends. May we all live long and be happy. And thank God it's over!" I proclaimed holding up my seltzer with lime.

We all laughed and raised our glasses.

"Friends!"

I'd never tell Chris or anyone else about what had happened back there in Vinnie's house. It's something I'd rather forget and it would serve no one's purpose to bring it up. Karen would pay for her sins, one way or another. I had no say in that, nor did I want it. That's God's job and he does it way better than I do. It was time to move on. It was over and I wanted to close the book.

Epilogue

I sat back in my worn, brown leather chair and looked at the computer screen with mixed feelings of sadness and elation as I typed the words, "The End." What a catharsis it was to finish a work. Emotions flooded my veins and the tears would come, they always did after I finished. I got up and stretched, standing with my hands clasped behind my back looking out over the place I'd come to love so much. I felt so content and so, so lucky. I knew that God always gave me what I needed. Not always what I thought I wanted at the time, but always just what I needed.

The bay was a deep rich blue with bold white caps standing out brightly like someone painted them on with a brush. There were dozens of small boats bobbing up and down with the rising tide in the perfect afternoon sun. I closed my eyes and smelled the beautiful salt air and heard the seagulls cry. I opened my eyes slowly and watched Chris, my loving wife, my partner, my best friend, playing with our Goldens, Rocky and Apollo, down on the beach below. It didn't get any better than this. This is where I made my stand and learned how to live and this will be where I'll rest when I'm gone. This was the place where Nick and Chris, Eddie, Peck, Mac, Ray and Jazz were born from within and live on in the pages of my novels. And they are very real to me.

The End. . . for now!

About The Author

Tom Rieber, his wife Kibbi and their Golden Retriever, Skyler, live on the beautiful southeastern coast of North Carolina but spend many quality moments of their lives on Cape Cod, Massachusetts. The Cape, alive with character, has become their second home and setting for the first several of his *Nick Thomas* series of novels. Rieber knows well the world of which he writes. He is a recovering alcoholic himself for many years and is still very active in helping others who are trying to claw their way back from their own personal hells. He is a true believer, not only in himself but others who want to try to turn their lives around. He truly is Nick Thomas.

Rieber has worked as a staff writer and sports columnist for a several newspapers in Central Connecticut. He has written and published numerous short stories and has won awards on both the local and collegiate levels for short fiction and poetry. His life experience includes a stint in the U.S. Navy during the Vietnam War, to working his way through college by tending bar, working in hospitals and building houses along with many more insignificant "short" careers in-between. Twenty something years ago Rieber settled into a career in real estate where he stayed and sometimes flourished until retirement this year.

As a direct result of these diverse endeavors he has become an incurable romantic and informal philosopher to those who will listen.

Rieber is also involved in many writers support groups that offers help and structure to those who wish to write but are caught up in the web of everyday procrastination.

Rieber's second novel, *The Devils Parody,* already under pen, uses the same core of colorful characters that make *The Nine Irony* come alive and he has drafts of two more additional Nick Thomas Novels.

Happy reading, and most of all
have fun and don't take yourself
too seriously!

Printed in the United States
216067BV00001B/3/P

9 781607 437482